SAX ROHMER

TITAN BOOKS

THE MYSTERY OF DR. FU-MANCHU
Print edition ISBN: 9780857686039
E-book edition ISBN: 9780857686695

Published by
Titan Books
A division of Titan Publishing Group Ltd
144 Southwark Street
London
SE1 0UP

First edition: February 2012
10 9 8 7 6 5 4 3 2 1

Visit our website: www.titanbooks.com

Did you enjoy this book? We love to hear from our readers. Please email us at readerfeedback@titanemail.com or write to us at Reader Feedback at the above address.

To receive advance information, news, competitions, and exclusive offers online, please sign up for the Titan newsletter on our website: www.titanbooks.com

Frontispiece illustration by J. C. Coll, detail from an illustration for "Kâramanèh," first appearing in *Collier's*, April 26, 1913. Special thanks to Dr. Lawrence Knapp for the illustrations from "The Page of Fu-Manchu" -- http://www.njedge.net/~knapp/FuFrames.htm

A CIP catalogue record for this title is available from the British Library.

Printed and bound in the United States.

"Don't stir!" said Smith savagely. "I warn you!"

CHAPTER ONE

MR. NAYLAND SMITH OF BURMA

"A gentleman to see you, Doctor."

From across the common a clock sounded the half-hour.

"Ten-thirty!" I said. "A late visitor. Show him up, if you please."

I pushed my writing aside and tilted the lampshade, as footsteps sounded on the landing. The next moment I had jumped to my feet, for a tall, lean man, with his square-cut, clean-shaven face sun-baked to the hue of coffee, entered and extended both hands with a cry:

"Good old Petrie! Didn't expect me, I'll swear!"

It was Nayland Smith—whom I had thought to be in Burma!

"Smith," I said, and gripped his hands hard, "this is a delightful surprise! Whatever—however—"

"Excuse me, Petrie!" he broke in. "Don't put it down to the sun!" And he put out the lamp, plunging the room into darkness.

I was too surprised to speak.

"No doubt you will think me mad," he continued, and, dimly, I could see him at the window, peering out into the road, "but before you are many hours older you will know that I have good reason to

be cautious. Ah, nothing suspicious! Perhaps I am first this time."
And, stepping back to the writing-table, he relighted the lamp.

"Mysterious enough for you?" he laughed, and glanced at my
unfinished MS. "A story, eh? From which I gather that the district
is beastly healthy—what, Petrie? Well, I can put some material in
your way that, if sheer uncanny mystery is a marketable commodity,
ought to make you independent of influenza and broken legs and
shattered nerves and all the rest."

I surveyed him doubtfully, but there was nothing in his
appearance to justify me in supposing him to suffer from delusions.
His eyes were too bright, certainly, and a hardness now had crept
over his face. I got out the whisky and siphon, saying:

"You have taken your leave early?"

"I am not on leave," he replied, and slowly filled his pipe. "I am
on duty."

"On duty!" I exclaimed. "What, are you moved to London or
something?"

"I have got a roving commission, Petrie, and it doesn't rest with
me where I am today nor where I shall be tomorrow."

There was something ominous in the words, and, putting down
my glass, its contents untasted, I faced around and looked him
squarely in the eyes.

"Out with it!" I said. "What is it all about?"

Smith suddenly stood up and stripped off his coat. Rolling back
his left shirt-sleeve, he revealed a wicked-looking wound in the
fleshy part of the forearm. It was quite healed, but curiously striated
for an inch or so around.

"Ever seen one like it?" he asked.

"Not exactly," I confessed. "It appears to have been deeply
cauterized."

"Right! Very deeply!" he rapped. "A barb steeped in the venom of a hamadryad went in there!"

A shudder I could not repress ran coldly through me at mention of that most deadly of all the reptiles of the East.

"There's only one treatment," he continued, rolling his sleeve down again, "and that's with a sharp knife, a match, and a broken cartridge. I lay on my back, raving, for three days afterwards in a forest that stank with malaria, but I should have been lying there now if I had hesitated. Here's the point. It was not an accident!"

"What do you mean?"

"I mean that it was a deliberate attempt on my life, and I am hard upon the tracks of the man who extracted that venom—patiently, drop by drop—from the poison-glands of the snake, who prepared that arrow, and who caused it to be shot at me."

"What fiend is this?"

"A fiend who, unless my calculations are at fault, is now in London, and who regularly wars with pleasant weapons of that kind. Petrie, I have travelled from Burma not in the interests of the British Government merely, but in the interests of the entire white race, and I honestly believe—though I pray I may be wrong—that its survival depends largely upon the success of my mission."

To say that I was perplexed conveys no idea of the mental chaos created by these extraordinary statements, for into my humdrum suburban life Nayland Smith had brought fantasy of the wildest. I did not know what to think, what to believe.

"I am wasting precious time!" he rapped decisively, and, draining his glass, he stood up. "I came straight to you, because you are the only man I dare to trust. Except the big chief at headquarters, you are the only person in England, I hope, who knows that Nayland Smith has quitted Burma. I must have someone with me, Petrie, all the time—it's imperative! Can you put me up here, and spare a few days to the strangest business, I promise you, that ever was recorded in fact or fiction?"

I agreed readily enough, for, unfortunately, my professional duties were not onerous.

"Good man!" he cried, wringing my hand in his impetuous way. "We start now."

"What, tonight?"

"Tonight! I have thought of turning in, I must admit. I have not dared to sleep for forty-eight hours, except in fifteen-minute stretches. But there is one move that must be made tonight and immediately. I must warn Sir Crichton Davey."

"Sir Crichton Davey—of the India—"

"Petrie, he is a doomed man! Unless he follows my instructions without question, without hesitation—before heaven, nothing can save him! I do not know when the blow will fall, how it will fall, nor from whence, but I know that my first duty is to warn him. Let us walk down to the corner of the common and get a taxi."

How strangely does the adventurous intrude upon the humdrum; for, when it intrudes at all, more often than not its intrusion is sudden and unlooked for. Today we may seek for romance and fail to find it: unsought, it lies in wait for us at most prosaic corners of life's highway.

The drive that night, though it divided the drably commonplace from the wildly bizarre—though it was the bridge between the ordinary and the outré—has left no impression upon my mind. Into the heart of a weird mystery the cab bore me; and in reviewing my memories of those days I wonder that the busy thoroughfares through which we passed did not display before my eyes signs and portents—warnings.

It was not so. I recall nothing of the route and little of import that passed between us (we both were strangely silent, I think) until we were come to our journey's end. Then:

"What's this?" muttered my friend hoarsely.

Constables were moving on a little crowd of curious idlers who pressed about the steps of Sir Crichton Davey's house and sought to peer in at the open door. Without waiting for the cab to draw up to the kerb, Nayland Smith recklessly leapt out, and I followed close at his heels.

"What has happened?" he demanded breathlessly of a constable.

The latter glanced at him doubtfully, but something in his voice and bearing commanded respect.

"Sir Crichton Davey has been killed, sir."

Smith lurched back as though he had received a physical blow, and clutched my shoulder convulsively. Beneath the heavy tan his face had blanched, and his eyes were set in a stare of horror.

"My God!" he whispered, "I am too late!"

With clenched fists he turned and, pressing through the group of loungers, bounded up the steps. In the hall a man who unmistakably was a Scotland Yard official stood talking to a footman. Other members of the household were moving about, more or less aimlessly, and the chilly hand of King Fear had touched one and all, for, as they came and went, they glanced ever over their shoulders, as if each shadow cloaked a menace, and listened, as it seemed, for some sound which they dreaded to hear.

Smith strode up to the detective and showed him a card, upon glancing at which the Scotland Yard man said something in a low voice, and, nodding, touched his hat to Smith in a respectful manner.

A few brief questions and answers, and, in gloomy silence, we followed the detective up the heavily carpeted stair, along a corridor lined with pictures and busts, and into a large library. A group of people were in this room, and one, in whom I recognized Chalmers Cleeve, of Harley Street, was bending over a motionless form stretched upon a couch. Another door communicated with a small study, and through the opening I could see a man on all fours examining the carpet. The uncomfortable sense of hush, the group about the physician, the bizarre figure crawling, beetle-like, across the inner room, and the grim hub around which all this ominous activity turned, made up a scene that etched itself indelibly on my mind.

As we entered, Dr. Cleeve straightened himself, frowning thoughtfully.

"Frankly, I do not care to venture any opinion at present regarding the immediate cause of death," he said. "Sir Crichton was addicted to cocaine, but there are indications which are not in accordance with cocaine-poisoning. I fear that only a post-mortem can establish the facts—if," he added, "we ever arrive at them. A most mysterious case!"

Smith stepped forward and engaged the famous pathologist in conversation. I seized the opportunity to examine Sir Crichton's body.

The dead man was in evening dress, but wore an old smoking-jacket. He had been of spare but hardy build, with thin, aquiline features, which now were oddly puffy, as were his clenched hands. I pushed back his sleeve, and saw the marks of the hypodermic syringe upon his left arm. Quite mechanically I turned my attention to the right arm. It was unscarred, but on the back of the hand was a faint red mark, not unlike the imprint of painted lips. I examined it closely, and even tried to rub it off, but it evidently was caused by some morbid process of local inflammation, if it were not a birthmark.

Turning to a pale young man whom I had understood to be Sir Crichton's private secretary, I drew his attention to this mark, and inquired if it were constitutional.

"It is not, sir," answered Dr. Cleeve, overhearing my question. "I have already made that inquiry. Does it suggest anything to your mind? I must confess that it affords me no assistance."

"Nothing," I replied. "It is most curious."

"Excuse me, Mr.. Burboyne," said Smith, now turning to the secretary, "but Inspector Weymouth will tell you that I act with authority. I understand that Sir Crichton was—seized with illness in his study?"

"Yes—at half-past ten. I was working here in the library, and he inside, as was our custom."

"The communicating door was kept closed?"

"Yes, always. It was open for minute or less at about ten twenty-five, when a message came for Sir Crichton. I took it in to him, and he then seemed in his usual health."

"What was the message?"

"I could not say. It was brought by a district messenger, and he placed it beside him on the table. It is there now, no doubt."

"And at half-past ten?"

"Sir Crichton suddenly burst open the door and threw himself, with a scream, into the library. I ran to him, but he waved me back. His eyes were glaring horribly. I had just reached his side when he fell, writhing, upon the floor. He seemed past speech, but as I raised him and laid him upon the couch, he gasped something that sounded like 'The red hand!' Before I could get to bell or telephone he was dead!"

Mr.. Burboyne's voice shook as he spoke the words, and Smith seemed to find this evidence confusing.

"You do not think he referred to the mark on his own hand?"

"I think not. From the direction of his last glance, I feel sure he referred to something in the study."

"What did you do?"

"Having summoned the servants, I ran into the study. But there was absolutely nothing unusual to be seen. The windows were closed and fastened. He worked with closed windows in the hottest weather. There is no other door, for the study occupies the end of a narrow wing, so that no one could possibly have gained access to it, whilst I was in the library, unseen by me. Had someone concealed himself in the study earlier in the evening—and I am convinced that it offers no hiding-place—he could only have come out again by passing through here."

Nayland Smith tugged at the lobe of his left ear, as was his habit when meditating.

"You had been at work here in this way for some time?"

"Yes. Sir Crichton was preparing an important book."

"Had anything unusual occurred prior to this evening?"

"Yes," said Mr. Burboyne, with evident perplexity, "though I attached no importance to it at the time. Three nights ago Sir Crichton came out to me, and appeared very nervous; but at times his nerves—you know? Well, on this occasion he asked me to search the study. He had an idea that something was concealed there."

"Something, or someone?"

" 'Something' was the word he used. I searched, but fruitlessly, and he seemed quite satisfied, and returned to his work."

"Thank you, Mr. Burboyne. My friend and I would like a few minutes' private investigation in the study."

CHAPTER TWO

THE PERFUMED ENVELOPES

Sir Crichton Davey's study was a small one, and a glance sufficed to show that, as the secretary had said, it offered no hiding-place. It was heavily carpeted, and over-full of Burmese and Chinese ornaments and curios, and upon the mantelpiece stood several framed photographs which showed this to be the sanctum of a wealthy bachelor who was no misogynist. A map of the Indian Empire occupied the larger part of one wall. The grate was empty, for the weather was extremely warm, and a green-shaded lamp on the littered writing-table afforded the only light. The air was stale, for both windows were closed and fastened.

Smith immediately pounced upon a large, square envelope that lay beside the blotting-pad. Sir Crichton had not even troubled to open it, but my friend did so. It contained a blank sheet of paper!

"Smell!" he directed, handing the letter to me.

I raised it to my nostrils. It was scented with some pungent perfume.

"What is it?" I asked.

"It is a rather rare essential oil," was the reply, "which I have met with before, though never in Europe. I begin to understand, Petrie."

He tilted the lampshade, and made a close examination of the scraps of paper, matches and other debris that lay in the grate and on the hearth. I took up a copper vase from the mantelpiece, and was examining it curiously, when he turned, a strange expression upon his face.

"Put that back, old man," he said quietly.

Much surprised, I did as he directed.

"Don't touch anything in the room. It may be dangerous."

Something in the tone of his voice chilled me, and I hastily replaced the vase, and stood by the door of the study, watching him search, methodically, every inch of the room—behind the books, in all the ornaments, in table drawers, in cupboards, on shelves.

"That will do," he said at last. "There is nothing here, and I have no time to search further."

We returned to the library.

"Inspector Weymouth," said my friend, "I have a particular reason for asking that Sir Crichton's body be removed from this room at once and the library locked. Let no one be admitted on any pretence whatever until you hear from me."

It spoke volumes for the mysterious credentials borne by my friend that the man from Scotland Yard accepted his orders without demur, and, after a brief chat with Mr. Burboyne, Smith passed briskly downstairs. In the hall a man who looked like a groom out of livery was waiting.

"Are you Wills?" asked Smith.

"Yes, sir."

"It was you who heard a cry of some kind at the rear of the house about the time of Sir Crichton's death?"

"Yes, sir. I was locking the garage door, and happening to look up at the window of Sir Crichton's study, I saw him jump out of his chair. Where he used to sit at his writing, sir, you could see his shadow on the blind. Next minute I heard a call out in the lane."

"What kind of call?"

The man, whom the uncanny happening clearly had frightened, seemed puzzled for a suitable description.

"A sort of wail, sir!" he said at last. "I never heard anything like it before, and don't want to again."

"Like this?" inquired Smith, and he uttered a low, wailing cry, impossible to describe.

Wills perceptibly shuddered; and, indeed, it was an eerie sound.

"The same, sir, I think," he said, "but much louder."

"That will do," said Smith, and I thought I detected a note of triumph in his voice. "But stay! Take us through to the back of the house."

The man bowed and led the way, so that shortly we found ourselves in a small, paved courtyard. It was a perfect summer's night, and the deep blue vault above was jewelled with myriads of starry points. How impossible it seemed to reconcile that vast, eternal calm with the hideous passions and fiendish agencies which that night had loosed a soul upon the infinite.

"Up yonder are the study windows, sir. Over that wall on your left is the back lane from which the cry came, and beyond is Regent's Park."

"Are the study windows visible from there?"

"Oh yes, sir."

"Who occupies the adjoining house?"

"Major-General Platt-Houston, sir; but the family is out of town."

"Those iron stairs are a means of communication between the

domestic offices and the servants' quarters, I take it?"

"Yes, sir."

"Then send someone to make my business known to the Major-General's housekeeper; I want to examine those stairs."

Singular though my friend's proceedings appeared to me, I had ceased to wonder at anything. Since Nayland Smith's arrival at my rooms I seemed to have been moving through the fitful phases of a nightmare. My friend's account of how he came by the wound in his arm; the scene on our arrival at the house of Sir Crichton Davey; the secretary's story of the dying man's cry, "The red hand!"; the hidden perils of the study; the wail in the lane—all were fitter incidents of delirium than of sane reality. So, when a white-faced butler made us known to a nervous old lady who proved to be the housekeeper of the next-door residence, I was not surprised at Smith's saying:

"Lounge up and down outside, Petrie. Everyone has cleared off now. It is getting late. Keep your eyes open and be on your guard. I thought I had the start, but *he* is here before me, and, what is worse, he probably knows by now that I am here, too."

With which he entered the house and left me out in the square, with leisure to think, to try to understand.

The crowd which usually haunts the scene of a sensational crime had been cleared away, and a report had been circulated that Sir Crichton had died from natural causes. The intense heat having driven most of the residents out of town, practically I was alone in the square, and I gave myself up to a brief consideration of the mystery in which I so suddenly had become involved.

By what agency had Sir Crichton met his death? Did Nayland Smith know? I rather suspected that he did. What was the hidden significance of the perfumed envelope? Who was that mysterious personage whom Smith so evidently dreaded, who had attempted his life, who, presumably, had murdered Sir Crichton? Sir Crichton Davey, during the time that he had held office in India, and during his long term of service at home, had earned the goodwill of all, British and native alike. Who was his secret enemy?

Something touched me lightly on the shoulder.

I turned, with my heart fluttering like a child's. This night's work had imposed a severe strain even upon my callous nerves.

A girl wrapped in a hooded opera-cloak stood at my elbow, and, as she glanced up at me, I thought that I never had seen a face so seductively lovely nor of so unusual a type. With the skin of a perfect blonde, she had eyes and lashes as black as a Creole's, which, together with her full red lips, told me that this beautiful stranger whose touch had so startled me was not a child of our Northern shores.

"Forgive me," she said, speaking with an odd, pretty accent, and laying a slim hand, with jewelled fingers, confidingly upon my arm, "if I startled you. But—is it true that Sir Crichton Davey has been—murdered?"

I looked into her big, questioning eyes, a harsh suspicion labouring in my mind, but could read nothing in their mysterious depths—only I wondered anew at my questioner's beauty. The grotesque idea momentarily possessed me that, were the bloom of her red lips due to art and not to nature, their kiss would leave—though not indelibly—just such a mark as I had seen upon the dead man's hand. But I dismissed the fantastic notion as bred out of the night's horrors, and worthy only of a medieval legend. No doubt she was some friend or acquaintance of Sir Crichton who lived close by.

"I cannot say that he has been murdered," I replied, acting upon the latter supposition, and seeking to tell her what she asked as gently as possible. "But he is —"

"Dead?"

I nodded.

She closed her eyes and uttered a low, moaning sound, swaying dizzily. Thinking she was about to swoon, I threw my arm around her shoulders to support her. But she smiled sadly, and pushed me gently away.

"I am quite well, thank you," she said.

"You are certain? Let me walk with you until you feel quite sure of yourself."

She shook her head, flashed a rapid glance at me with her beautiful eyes, and looked away in a sort of sorrowful embarrassment for which I was entirely at a loss to account. Suddenly she resumed:

"I cannot let my name be mentioned in this dreadful matter, but—I think I have some information—for the police. Will you give this to—whomever you think proper?"

She handed me a sealed envelope, again met my eyes with one of her dazzling glances, and hurried away. She had gone no more than ten or twelve yards, and I still was standing bewildered, watching her graceful, retreating figure, when she turned abruptly and came back. Without looking directly at me, but alternately glancing towards a distant corner of the square and towards the house of Major-General Platt-Houston, she made the following extraordinary request:

"If you would do me a very great service, for which I always would be grateful"—she glanced at me with passionate intentness—"when you have given my message to the proper person, leave him and do not go near him any more tonight!"

Before I could find words to reply she gathered up her cloak and ran. Before I could determine whether or not to follow her (for her words had aroused anew all my worst suspicions) she had disappeared! I heard the whir of a re-started motor at no great distance, and, in the instant that Nayland Smith came running down the steps, I knew that I had nodded at my post.

"Smith!" I cried, as he joined me, "tell me what we must do!"

And rapidly I acquainted him with the incident.

My friend looked very grave; then a grim smile crept around his lips.

"She was a big card to play," he said, "but he did not know that I held one to beat it."

"What! You know this girl! Who is she?"

"She is one of the finest weapons in the enemy's armoury, Petrie. But a woman is a two-edged sword, and treacherous. To our great good fortune she has formed a sudden predilection, characteristically Oriental, for yourself. Oh, you may scoff, but it is evident. She was employed to get this letter placed in my hands. Give it to me."

I did so.

"She has succeeded. Smell."

He held the envelope under my nose, and with a sudden sense of nausea I recognized the strange perfume.

"You know what this presaged in Sir Crichton's case? Can you doubt any longer? She did not want you to share my fate, Petrie."

"Smith," I said unsteadily, "I have followed your lead blindly in this horrible business, and have not pressed for an explanation, but I must insist before I go one step further upon knowing what it all means."

"Just a few steps further," he rejoined, "as far as a cab. We are hardly safe here. Oh, you need not fear shots or knives. The man whose servants are watching us now scorns to employ such clumsy, tell-tale weapons."

Only three cabs were on the rank, and, as we entered the first, something hissed past my ear, missed both Smith and myself by a miracle, and, passing over the roof of the taxi, presumably fell in the enclosed garden occupying the centre of the square!

"What was that?" I cried.

"Get in—quickly!" Smith rapped back. "It was attempt number one! More than that I cannot say. Don't let the man hear. He has noticed nothing. Pull up the window on your side, Petrie, and look out behind. Good! We've started."

The cab moved off with a metallic jerk, and I turned and looked back through the little window in the rear.

"Some one has got into another cab. It is following ours, I think."

Nayland Smith lay back and laughed unmirthfully.

"Petrie," he said, "if I escape alive from this business I shall know that I bear a charmed life."

I made no reply, as he pulled out the dilapidated pouch and filled his pipe.

"You have asked me to explain matters," he continued, "and I will do so to the best of my ability. You no doubt wonder why a servant of the British Government, lately stationed in Burma, suddenly appears in London in the character of a detective. I am here, Petrie— and I bear credentials from the very highest sources—because, quite by accident, I came upon a clue. Following it up, in the ordinary course of routine, I obtained evidence of the existence and malignant activity of a certain man. At the present stage of the case I should not be justified in terming him the emissary of an Eastern Power, but I may say that representations are shortly to be made to that Power's ambassador in London."

He paused, and glanced back towards the pursuing cab.

'There is little to fear until we arrive home," he said calmly. "Afterwards there is much. To continue. This man, whether a fanatic, or a duly appointed agent, is, unquestionably, the most malign and formidable personality existing in the known world today. He is a linguist who speaks with almost equal facility in any of the civilized languages, and in most of the barbaric. He is an adept in all the arts and sciences which a great university could teach him. He also is an adept in certain obscure arts and sciences which *no* university of today can teach. He has the brains of any three men of genius. Petrie, he is a mental giant."

"You amaze me!" I said.

"As to his mission among men. Why did M. Jules Furneaux fall dead in a Paris opera-house? Because of heart failure? No! Because his last speech had shown that he held the key to the secret of Tongking. What became of the Grand Duke Stanislaus? Elopement? Suicide? Nothing of the kind. He alone was fully alive to Russia's growing peril. He alone knew the truth about Mongolia. Why was Sir Crichton Davey murdered? Because, had the work he was engaged upon ever seen the light, it would have shown him to be the only living Englishman who understood the importance of the Tibetan frontiers. I say to you solemnly, Petrie, that these are but a few. Is there a man who would arouse the West to a sense of the awakening of the East, who would teach the deaf to hear, the blind to see, that the millions only await their leader? He will die. And this is only one phase of the devilish campaign. The others I can merely surmise."

"But, Smith, this is almost incredible! What perverted genius controls this awful secret movement?"

"Imagine a person, tall, lean and feline, high-shouldered, with a brow like Shakespeare and a face like Satan, a close-shaven skull, and long, magnetic eyes of the true cat-green. Invest him with all the cruel cunning of an entire Eastern race, accumulated in one giant intellect, with all the resources of science past and present, with all the resources, if you will, of a wealthy government—which, however, already has denied all knowledge of his existence. Imagine that awful being, and you have a mental picture of Dr. Fu-Manchu, the yellow peril incarnate in one man."

CHAPTER THREE

THE ZAYAT KISS

I sank into an armchair in my rooms and gulped down a strong peg of brandy.

"We have been followed here," I said. "Why did you make no attempt to throw the pursuers off the track, to have them intercepted?"

Smith laughed.

"Useless, in the first place. Wherever we went, *he* would find us. And of what use to arrest his creatures? We could prove nothing against them. Further, it is evident that an attempt is to be made upon my life tonight—and by the same means that proved so successful in the case of poor Sir Crichton."

His square jaw grew truculently prominent, and he leapt stormily to his feet, shaking his clenched fists towards the window.

"The villain!" he cried. "The fiendishly clever villain! I suspected that Sir Crichton was next, and I was right. But I came too late, Petrie! That hits me hard, old man. To think that I knew and yet failed to save him!"

He resumed his seat, smoking vigorously.

"Fu-Manchu has made the blunder common to all men of unusual genius," he said. "He has underrated his adversary. He has not given me credit for perceiving the meaning of the scented messages. He has thrown away one powerful weapon—to get such a message into my hands—and he thinks that, once safe within doors, I shall sleep, unsuspecting, and die as Sir Crichton died. But, without the indiscretion of your charming friend, I should have known what to expect when I received her 'information'—which, by the way, consists of a blank sheet of paper."

"Smith," I broke in, "who is she?"

"She is either Fu-Manchu's daughter, his wife, or his slave. I am inclined to believe the latter, for she has no will but his will, except"—with a quizzical glance—"in a certain instance."

"How can you jest with some awful thing—heaven knows what— hanging over your head? What is the meaning of these perfumed envelopes? How did Sir Crichton die?"

"He died of the Zayat Kiss. Ask me what that is, and I reply, 'I do not know'. The zayats are the Burmese caravanserais, or rest-houses. Along a certain route—in which I set eyes, for the first and only time, upon Dr. Fu-Manchu—travellers who use them sometimes die as Sir Crichton died, with nothing to show the cause of death but a little mark upon the neck, face, or limb, which has earned, in those parts, the title of the 'Zayat Kiss'. The rest-houses along that route are shunned now. I have my theory, and I hope to prove it tonight, if I live. It will be one more broken weapon in his fiendish armoury, and it is thus, and thus only, that I can hope to crush him. This was my principal reason for not enlightening Dr. Cleeve. Even walls have ears where Fu-Manchu is concerned, so I feigned ignorance of the meaning of the mark, knowing that he would be almost certain to employ the same methods upon some other victim. I wanted an opportunity to study the Zayat Kiss in operation, and I shall have one."

"But the scented envelopes?"

"In the swampy forest of the district I have referred to a rare species of orchid, almost green, and with a peculiar scent, is sometimes met with. I recognized the heavy perfume at once. I take it that the thing which kills the travellers is attracted by this orchid. You will notice that the perfume clings to whatever it touches. I doubt if it can be washed off in the ordinary way. After at least one unsuccessful attempt to kill Sir Crichton—you recall that he thought there was something concealed in his study on a previous occasion?—Fu-Manchu hit upon the perfumed envelopes. He may have a supply of these green orchids in his possession—possibly to feed the creature."

"What creature? How could any creature have got into Sir Crichton's room tonight?"

"You no doubt observed that I examined the grate of the study. I found a fair quantity of fallen soot. I at once assumed, since it appeared to be the only means of entrance, that something had been dropped down; and I took it for granted that the thing, whatever it was, must still be concealed either in the study or in the library. But when I had obtained the evidence of the groom, Wills, I perceived that the cry from the lane or from the park was a signal. I noted that the movements of anyone seated at the study table were visible, in shadow, on the blind, and that the study occupied the corner of a two-storied wing, and therefore had a short chimney. What did the signal mean? That Sir Crichton had leapt up from his chair, and either had received the Zayat Kiss or had seen the thing which someone on the roof had lowered down the straight chimney. It was the signal to withdraw that deadly thing. By means of the iron stairway at the rear of Major-General Platt-Houston's, I quite easily gained access to the roof above Sir Crichton's study—and I found this."

Out from his pocket Nayland Smith drew a tangled piece of silk, mixed up with which were a brass ring and a number of unusually large-sized split-shot, nipped on in the manner usual on a fishing-line.

"My theory proven," he resumed. "Not anticipating a search on the roof, they had been careless. This was to weigh the line and to prevent the creature clinging to the walls of the chimney. Directly it had dropped in the grate, however, by means of this ring, I assume that the weighted line was withdrawn and the thing was only held by one slender thread, which sufficed, though, to draw it back again when it had done its work. It might have got tangled, of course, but they reckoned on its making straight up the carved leg of the writing-table for the prepared envelope. From there to the hand of Sir Crichton—which, from having touched the envelope, would also be scented with the perfume—was a certain move."

"My God! How horrible!" I exclaimed, and glanced apprehensively into the dusky shadows of the room. "What is your theory respecting this creature—what shape, what colour—?"

"It is something that moves rapidly and silently, I will venture no more at present, but I think it works in the dark, The study was dark, remember, save for the bright patch beneath the reading-lamp. I have observed that the rear of this house is ivy-covered right up to, and above, your bedroom. Let us make ostentatious preparations to retire, and I think we may rely upon Fu-Manchu's servants to attempt my removal, at any rate—if not yours."

"But, my dear fellow, it is a climb of thirty-five feet at the very least."

"You remember the cry in the back lane? It suggested something to me, and I tested my idea—successfully. It was the cry of a dacoit. Oh, dacoity, though quiescent, is by no means extinct. Fu-Manchu has dacoits in his train, and probably it is one who operates the Zayat Kiss, since it was a dacoit who watched the window of the study this evening. To such a man an ivy-covered wall is a grand staircase."

The horrible events that followed are punctuated in my mind, by the striking of a distant clock. It is singular how trivialities thus assert themselves in moments of high tension. I will proceed, then, by these punctuations, to the coming of the horror that it was written we should encounter.

The clock across the common struck two.

Having removed all traces of the scent of the orchid from our hands with a solution of ammonia, Smith and I had followed the programme laid down. It was an easy matter to reach the rear of the house, by simply climbing a fence, and we did not doubt that, seeing the light go out in the front, our unseen watcher would proceed to the back.

The room was a large one, and we had made up my camp-bed at one end, stuffing odds and ends under the clothes to lend the appearance of a sleeper, which device we also had adopted in the case of the larger bed. The perfumed envelope lay upon a little coffee-table in the centre of the floor, and Smith, with an electric pocket-lamp, a revolver and a brassy beside him, sat on cushions in the shadow of the wardrobe. I occupied a post between the windows.

No unusual sound, so far, had disturbed the stillness of the night. Save for the muffled throb of the rare all-night cars passing the front of the house, our vigil had been a silent one. The full moon had painted about the floor weird shadows of the clustering ivy, spreading the design gradually from the door, across the room, past the little table where the envelope lay, and finally to the foot of the bed.

The distant clock struck a quarter-past two.

A slight breeze stirred the ivy, and a new shadow added itself to the extreme edge of the moon's design.

Something rose, inch by inch, above the sill of the westerly window. I could see only its shadow, but a sharp, sibilant breath from Smith told me that he, from his post, could see the cause of the shadow.

Every nerve in my body seemed to be strung tensely. I was icily cold, expectant, and prepared for whatever horror was upon us.

The shadow became stationary. The dacoit was studying the interior of the room.

Then it suddenly lengthened, and, craning my head to the left, I saw a lithe, black-clad form, surmounted by a yellow face, sketchy in the moonlight, pressed against the window-panes!

One thin, brown hand appeared over the edge of the lowered sash, which it grasped—and then another. The man made absolutely no sound whatever. The second hand disappeared—and reappeared. It held a small, square box.

There was a very faint *click*.

The dacoit swung himself below the window with the agility of an ape, as, with a dull, sickening thud, *something* dropped upon the carpet!

"Stand still, for your life!" came Smith's voice, high-pitched.

A beam of white light leapt out across the room and played fully upon the coffee-table in the centre.

Prepared as I was for something horrible, I know that I paled at sight of the thing that was running around the edge of the envelope.

It was an insect, full six inches long, and of a vivid, venomous red colour! It had something of the appearance of a great ant, with its long, quivering antennae and its febrile, horrible vitality; but it was proportionately longer of body and smaller of head, and had numberless rapidly moving legs. In short, it was a giant centipede, apparently of the *scolopendra* group, but of a form quite new to me.

These things I realized in one breathless instant; in the next— Smith had dashed the thing's poisonous life out with one straight, true blow of the golf club!

I leapt to the window and threw it widely open feeling a silk thread brush my hand as I did so. A black shape was dropping, with incredible agility, from branch to branch of the ivy, and, without once offering a mark for a revolver-shot, it merged into the shadows beneath the trees of the garden.

As I turned and switched on the light Nayland Smith dropped limply into a chair, leaning his head upon his hands. Even that grim courage had been tried sorely.

"Never mind the dacoit, Petrie," he said. "Nemesis will know where to find him. We know now what causes the mark of the Zayat Kiss. Therefore science is richer for our first brush with the enemy, and the enemy is poorer—unless he has any more unclassified centipedes. I understand now something that has been puzzling me since I heard of it—Sir Crichton's stifled cry. When we remember that he was almost past speech, it is reasonable to suppose that his cry was not 'The red hand!' but 'The red *ant*!' Petrie, to think that I failed, by less than an hour, to save him from such an end!"

CHAPTER FOUR

THE CLUE OF THE PIGTAIL

"The body of a lascar dressed in the manner usual on the P & O boats, was recovered from the Thames off Tilbury by the river police at six a.m. this morning. It is supposed that the man met with an accident in leaving his ship."

Nayland Smith passed me the evening paper, and pointed to the above paragraph.

"For 'lascar' read 'dacoit'," he said. "Our visitor, who came by way of the ivy, fortunately for us failed to follow his instructions. Also, he lost the centipede and left a clue behind him. Dr. Fu-Manchu does not overlook such lapses."

It was a sidelight upon the character of the awful being with whom we had to deal. My very soul recoiled from bare consideration of the fate that would be ours if ever we fell into his hands.

The telephone bell rang. I went out and found that Inspector Weymouth of New Scotland Yard had called us up.

"Will Mr. Nayland Smith please come to the Wapping River Police Station at once?" was the message.

Peaceful interludes were few enough throughout that wild pursuit.

"It is certainly something important," said my friend, "and, if Fu-Manchu is at the bottom of it—as we must presume him to be— probably something ghastly."

A brief survey of the timetables showed us that there were no trains to serve our haste. We accordingly chartered a cab and proceeded east.

Smith, throughout the journey, talked entertainingly about his work in Burma. Of intent, I think, he avoided any reference to the circumstances which first had brought him in contact with the sinister genius of the Yellow movement. His talk was rather of the sunshine of the East than of its shadows.

But the drive concluded—and all too soon. In a silence which neither of us seemed disposed to break, we entered the police depôt, and followed an officer, who received us, into the room where Weymouth waited.

The inspector greeted us briefly, nodding toward the table.

"Poor Cadby, the most promising lad at the Yard," he said; and his usually gruff voice had softened strangely.

Smith struck his right fist into the palm of his left hand and swore under his breath, striding up and down the neat little room. No one spoke for a moment, and in the silence I could hear the whispering of the Thames outside—of the Thames which had so many strange secrets to tell, and now was burthened with another.

He lay prone upon the deal table—this latest of the river's dead— dressed in rough sailor garb, and, to all outward seeming, a seaman of nondescript nationality—such as is no stranger in Wapping and Shadwell. His dark, curly hair clung clammily about the brown forehead; his skin was stained, they told me. He wore a gold ring in one ear, and three fingers of the left hand were missing.

"It was almost the same with Mason." The river police inspector was speaking. "A week ago, on a Wednesday, he went off in his own time on some funny business down St. George's way—and Thursday night the ten o'clock boat got the grapnel on him off Hanover Hole. His first two fingers on the right hand were clean gone, and his left hand was mutilated frightfully."

He paused and glanced at Smith.

"That lascar, too," he continued, "that you came down to see, sir; you remember his hands?"

Smith nodded.

"He was not a lascar," he said shortly. "He was a dacoit."

Silence fell again.

I turned to the array of objects lying on the table—those which had been found in Cadby's clothing. None of them were noteworthy, except that which had been found thrust into the loose neck of his shirt. This last it was which had led the police to send for Nayland Smith, for it constituted the first clue which had come to light pointing to the authors of these mysterious tragedies.

It was a Chinese pigtail. That alone was sufficiently remarkable; but it was rendered more so by the fact that the plaited queue was a false one, being attached to a most ingenious bald wig.

"You're sure it wasn't part of a Chinese make-up?" questioned Weymouth, his eye on the strange relic. "Cadby was clever at disguise."

Smith snatched the wig from my hands with a certain irritation, and tried to fit it on the dead detective.

"Too small by inches!" he jerked. "And look how it's padded in the crown. This thing was made for a most abnormal head."

He threw it down, and fell to pacing the room again.

"Where did you find him—exactly?" he asked.

"Limehouse Reach—under Commercial Dock Pier—exactly an hour ago."

"And you last saw him at eight o'clock last night?"—to Weymouth.

"Eight to a quarter-past."

"You think he has been dead nearly twenty-four hours, Petrie?"

"Roughly, twenty-four hours," I replied.

"Then, we know that he was on the track of the Fu-Manchu group, that he followed up some clue which led him to the neighbourhood of old Ratcliff Highway, and that he died the same night. You are sure that is where he was going?"

"Yes," said Weymouth. "He was jealous of giving anything away, poor chap; it meant a big lift for him if he pulled the case off. But he gave me to understand that he expected to spend last night in that district. He left the Yard about eight, as I've said, to go to his rooms and dress for the job."

"Did he keep any record of his cases?"

"Of course! He was most particular. Cadby was a man with ambitions, sir! You'll want to see his book. Wait while I get his address, it's somewhere in Brixton."

He went to the telephone, and Inspector Ryman covered up the dead man's face.

Nayland Smith was palpably excited.

"He almost succeeded where we have failed, Petrie," he said. "There is no doubt in my mind that he was hot on the track of Fu-Manchu! Poor Mason had probably blundered on the scent, too, and he met with a similar fate. Without other evidence, the fact that they both died in the same way as the dacoit would be conclusive, for we know that Fu-Manchu killed the dacoit!"

"What is the meaning of the mutilated hands, Smith?"

"God knows! Cadby's death was from drowning, you say?"

"There are no other marks of violence."

"But he was a very strong swimmer, doctor," interrupted Inspector Ryman. "Why, he pulled off the quarter-mile championship at the Crystal Palace last year! Cadby wasn't a man easy to drown. And as for Mason, he was an R.N.R., and like a fish in the water!"

Smith shrugged his shoulders helplessly.

"Let us hope that one day we shall know how they died," he said simply.

Weymouth returned from the telephone,

"The address is No.—Coldharbour Lane," he reported. "I shall not be able to come along, but you can't miss it; it's close by the Brixton Police Station. There's no family, fortunately; he was quite alone in the world. His case-book isn't in the American desk which you'll find in his sitting-room; it's in the cupboard in the corner—top shelf. Here are his keys, all intact. I think this is the cupboard key."

Smith nodded.

"Come on, Petrie," he said. "We haven't a second to waste."

Our cab was waiting, and in a few seconds we were speeding along Wapping High Street. We had gone no more than a few hundred yards, I think, when Smith suddenly slapped his open hand down on his knee.

"That pigtail!" he cried. "I have left it behind! We must have it, Petrie! Stop! Stop!"

The cab was pulled up, and Smith alighted.

"Don't wait for me," he directed hurriedly. "Here, take Weymouth's card. Remember where he said the book was? It's all we want. Come straight on to Scotland Yard and meet me there."

"But, Smith," I protested, "a few minutes can make no difference!"

"Can't it!" he snapped. "Do you suppose Fu-Manchu is going to leave evidence like that lying about? It's a thousand to one he has it already, but there is just a bare chance."

It was a new aspect of the situation, and one that afforded no room for comment; and so lost in thought did I become that the cab was outside the house for which I was bound ere I realized that we had quitted the purlieus of Wapping. Yet I had had leisure to review the whole troop of events which had crowded my life since the return of Nayland Smith from Burma. Mentally, I had looked again upon the dead Sir Crichton Davey, and with Smith had waited in the dark for the dreadful thing that had killed him. Now, with those remorseless memories jostling in my mind, I was entering the house of Fu-Manchu's last victim, and the shadow of that giant evil seemed to lie upon it like a palpable cloud.

Cadby's old landlady greeted me with a queer mixture of fear and embarrassment in her manner.

"I am Dr. Petrie," I said, "and I regret that I bring bad news respecting Mr. Cadby."

"Oh, sir!" she cried. "Don't tell me that anything has happened to him!" And divining something of the mission on which I was come, for such sad duty often falls to the lot of the medical man, "Oh, the poor, brave lad!"

Indeed, I respected the dead man's memory more than ever from that hour, since the sorrow of the worthy old soul was quite pathetic, and spoke eloquently for the unhappy cause of it.

"There was a terrible wailing at the back of the house last night, Doctor, and I heard it again tonight, a second before you knocked. Poor lad! It was the same when his mother died."

At the moment I paid little attention to her words, for such beliefs are common, unfortunately; but when she was sufficiently composed I went on to explain what I thought necessary. And now the old lady's embarrassment took precedence of her sorrow, and presently the truth came out:

"There's a—young lady—in his rooms, sir."

I started. This might mean little or might mean much.

"She came and waited for him last night, Doctor—from ten until half-past—and this morning again. She came the third time about an hour ago, and has been upstairs since."

"Do you know her, Mrs. Dolan?"

Mrs. Dolan grew embarrassed again.

"Well, Doctor," she said, wiping her eyes the while, "I *do*. And God knows he was a good lad, and I like a mother to him; but she is not the girl I should have liked a son of mine to take up with."

At any other time, this would have been amusing; now, it might be serious. Mrs. Dolan's account of the wailing became suddenly significant, for perhaps it meant that one of Fu-Manchu's dacoit followers was watching the house, to give warning of any stranger's approach! Warning to whom? It was unlikely that I should forget the dark eyes of another of Fu-Manchu's servants. Was that lure of men even now in the house, completing her evil work?

"I should never have allowed her in his rooms—" began Mrs. Dolan again. Then there was an interruption.

A soft rustling reached my ears—intimately feminine. The girl was stealing down!

I leapt out into the hall, and she turned and fled blindly before me—back up the stairs! Taking three steps at a time, I followed her, bounded into the room above almost at her heels, and stood with my back to the door.

She cowered against the desk by the window, a slim figure in a clinging silk gown, which alone explained Mrs. Dolan's distrust. The gaslight was turned very low, and her hat shadowed her face, but could not hide its startling beauty, could not mar the brilliancy of the skin, nor dim the wonderful eyes of this modern Delilah. For it was she!

"So I came in time," I said grimly, and turned the key in the lock.

"Oh!" she panted at that, and stood facing me, leaning back with her jewel-laden hands clutching the desk edge.

"Give me whatever you have removed from here," I said sternly, "and then prepare to accompany me."

She took a step forward, her eyes wide with fear, her lips parted.

"I have taken nothing," she said. Her breast was heaving tumultuously. "Oh, let me go! Please, let me go!" And impulsively she threw herself forward, pressing clasped hands against my shoulders, and looking up into my face with passionate, pleading eyes.

It is with some shame that I confess how her charm enveloped me like a magic cloud. Unfamiliar with the complex Oriental temperament, I had laughed at Nayland Smith when he had spoken of this girl's infatuation. "Love in the East," he had said, "is like the conjurer's mango-tree; it is born, grows and flowers at the touch of a hand." Now, in those pleading eyes I read confirmation of his words. Her clothes or her hair exhaled a faint perfume. Like all Fu-Manchu's servants, she was perfectly chosen for her peculiar duties. Her beauty was wholly intoxicating.

But I thrust her away.

"You have no claim to mercy," I said. "Do not count upon any. What have you taken from here?"

She grasped the lapels of my coat.

"I will tell you all I can—all I dare," she panted eagerly, fearfully. "I should know how to deal with your friend, but with you I am lost! If you could only understand you would not be so cruel." Her slight accent, added charm to the musical voice. "I am not free, as your English women are. What I do I must do, for it is the will of my master, and I am only a slave. Ah, you are not a man if you can give me to the police. You have no heart if you can forget that I tried to save you once."

I had feared that plea, for, in her own Oriental fashion, she certainly had tried to save me from a deadly peril—at the expense of my friend. But I had feared the plea, for I did not know how to meet it. How could I give her up, perhaps to stand her trial for murder? And now I fell silent, and she saw why I was silent.

"I may deserve no mercy; I may be even as bad as you think; but what have *you* to do with the police? It is not your work to hound a woman to death. Could you ever look another woman in the eyes— one that you loved, and know that she trusted you—if you had done such a thing? Ah, I have no friend in all the world, or I should not be here. Do not be my enemy, my judge, and make me worse than I am; be my friend, and save me—from *him*." The tremulous lips were close to mine, her breath fanned my cheek. "Have mercy on me."

At that moment I honestly would have given half of my worldly possessions to have been spared the decision which I knew I must come to. After all, what proof had I that she was a willing accomplice of Dr. Fu-Manchu? Furthermore, she was an Oriental, and her code must necessarily be different from mine. Irreconcilable as the thing may be with Western ideas, Nayland Smith had really told me that he believed the girl to be a slave. Then there remained that other reason why I loathed the idea of becoming her captor. It was almost tantamount to betrayal! Must I soil my hands with such work?

Thus—I suppose—her seductive beauty argued against my sense of right. The jewelled fingers grasped my shoulders nervously, and her slim body quivered against mine as she watched me, with all her soul in her eyes, in an abandonment of pleading despair. Then I remembered the fate of the man in whose room we stood.

"You lured Cadby to his death," I said, and shook her off.

"No, no!" she cried wildly, clutching at me. "No, I swear by the holy name I did not! I did not! I watched him, spied upon him—yes! But, listen: it was because he would not be warned that he met his death. *I* could not save him! Ah, I am not so bad as that. I will tell you. I have taken his notebook and torn out the last pages and burnt them. Look! in the grate. The book was too big to steal away. I came twice and could not find it. There, will you let me go?"

"If you will tell me where and how to seize Dr. Fu-Manchu—yes."

Her hands dropped, and she took a backward step. A new terror was to be read in her face.

"I dare not! I dare not!"

"Then you would—if you dared?"

She was watching me intently.

"Not if *you* would go to find him," she said.

And, with all that I thought her to be, the stern servant of justice that I would have had myself, I felt the hot blood leap to my cheek at all which the words implied. She grasped my arm.

"Could you hide me from him if I came to you, and told you all I know?"

"The authorities—"

"Ah!" Her expression changed. "They can put me on the rack if they choose, but never one word would I speak—never one little word."

She threw up her head scornfully. Then the proud glance softened again.

"But I will speak for you."

Closer she came, and closer, until she could whisper in my ear.

"Hide me from your police, from *him*, from everybody, and I will no longer be his slave."

My heart was beating with painful rapidity. I had not counted on this warring with a woman; moreover, it was harder than I could have dreamt of. For some time I had been aware that by the charm of her personality and the art of her pleading she had brought me down from my judgment-seat—had made it all but impossible for me to give her up to justice. Now, I was disarmed—but in a quandary. What should I do? What *could* I do? I turned away from her and walked to the hearth, in which some paper ash lay and yet emitted a faint smell.

Not more than ten seconds elapsed, I am confident, from the time that I stepped across the room until I glanced back. But she was gone!

As I leapt to the door the key turned gently from the outside.

"*Ma'alesh!*" came her soft whisper, "but I am afraid to trust you—yet. Be comforted, for there is one near who would have killed you had I wished it. Remember, I will come to you whenever you will take me and hide me."

Light footsteps pattered down the stairs. I heard a stifled cry from Mrs. Dolan as the mysterious visitor ran past her. The front door opened, and closed.

CHAPTER FIVE

A THAMES-SIDE NOCTURNE

"Shen-Yan's is a dope shop in one of the burrows off the old Ratcliff highway," said Inspector Weymouth. " 'Singapore Charlie's,' they call it. It's a centre for some of the Chineses societies, I believe, but all sorts of opium-smokers use it. There have never been any complaints that I know of. I don't understand this."

We stood in his room at New Scotland Yard, bending over a sheet of foolscap upon which were arranged some burnt fragments from poor Cadby's grate, for so hurriedly had the girl done her work that combustion had not been complete.

"What do we make of this?" said Smith. " '... Hunchback ... lascar went up ... unlike others ... not return ... till Shen-Yan' (there is no doubt about the name, I think) 'turned me out ... booming sound ... lascar in ... mortuary I could ident ... not for days, or suspici ... Tuesday night in a different make ... snatch ... pigtail ...' "

"The pigtail again!" rapped Weymouth.

"She evidently burned the torn-out pages all together," continued Smith. "They lay flat, and this was in the middle. I see the hand

45

of retributive justice in that, Inspector. Now we have a reference to a hunchback, and what follows amounts to this: A lascar (amongst several other persons) went up somewhere—presumably upstairs—at Shen-Yan's, and did not come down again. Cadby, who was there disguised, noted a booming sound. Later, he identified the lascar in some mortuary. We have no means of fixing the date of this visit to Shen-Yan's, but I feel inclined to put down the 'lascar' as the dacoit who was murdered by Fu-Manchu! It is sheer supposition, however. But that Cadby meant to pay another visit to the place in a different 'make-up', or disguise, is evident, and that the Tuesday night proposed was last night is a reasonable deduction. The reference to a pigtail is principally interesting because of what was found on Cadby's body."

Inspector Weymouth nodded affirmatively, and Smith glanced at his watch.

"Exactly ten twenty-three," he said. "I will trouble you, Inspector, for the freedom of your fancy wardrobe. There is time to spend an hour in the company of Shen-Yan's opium fiends."

Weymouth raised his eyebrows.

"It might be risky. What about an official visit?"

Nayland Smith laughed.

"Worse than useless! By your own showing, the place is open to inspection. No; guile against guile? We are dealing with a Chinaman, with the incarnate essence of Eastern subtlety, with the most stupendous genius that the modern Orient has produced."

"I don't believe in disguises," said Weymouth, with a certain truculence. "It's mostly played out, that game, and generally leads to failure. Still, if you're determined, sir, there's an end of it. Foster will make your face up. What disguise do you propose to adopt?"

"A sort of Dago seaman, I think; something like poor Cadby. I can rely on my knowledge of the brutes, if I am sure of my disguise."

"You are forgetting me, Smith," I said.

He turned to me quickly.

"Petrie," he replied, "it is *my* business, unfortunately, but it is no sort of hobby."

"You mean that you can no longer rely upon me?" I said angrily.

Smith grasped my hand and met my rather frigid stare with a look of real concern on his gaunt, bronzed face.

"My dear old chap," he answered, "that was really unkind. You know that I meant something totally different."

"It's all right Smith," I said, immediately ashamed of my choler, and wrung his hand heartily "I can pretend to smoke opium as well as another. I shall be going, too, Inspector."

As a result of this little passage of words, some twenty minutes later two dangerous looking seafaring ruffians entered a waiting cab, accompanied by Inspector Weymouth, and were driven off into the wilderness of London's night. In this theatrical business there was, to my mind, something ridiculous—almost childish—and I could have laughed heartily had it not been that grim tragedy lurked so near to farce.

The mere recollection that somewhere at our journey's end Fu-Manchu awaited us was sufficient to sober my reflections— Fu-Manchu, who, with all the powers represented by Nayland Smith pitted against him, pursued his dark schemes triumphantly and lurked in hiding within this very area which was so sedulously patrolled—Fu-Manchu, whom I had never seen, but whose name stood for horrors indefinable! Perhaps I was destined to meet the terrible Chinese doctor tonight.

I ceased to pursue a train of thought which promised to lead to morbid depths, and directed my attention to what Smith was saying.

"We will drop down from Wapping and reconnoitre, as you say the place is close to the riverside. Then you can put us ashore somewhere below. Ryman can keep the launch close to the back of the premises, and your fellows will be hanging about near the front, near enough to hear the whistle."

"Yes," assented Weymouth, "I've arranged for that. If you are suspected, you shall give the alarm?"

"I don't know," said Smith thoughtfully. "Even in that event I might wait a while."

"Don't wait too long," advised the inspector. "We shouldn't be much wiser if your next appearance was on the end of a grapnel, somewhere down Greenwich Reach, with half your fingers missing."

The cab pulled up outside the river police depôt, and Smith and I entered without delay, four shabby-looking fellows who had been seated in the office springing up to salute the inspector, who followed us in.

"Guthrie and Lisle," he said briskly, "get along and find a dark corner which commands the door of Singapore Charlie's off the old Highway. You look the dirtiest of the troupe, Guthrie; you might drop asleep on the pavement, and Lisle can argue with you about getting home. Don't move till you hear the whistle inside or have my orders, and note everybody that goes in and comes out. You other two belong to this division?"

The C.I.D. men having departed, the remaining pair saluted again.

"Well, you're on special duty tonight. You've been prompt, but don't stick your chests out so much. Do you know of a back way to Shen-Yan's?"

The men looked at one another, and both shook thier heads.

"There's an empty shop nearly opposite, sir," replied one of them.

"I know a broken window at the back where we could climb in. Then we could get through to the front and watch from there."

"Good!" cried the inspector. "See you are not spotted, though; and if you hear the whistle, don't mind doing a bit of damage, but be inside Shen-Yan's like lightning. Otherwise, wait for orders."

Inspector Ryman came in, glancing at the clock.

"Launch is waiting," he said.

"Right," replied Smith thoughtfully. "I am half afraid, though, that the recent alarms may have scared our quarry—your man, Mason, and then Cadby. Against which we have that, so far as he is likely to know, there has been no clue pointing to this opium den. Remember, he thinks Cadby's notes are destroyed."

"The whole business is an utter mystery to me," confessed Ryman. "I'm told that there's some dangerous Chinese devil hiding somewhere in London, and that you expect to find him at Shen-Yan's. Supposing he uses that place, which is possible, how do you know he's there tonight?"

"I don't," said Smith, "but it is the first clue we have had pointing to one of his haunts, and time means precious lives where Dr. Fu-Manchu is concerned"

"Who is he, sir, exactly, this Dr. Fu-Manchu?"

"I have only the vaguest idea, Inspector; but he is no ordinary criminal. He is the greatest genius which the powers of evil have put on earth for centuries. He has the backing of a political group whose wealth is enormous, and his mission in Europe is *to pave the way*! Do you follow me? He is the advance-agent of a movement so epoch-making that not one Britisher, and not one American, in fifty thousand has ever dreamed of it."

Ryman stared, but made no reply, and we went out, passing down to the breakwater and boarding the waiting launch. With her crew of three, the party numbered seven that swung out into the Pool, and, clearing the pier, drew in again and hugged the murky shore.

The night had been clear enough hitherto, but now came scudding rainbanks to curtain the crescent moon, and anon to unveil her again and show the muddy swirls about us. The view was not extensive from the launch. Sometimes a deepening of the near shadows would tell of a moored barge, or lights high above our heads mark the deck of a large vessel. In the floods of moonlight gaunt shapes towered above; in the ensuing darkness only the oily glitter of the tide occupied the foreground of the night-piece.

The Surrey shore was a broken wall of blackness, patched with lights about which moved hazy suggestions of human activity. The bank we were following offered a prospect even more gloomy—a dense, dark mass, amid which, sometimes, mysterious half-tones told of a dock gate, or sudden high light leapt flaring to the eye.

Then, out of the mystery ahead, a green light grew and crept down upon us. A giant shape loomed up, and frowned crushingly upon the little craft. A blaze of light, the jangle of a bell, and it was past. We were dancing in the wash of one of the Scotch steamers, and the murk had fallen again.

Discords of remote activity rose above the more intimate throbbing of our screw, and we seemed a pigmy company floating past the workshops of Brobdingnagian toilers. The chill of near water communicated itself to me, and I felt the protection of my shabby garments inadequate against it.

Far over of the Surrey shore a blue light—vaporous, mysterious— flicked translucent tongues against the night's curtain. It was a weird, elusive flame, leaping, wavering, changing from blue to a yellowed violet, rising, falling.

"Only a gasworks," came Smith's voice, and I knew that he, too, had been watching those elfin fires. "But it always reminds me of a Mexican teocalli, and the altar of sacrifice."

The simile was apt, but gruesome. I thought of Dr. Fu-Manchu and the severed fingers, and could not repress a shudder.

"On your left, past the wooden pier! Not where the lamp is— beyond that; next to the dark, square building—Shen-Yan's."

It was Inspector Ryman speaking.

"Drop us somewhere handy, then," replied Smith, "and lie close in, with your ears wide open. We may have to run for it, so don't go far away."

From the tone of his voice I knew that the night mystery of the Thames had claimed at least one other victim.

"Dead slow," came Ryman's order. "We'll put in to the Stone Stairs."

CHAPTER SIX

THE OPIUM DEN

A seemingly drunken voice was droning from a neighbouring alleyway as Smith lurched in hulking fashion to the door of a little shop above which, crudely painted, were the words:

"SHEN-YAN, Barber."

I shuffled along behind him, and had time to note the box of studs, German shaving tackle and rolls of twist which lay untidily in the window, ere Smith kicked the door open, clattered down three wooden steps, and pulled himself up with a jerk, seizing my arm for support.

We stood in a bare and very dirty room, which could only claim kinship with a civilized shaving-saloon by virtue of the grimy towel thrown across the back of the solitary chair. A Yiddish theatrical bill of some kind, illustrated, adorned one of the walls, and another bill, in what may have been Chinese, completed the decorations. From behind a curtain heavily brocaded with filth a little Chinaman appeared, dressed in a loose smock, black trousers and thick-soled slippers, and, advancing, shook his head vigorously.

"No shavee—no shavee," he chattered, simian fashion, squinting from one to the other of us with his twinkling eyes. "Too late! Shuttee shop!"

"Don't you come none of it wi' me!" roared Smith, in a voice of amazing gruffness, and shook an artificially dirtied fist under the Chinaman's nose. "Get inside and gimme an' my mate a couple o' pipes. Smokee pipe, you yellow scum—savvy?"

My friend bent forward and glared into the other's eyes with a vindictiveness that amazed me, unfamiliar as I was with this form of gentle persuasion.

"Kop 'old o' that," he said, and thrust a coin into the Chinaman's yellow paw. "Keep me waitin' an' I'll pull the dam' shop down, Charlie. You can lay to it."

"No habe got pipee—" began the other.

Smith raised his fist, and Yan capitulated.

"Allee lightee," he said. "Full up—no loom. You come see see."

He dived behind the dirty curtain, Smith and I following, and ran up a dark stair. The next moment I found myself in an atmosphere which was literally poisonous. It was all but unbreathable, being loaded with opium fumes. Never before had I experienced anything like it. Every breath was an effort. A tin oil-lamp on a box in the middle of the floor dimly illuminated the horrible place, about the walls of which ten or twelve bunks were ranged and all of them occupied. Most of the occupants were lying motionless but one or two were squatting in their bunks noisily sucking at the little metal pipes. These had not yet attained to the opium-smoker's Nirvana.

"No loom—samee tella you," said Shen-Yan, complacently testing Smith's shilling with his yellow, decayed teeth.

Smith walked to a corner and dropped, cross-legged, on the floor, pulling me down with him.

"Two pipe quick," he said. "Plenty room. Two piecee pipe—or plenty heap trouble."

A dreary voice from one of the bunks came:

"Give 'im a pipe, Charlie, curse yer! An' stop 'is palaver."

Yan performed a curious little shrug, rather of the back than of the shoulders, and shuffled to the box which bore the smoky lamp. Holding a needle in the flame, he dipped it, when red-hot, into an old cocoa tin, and withdrew it with a bead of opium adhering to the end. Slowly roasting this over the lamp, he dropped it into the bowl of the metal pipe which he held ready, where it burned with a spirituous blue flame.

"Pass it over," said Smith huskily, and rose on his knees with the assumed eagerness of a slave to the drug.

Yan handed him the pipe, which he promptly put to his lips, and prepared another for me.

"Whatever you do, don't inhale any," came Smith's whispered injunction.

It was with a sense of nausea greater even than that occasioned by the disgusting atmosphere of the den that I took the pipe and pretended to smoke. Taking my cue from my friend, I allowed my head gradually to sink lower and lower, until, within a few minutes, I sprawled sideways on the floor, Smith lying close beside me.

"The ship's sinkin'," droned a voice from one of the bunks. "Look at the rats."

Yan had noiselessly withdrawn, and I experienced a curious sense of isolation from my fellows—from the whole of the Western world. My throat was parched with the fumes, my head ached. The vicious atmosphere seemed contaminating. I was as one dropped

Somewhere East of Suez, where the best is like the worst,

And there ain't no Ten Commandments, …

Smith began to whisper softly.

"We have carried it through successfully so far," he said. "I don't know if you have observed it, but there is a stair just behind you, half concealed by a ragged curtain. We are near that, and well in the dark. I have seen nothing suspicious so far—or nothing much. But if there was anything going forward it would no doubt be delayed until we new arrivals were well doped. *S-sh!*"

He pressed my arm to emphasize the warning. Through my half-closed eyes I perceived a shadowy form near the curtain to which he had referred. I lay like a log, but my muscles were tensed nervously.

The shadow materialized as the figure moved forward into the room with a curiously lithe movement.

The smoky lamp in the middle of the place afforded scant illumination, serving only to indicate sprawling shapes—here an extended hand, brown or yellow, there a sketchy, corpse-like face; whilst from all about rose obscene sighings and murmurings in far-away voices—an uncanny, animal chorus. It was like a glimpse of the Inferno seen by some Chinese Dante. But so close to us stood the newcomer that I was able to make out a ghastly parchment face, with small, oblique eyes, and a misshapen head crowned with a coiled pigtail, surmounting a slight, hunched body. There was something unnatural, inhuman, about that mask-like face, and something repulsive in the bent shape and the long, yellow hands clasped one upon the other.

Fu-Manchu, from Smith's account, in no way resembled this crouching apparition with the death's-head countenance and lithe movements; but an instinct of some kind told me that we were on the right scent—that this was one of the Doctor's servants. How I came to that conclusion, I cannot explain; but with no doubt in my mind that this was a member of the formidable murder group, I saw the yellow man creep nearer, nearer, silently bent and peering. He was watching *us*.

Of another circumstance I became aware, and a disquieting circumstance. There were fewer murmurings and sighings from the surrounding bunks. The presence of the crouching figure had created a sudden semi-silence in the den, which could only mean that some of the supposed opium-smokers had merely feigned coma and the approach of coma.

Nayland Smith lay like a dead man, and, trusting to the darkness, I, too, lay prone and still, but watched the evil face bending lower and lower, until it came within a few inches of my own. I completely closed my eyes.

Delicate fingers touched my right eyelid. Divining what was coming, I rolled my eyes up, as the lid was adroitly lifted and lowered again. The man moved away.

I had saved the situation! And noting anew the hush about me—a hush in which I fancied many pairs of ears listened—I was glad. For just a moment I realized fully how, with the place watched back and front, we yet were cut off, were in the hands of Far Easterns, to some extent in the power of members of that most inscrutably mysterious race, the Chinese.

"Good," whispered Smith at my side. "I don't think I could have done it. He took me on trust after that. My God! what an awful face. Petrie, it's the hunchback of Cadby's notes. Ah, I thought so. Do you see that?"

I turned my eyes around as far as was possible. A man had scrambled down from one of the bunks and was following the bent figure across the room.

They passed around us quietly, the little yellow man leading, with his curious, lithe gait, and the other, an impassive Chinaman, following. The curtain was raised, and I heard footsteps receding on the stairs.

"Don't stir," whispered Smith.

An intense excitement was clearly upon him, and he communicated it to me. Who was the occupant of the room above?

Footsteps on the stair, and the Chinaman reappeared, recrossed the floor, and went out. The little, bent man went over to another bunk, this time leading up the stair one who looked like a lascar.

"Did you see his right hand?" whispered Smith. "A dacoit! They come here to report and to take orders. Petrie, Dr. Fu-Manchu is up there."

"What shall we do?"—softly.

"Wait. Then we must try to rush the stairs. It would be futile to bring in the police first. He is sure to have some other exit. I will give the word while the little yellow devil is down here. You are nearer and will have to go first, but if the hunchback follows, I can then deal with him."

Our whispered colloquy was interrupted by the return of the dacoit, who recrossed the room as the Chinaman had done, and immediately took his departure. A third man, whom Smith identified as a Malay, ascended the mysterious stairs, descended, and went out; and a fourth, whose nationality it was impossible to determine, followed. Then, as the softly moving usher crossed to a bunk on the right of the outer door—

"Up you go, Petrie!" cried Smith, for further delay was dangerous and further dissimulation useless.

I leapt to my feet. Snatching my revolver from the pocket of the rough jacket I wore, I bounded to the stair and went blundering up in complete darkness. A chorus of brutish cries clamoured from behind, with a muffled scream rising above them all. But Nayland Smith was close behind as I raced along a covered gangway, in a purer air, and at my heels when I crashed open a door at the end and almost fell into the room beyond.

What I saw were merely a dirty table, with some odds and ends upon it of which I was too excited to take note, an oil-lamp swung by a brass chain above, and a man sitting behind the table. But from the moment that my gaze rested upon the one who sat there, I think if the place had been an Aladdin's palace I should have had no eyes for any of its wonders.

He wore a plain yellow robe, of a hue almost identical with that of his smooth, hairless countenance. His hands were large, long and bony, and he held them knuckles upward and rested his pointed chin upon their thinness. He had a great, high brow, crowned with sparse, neutral-coloured hair.

Of his face, as it looked out at me over the dirty table, I despair of writing convincingly. It was that of an archangel of evil, and it was wholly dominated by the most uncanny eyes that ever reflected a human soul, for they were narrow and long, very slightly oblique, and of a brilliant green. But their unique horror lay in a certain filminess (it made me think of the *membrana nictitans* in a bird) which, obscuring them as I threw awide the door, seemed to lift as I actually passed the threshold, revealing the eyes in all their brilliant viridescence.

I know that I stopped dead, one foot within the room, for the malignant force of the man was something surpassing my experience. He was surprised by this sudden intrusion—yes, but no trace of fear showed upon that wonderful face, only a sort of pitying contempt. And, as I paused, he rose slowly to his feet, never removing his gaze from mine.

"It's Fu-Manchu!" cried Smith over my shoulder, in a voice that was almost a scream. *"It's Fu-Manchu!* Cover him! Shoot him dead if—"

The conclusion of that sentence I never heard.

Dr. Fu-Manchu reached down beside the table, and the floor slipped from under me.

One last glimpse I had of the fixed green eyes, and with a scream I was unable to repress I dropped—dropped—dropped—and plunged into icy water, which closed over my head.

Vaguely I had seen a spurt of flame, had heard another cry following my own, a booming sound (the trap), the flat note of a police whistle. But when I rose to the surface impenetrable darkness enveloped me; I was spitting filthy, oily liquid from my mouth, and fighting down the black terror that had me by the throat—terror of the darkness about me, of the unknown depths beneath me, of the pit into which I was cast amid stifling stenches and the lapping of tidal water.

"Smith!" I cried ... "Help! Help!"

My voice seemed to beat back upon me, yet I was about to cry out again, when, mustering all my presence of mind and all my failing courage, I recognized that I had better employment for my energies, and began to swim straight ahead, desperately determined to face all the horrors of this place—to die hard if die I must.

A drop of liquid fire fell through the darkness and hissed into the water beside me!

I felt that, despite my resolution, I was going mad.

Another fiery drop—and another!

I touched a rotting wooden post and slimy timbers. I had reached one bound of my watery prison. More fire fell from above, and the scream of hysteria quivered, unuttered in my throat.

Keeping myself afloat with increasing difficulty in my heavy garments, I threw my head back and raised my eyes.

No more drops fell, and no more drops would fall; but it was merely a question of time for the floor to collapse. For it was beginning to emit a dull, red glow.

The room above me was in flames!

It was drops of burning oil from the lamp, finding passage through the cracks in the crazy flooring, which had fallen about me—for the death trap had reclosed, I suppose, mechanically.

My saturated garments were dragging me down, and now I could hear the flames hungrily eating into the ancient rottenness overhead. Shortly that cauldron would be loosed upon my head. The glow of the flames grew brighter ... and showed me the half-rotten piles upholding the building, showed me the tidal mark upon the slime-coated walls—showed me that there was no escape!

By some subterranean duct the foul place was fed from the Thames. By that duct, with the out-going tide, my body would pass, in the wake of Mason, Cadby, and many another victim!

Rusty iron rungs were affixed to one of the walls communicating with a trap—but the bottom three were missing!

Brighter and brighter grew the awesome light—the light of what should be my funeral pyre—reddening the oily water and adding a new dread to the whispering, clammy horror of the pit. But something it showed me ... a projecting beam a few feet above the water ... and directly below the iron ladder!

"Merciful heaven!" I breathed. "Have I the strength?"

A desire for laughter claimed me with sudden, all but irresistible force. I knew what it portended and fought it down—grimly, sternly.

My garments weighed upon me like a suit of mail; with my chest aching dully, my veins throbbing to bursting, I forced tired muscles to work, and, every stroke an agony, approached the beam. Nearer I swam ... nearer. Its shadow fell black upon the water, which now had all the seeming of a pool of blood. Confused sounds—a remote uproar—came to my ears. I was nearly spent ... I was in the shadow of the beam! If I could throw up one arm ...

A shrill scream sounded far above me!

"Petrie! Petrie!" (That voice must be Smith's!) "Don't touch the beam! For God's sake *don't touch the beam!* Keep afloat another few seconds and I can get to you!"

Another few seconds! Was that possible?

I managed to turn, to raise my throbbing head; and I saw the strangest sight which that night yet had offered Nayland Smith stood upon the lowest iron rung ... supported by the hideous, crook-backed Chinaman, who stood upon the rung above!

"I can't reach him!"

It was as Smith hissed the words despairingly that I looked up—and saw the Chinaman snatch at his coiled pigtail and pull it off! With it came the wig to which it was attached; and the ghastly yellow mask, deprived of its fastenings, fell from position!

"Here! Here! Be quick! Oh! Be quick! You can lower this to him! Be quick! Be quick!"

A cloud of hair came falling about the slim shoulders as the speaker bent to pass this strange life-line to Smith; and I think it was my wonder at knowing her for the girl whom that day I had surprised in Cadby's rooms which saved my life.

For I not only kept afloat, but kept my gaze upturned to that beautiful, flushed face, and my eyes fixed upon hers—which were wild with fear ... for me!

Smith, by some contortion, got the false queue into my grasp, and I, with the strength of desperation, by that means seized hold upon the lowest rung. With my friend's arm around me I realized that exhaustion was even nearer than I had supposed. My last distinct memory is of the bursting of the floor above and the big burning joist hissing into the pool beneath us. Its fiery passage striated with light two sword blades, riveted, edges up, along the top of the beam which I had striven to reach.

"The severed fingers—" I said; and swooned.

How Smith got me through the trap I do not know—nor how we made our way through the smoke and flames of the narrow passage it opened upon. My next recollection is of sitting up, with my friend's arm supporting me and Inspector Ryman holding a glass to my lips.

A bright glare dazzled my eyes. A crowd surged about us, and a clangour and shouting drew momentarily nearer.

"It's the engines coming," explained Smith, seeing my bewilderment, "Shen-Yan's is in flames. It was your shot as you fell through the trap, broke the oil-lamp."

"Is everybody out?"

"So far as we know."

"Fu-Manchu?"

Smith shrugged his shoulders.

"No one has seen him. There was some door at the back—"

"Do you think he may—"

"No," he said tensely. "Not until I see him lying dead before me shall I believe it."

Then memory resumed its sway. I struggled to my feet.

"Smith, where is she?" I cried. "Where is she?"

"I don't know," he answered.

"She's given us the slip, Doctor," said Inspector Weymouth, as a fire-engine came swinging around the corner of the narrow lane. "So has Mr. Singapore Charlie—and, I'm afraid, somebody else. We've got six or eight all-sorts, some awake and some asleep, but I suppose we shall have to let 'em go again. Mr. Smith tells me that the girl was disguised as a Chinaman. I expect that's why she managed to slip away."

I recalled how I had been dragged from the pit by the false queue, how the strange discovery which had brought death to poor Cadby had brought life to me, and I seemed to remember, too, that Smith had dropped it as he threw his arm about me on the ladder. Her mask the girl might have retained, but her wig, I felt certain, had been dropped into the water.

It was later that night, when the brigade still were playing upon the blackened shell of what had been Shen-Yan's opium-shop and Smith and I were speeding away in a cab from the scene of God knows how many crimes, that I had an idea.

"Smith," I said, "did you bring the pigtail with you that was found on Cadby?"

"Yes. I had hoped to meet the owner."

"Have you got it now?"

"No. I met the owner."

I thrust my hands deep into the pockets of the big pea-jacket lent to me by Inspector Ryman, leaning back in my corner.

"We shall never really excel at this business," continued Nayland Smith. "We are far too sentimental. I knew what it meant to us, Petrie, what it meant to the world, but I hadn't the heart. I owed her your life—I had to square the account."

CHAPTER SEVEN

REDMOAT

Night fell on Redmoat. I glanced from the window at the nocturne in silver and green which lay beneath me. To the west of the shrubbery, with its broken canopy of elms and beyond the copper beech which marked the centre of its mazes, a gap offered a glimpse of the Waveney where it swept into a broad. Faint bird-calls floated over the water. These, with the whisper of leaves, alone claimed the ear.

Ideal rural peace, and the music of an English summer evening; but to my eyes, every shadow holding fantastic terrors; to my ears, every sound a signal of dread. For the deathful hand of Fu-Manchu was stretched over Redmoat, at any hour to loose strange, Oriental horrors upon its inmates.

"Well," said Nayland Smith, joining me at the window, "we had dared to hope him dead, but we know now that he lives!"

The Rev. J. D. Eltham coughed nervously, and I turned, leaning my elbow upon the table, and studied the play of expression upon the refined, sensitive face of the clergyman.

"You think I acted rightly in sending for you, Mr. Smith?"

Nayland Smith smoked furiously.

"Mr. Eltham," he replied, "you see in me a man groping in the dark. I am today no nearer to the conclusion of my mission than upon the day when I left Mandalay. You offer me a clue; I am here. Your affair, I believe, stands thus. A series of attempted burglaries, or something of the kind, has alarmed your household. Yesterday, returning from London with your daughter, you were both drugged in some way, and, occupying a compartment to yourselves, you both slept. Your daughter awoke, and saw someone else in the carriage—a yellow-faced man who held a case of instruments in his hands."

"Yes. I was, of course, unable to enter into particulars over the telephone. The man was standing by one of the windows. Directly he observed that my daughter was awake, he stepped towards her."

"What did he do with the case in his hands?"

"She did not notice—or did not mention having noticed. In fact, as was natural, she was so frightened that she recalls nothing more, beyond the fact that she strove to arouse me, without succeeding, felt hands grasp her shoulders—and swooned."

"But someone used the emergency cord, and stopped the train."

"Greba has no recollection of having done so."

"H'm! Of course no yellow-faced man was on the train. When did you awake?"

"I was aroused by the guard, but only when he had repeatedly shaken me."

"Upon reaching Great Yarmouth you immediately called up Scotland Yard? You acted very wisely, sir. How long were you in China?"

Mr. Eltham's start of surprise was almost comical.

"It is perhaps not strange that you should be aware of my residence in China, Mr. Smith," he said; "but my not having mentioned it may seem so. The fact is"—his sensitive face flushed in palpable embarrassment—"I left China under what I may term an episcopal cloud. I have lived in retirement ever since. Unwittingly—I solemnly declare to you, Mr. Smith, unwittingly—I stirred up certain deep-seated prejudices in my endeavours to do my duty—my duty. I think you asked me how long ago I was in China? I was there from 1896 until 1900—four years."

"I recall the circumstances, Mr. Eltham," said Smith, with an odd note in his voice. "I have been endeavouring to think where I had come across the name, and a moment ago I remembered. I am happy to have met you, sir."

The clergyman blushed again like a girl, and slightly inclined his head, with its scanty, fair hair.

"Had Redmoat, as its name implies, a moat around it? I was unable to see in the dusk."

"It remains. Redmoat—a corruption of Round Moat—was formerly a priory, disestablished by the eighth Henry in 1536." His pedantic manner was quaint at times. "But the moat is no longer flooded. In fact, we grow cabbages in part of it. If you refer to the strategic strength of the place"—he smiled, but his manner was embarrassed again—"it is considerable. I have barbed-wire fencing, and—other arrangements. You see, it is a lonely spot," he added apologetically. "And now, if you will excuse me, we will resume these gruesome inquiries after the more pleasant affairs of dinner."

He left us.

"Who is our host?" I asked, as the door closed.

Smith smiled.

"You are wondering what caused the 'episcopal cloud'?" he suggested. "Well, the deep-seated prejudices which our reverend friend stirred up culminated in the Boxer Risings."

"Good heavens, Smith!" I said; for I could not reconcile the diffident personality of the clergyman with the memories which those words awakened.

"He evidently should be on our danger list," my friend continued quickly; "but he has so completely effaced himself of recent years that I think it probable that someone else has only just recalled his existence to mind. The Rev. J. D, Eltham, my dear Petrie, though he may be a poor hand at saving souls, at any rate has saved a score of Christian women from death— and worse."

"J.D. Eltham—" I began.

"Is 'Parson Dan'!" rapped Smith, "the 'Fighting Missionary', the man who with a garrison of a dozen cripples and a German doctor held the hospital at Nan-Yang against two hundred Boxers. That's who the Rev. J. D. Eltham is! But what he is up to now, I have yet to find out. He is keeping something back—something which has made him an object of interest to Young China!"

During dinner the matters responsible for our presence there did not hold priority in the conversation. In fact, this, for the most part, consisted in light talk of books and theatres.

Greba Eltham, the clergyman's daughter, was a charming young hostess, and she, with Vernon Denby, Mr. Eltham's nephew, completed the party. No doubt the girl's presence, in part, at any rate, led us to refrain from the subject uppermost in our minds.

These little pools of calm dotted along the torrential course of the circumstances which were bearing my friend and myself onward to unknown issues form pleasant, sunny spots in my dark recollections.

So I shall always remember, with pleasure, that dinner-party at Redmoat, in the old-world dining-room; it was so very peaceful, so almost grotesquely calm. For I, within my very bones, felt it to be the calm before the storm.

When, later, we men passed to the library, we seemed to leave that atmosphere behind us.

"Redmoat," said the Rev. J. D. Eltham, "has latterly become the theatre of strange doings."

He stood on the hearthrug. A shaded lamp upon the big table and candles in ancient sconces upon the mantelpiece afforded dim illumination. Mr. Eltham's nephew, Vernon Denby, lolled smoking on the window-seat, and I sat near to him. Nayland Smith paced restlessly up and down the room.

"Some months ago, almost a year," continued the clergyman, "a burglarious attempt was made upon the house. There was an arrest, and the man confessed that he had been tempted by my collection." He waved his hand vaguely towards the several cabinets about the shadowed room.

"It was shortly afterwards that I allowed my hobby for—playing at forts, to run away with me." He smiled an apology. "I virtually fortified Redmoat—against trespassers of any kind, I mean. You have seen that the house stands upon a kind of large mound. This is artificial, being the buried ruins of a Roman outwork; a portion of the ancient *castrum*." Again he waved indicatively, this time towards the window.

"When it was a priory it was completely isolated and defending by its environing moat. Today it is completely surrounded by barbed-wire fencing. Below this fence, on the east, is a narrow stream, a tributary of the Waveney; on the north and west, the highroad, but nearly twenty feet below, the banks being perpendicular. On the south is the remaining part of the moat—now my kitchen garden; but from there up to the level of the house is nearly twenty feet again, and the barbed wire must be counted with.

"The entrance, as you know, is by way of a kind of cutting. There is a gate of the foot of the steps (they are some of the original steps of the priory, Dr. Petrie), and another gate at the head."

He paused, and smiled around upon us boyishly.

"My secret defences remain to be mentioned," he resumed; and, opening a cupboard, he pointed to a row of batteries, with a number of electric bells upon the wall behind. "The more vulnerable spots are connected at night with these bells," he said triumphantly. "Any attempt to scale the barbed wire or to force either gate would set two or more of these ringing. A stray cow raised one false alarm," he added, "and a careless rook threw us into a perfect panic on another occasion."

He was so boyish—so nervously brisk and acutely sensitive—that it was difficult to see in him the hero of the Nan-Yang hospital. I could only suppose that he had treated the Boxers' raid in the same spirit wherein he met would-be trespassers within the precincts of Redmoat. It had been an escapade, of which he was afterwards ashamed, as, faintly, he was ashamed of his "fortifications".

"But," rapped Smith, "it was not the visit of the burglar which prompted these elaborate precautions."

Mr. Eltham coughed nervously.

"I am aware," he said, "that, having invoked official aid, I must be perfectly frank with you, Mr. Smith. It was the burglar who was responsible for my continuing the wire fence all around the grounds, but the electrical contrivance followed, later, as a result of several disturbed nights. My servants grew uneasy about some one who came, they said, after dusk. No one could describe this nocturnal visitor, but certainly we found traces. I must admit that.

"Then—I received what I may term a warning. My position is a peculiar one—a peculiar one. My daughter, too, saw this prowling person, over by the Roman *castrum*, and described him as a yellow man. It was the incident in the train, following closely upon this other, which led me to speak to the police, little as I desired to—er—court publicity."

Nayland Smith walked to a window, and looked out across the sloping lawn to where the shadows of the shrubbery lay. A dog was howling dismally somewhere.

"Your defences are not impregnable, after all, then?" he jerked. "On our way up this evening Mr. Denby was telling us about the death of his collie a few nights ago."

The clergyman's face clouded.

"That, certainly, was alarming," he confessed. "I had been in London for a few days, and during my absence Vernon came down, bringing the dog with him. On the night of his arrival it ran, barking, into the shrubbery yonder, and did not come out. He went to look for it with a lantern, and found it lying among the bushes, quite dead. The poor creature had been dreadfully beaten about the head."

"The gates were locked," Denby interrupted, "and no one could have got out of the grounds without a ladder and someone to assist him. But there was no sign of a living thing about. Edwards and I searched every corner."

"How long has that other dog taken to howling?" inquired Smith.

"Only since Rex's death," said Denby quickly.

"It is my mastiff," explained the clergyman, "and he is confined in the yard. He is never allowed on this side of the house."

Nayland Smith wandered aimlessly about the library.

"I am sorry to have to press you, Mr. Eltham," he said, "but what was the nature of the warning to which you referred, and from whom did it come?"

Mr. Eltham hesitated for a long time.

"I have been so unfortunate," he said at last, "in my previous efforts, that I feel assured of your hostile criticism when I tell you that I am contemplating an immediate return to Ho-Nan!"

Smith jumped round upon him as though moved by a spring.

"Then you are going back to Nan-Yang?" he cried. "Now I understand! Why have you not told me before? That is the key for which I have been vainly seeking. Your troubles date from the time of your decision to return?"

"Yes, I must admit it," confessed the clergyman diffidently.

"And your warning came from China?"

"It did."

"From a Chinaman?"

"From the Mandarin Yen Sun Yat."

"Yen Sun Yat! My good sir! He warned you to abandon your visit? And you reject his advice? Listen to me." Smith was intensely excited now, his eyes bright, his lean figure curiously strung up, alert. "The Mandarin Yen Sun Yat is one of the Seven!"

"I do not follow you, Mr. Smith."

"Possibly. China today is not the China of '98. It is a huge secret machine, and Ho-Nan one of its most important wheels! But if, as I understand, this official is a friend of yours, believe me, he has saved your life! You would be a dead man now if it were not for your friend in China! My dear sir, you must accept his counsel."

Then, for the first time since I had made his acquaintance, "Parson Dan" showed through the surface of the Rev. J.D. Eltham.

"No, sir!" replied the clergyman—and the change in his voice was startling. "I am called to Nan-Yang. Only One may deter my going."

The admixture of deep spiritual reverence with intense truculence in his voice was dissimilar from anything I ever had heard.

"Then only One can protect you," cried Smith, "for by heaven, no *man* will be able to do so! Your presence in Ho-Nan can do no possible good at present. It must do harm. Your experience in 1900 should be fresh in your memory."

"Hard words, Mr. Smith."

"The class of missionary work which you favour, sir, is injurious to international peace. At the present moment, Ho-Nan is a barrel of gunpowder; you would be the lighted match. I do not willingly stand between any man and what he chooses to consider his duty, but I insist that you abandon your visit to the interior of China!"

"You insist, Mr. Smith?"

"As your guest, I regret the necessity for reminding you that I hold authority to enforce it."

Denby fidgeted uneasily. The tone of the conversation was growing harsh and the atmosphere of the library portentous with brewing storms.

There was a short, silent interval.

"This is what I had feared and expected," said the clergyman. "This was my reason for not seeking official protection."

"The phantom Yellow Peril," said Nayland Smith, "today materializes under the very eyes of the Western world."

"The 'Yellow Peril'!"

"You scoff, sir, and so do others. We take the proffered right hand of friendship but do not inquire if the hidden left holds a knife? The peace of the world is at stake, Mr. Eltham. Unknowingly, you tamper with tremendous issues."

Mr. Eltham drew a deep breath, thrusting both hands in his pockets.

"You are painfully frank, Mr. Smith," he said; "but I like you for it. I will reconsider my position and talk this matter over again with you tomorrow."

Thus, then, the storm blew over. Yet I had never experienced such an overwhelming sense of imminent peril—of a sinister presence—as oppressed me at that moment. The very atmosphere of Redmoat was impregnated with Eastern devilry; it loaded the air like some evil perfume. And then through the silence cut a throbbing scream—the scream of a woman in direst fear.

"My God, it's Greba!" whispered Mr. Eltham.

CHAPTER EIGHT

THE THING IN THE SHRUBBERY

In what order we dashed down to the drawing-room I cannot recall. But none was before me when I leapt over the threshold and saw Miss Eltham prone by the French windows.

These were closed and bolted, and she lay, with hands outstretched, in the alcove which they formed. I bent over her. Nayland Smith was at my elbow.

"Get my bag," I said. "She has swooned. It is nothing serious."

Her father, pale and wide-eyed, hovered about me, muttering incoherently, but I managed to reassure him; and his gratitude when, I having administered a simple restorative, the girl sighed shudderingly and opened her eyes, was quite pathetic.

I would permit no questioning at that time, and on her father's arm she retired to her own rooms.

It was some fifteen minutes later that her message was brought to me. I followed the maid to a quaint little octagonal apartment, and Greba Eltham stood before me, the candlelight caressing the soft curves of her face and gleaming in the meshes of her rich brown hair.

When she had answered my first question she hesitated in pretty confusion.

"We are anxious to know what alarmed you, Miss Eltham."

She bit her lip and glanced with apprehension toward the window.

"I am almost afraid to tell Father," she began rapidly. "He will think me imaginative, but you have been so kind. It was two green eyes! Oh! Dr. Petrie, they looked up at me from the steps leading to the lawn. And they shone like the eyes of a cat."

The words thrilled me strangely.

"Are you sure it was not a cat, Miss Eltham?"

"The eyes were too large, Dr. Petrie. There was something dreadful, most dreadful, in their appearance. I feel foolish and silly for having fainted twice in two days! But the suspense is telling upon me, I suppose. Father thinks"—she was becoming charmingly confidential, as a woman often will with a tactful physician—"that shut up here we are safe from—whatever threatens us." I noted, with concern, a repetition of the nervous shudder. "But since our return some one else has been in Redmoat!"

"Whatever do you mean, Miss Eltham?"

"Oh! I don't quite know what I do mean, Dr. Petrie. What does it all mean? Vernon has been explaining to me that some awful Chinaman is seeking the life of Mr. Nayland Smith. But if the same man wants to kill my father, why has he not done so?"

"I am afraid you puzzle me."

"Of course, I must do so. But—the man in the train. He could have killed us both quite easily! And—last night someone was in Father's room."

"In his room!"

"I could not sleep, and I heard something moving. My room is the next one. I knocked on the wall and woke Father. There was nothing; so I said it was the howling of the dog that had frightened me."

"How could any one get into his room?"

"I cannot imagine. But I am not sure it was a man."

"Miss Eltham, you alarm me. What do you suspect?"

"You must think me hysterical and silly, but whilst Father and I have been away from Redmoat perhaps the usual precautions have been neglected. Is there any creature, any large creature, which could climb up the wall to the window? Do you know of anything with a long, thin body?"

For a moment I offered no reply, studying the girl's pretty face, her eager, blue-grey eyes widely opened and fixed upon mine. She was not of the neurotic type, with her clear complexion and sunkissed neck; her arms, healthily toned by exposure to the country airs, were rounded and firm, and she had the agile shape of a young Diana, with none of the anæmic languor which breeds morbid dreams. She was frightened; yes, who would not have been? But the mere idea of this thing which she believed to be in Redmoat, without the apparition of the green eyes, must have prostrated a victim of "nerves".

"Have you seen such a creature, Miss Eltham?"

She hesitated again, glancing down and pressing her finger-tips together.

"As Father awoke and called out to know why I knocked, I glanced from my window. The moonlight threw half the lawn into shadow, and just disappearing in this shadow was something— something of a brown colour, marked with sections!"

"What size and shape?"

"It moved so quickly I could form no idea of its shape; I saw quite six feet of it flash across the grass!"

"Did you hear anything?"

"A swishing sound in the shrubbery, then nothing more."

She met my eyes expectantly. Her confidence in my powers of understanding and sympathy was gratifying, though I knew that I but occupied the position of a father-confessor.

"Have you any idea," I said, "how it came about that you awoke in the train yesterday whilst your father did not?"

"We had coffee at a refreshment-room; it must have been drugged in some way. I scarcely tasted mine, the flavour was so awful; but father is an old traveller and drank the whole of his cupful!"

Mr. Eltham's voice called from below.

"Dr. Petrie," said the girl quickly, "what do you think they want to do to him?"

"Ah!" I replied, "I wish I knew that."

"Will you think over what I have told you? For I do assure you there is something here in Redmoat—something that comes and goes in spite of father's 'fortifications'! Caesar knows there is. Listen to him. He drags at his chain so that I wonder he does not break it."

As we passed downstairs the howling of the mastiff sounded eerily through the house, as did the *clank-clank* of the tightening chain as he threw the weight of his big body upon it.

I sat in Smith's room that night for some time, he pacing the floor smoking and talking.

"Eltham has influential Chinese friends," he said; "but they dare not have him in Nan-Yang at present. He knows the country as he knows Norfolk; he would see things!"

"His precautions here have baffled the enemy, I think. The attempt in the train points to an anxiety to waste no opportunity. But whilst Eltham was absent (he was getting his outfit in London, by the way) they have been fixing some second string to their fiddle here. In case no opportunity offered before he returned, they provided for getting at him here!"

"But how, Smith?"

"That's the mystery. But the dead dog in the shrubbery is significant."

"Do you think some emissary of Fu-Manchu is actually inside Redmoat?"

"It's impossible, Petrie. You are thinking of secret passages, and so forth. There are none. Eltham has measured up every foot of the place. There isn't a rat-hole left unaccounted for; and as for a tunnel under the moat, the house stands on a solid mass of Roman masonry, a former camp of Hadrian's time. I have seen a very old plan of the Round Moat Priory, as it was called. There are no entrance and no exit save by the steps. So how was the dog killed?"

I knocked out my pipe on a bar of the grate.

"We are in the thick of it here," I said.

"We are always in the thick of it," replied Smith. "Our danger is no greater in Norfolk than in London. But what do they want to do? That man in the train with the case of instruments—*what* instruments? Then the apparition of the green eyes tonight. Can they have been the eyes of Fu-Manchu? Is some peculiarly unique outrage contemplated—something calling for the presence of the master?"

"He may have to prevent Eltham's leaving England without killing him."

"Quite so. He probably has instructions to be merciful. But God help the victim of Chinese mercy!"

I went to my own room then. But I did not even undress, refilling my pipe and seating myself at the open window. Having looked upon the awful Chinese doctor, the memory of his face, with its filmed green eyes, could never leave me. The idea that he might be near at that moment was a poor narcotic.

The howling and baying of the mastiff was almost continuous.

When all else in Redmoat was still the dog's mournful note yet rose on the night with something menacing in it. I sat looking out across the sloping turf to where the shrubbery showed as a black island in a green sea. The moon swam in a cloudless sky, and the air was warm and fragrant with country scents.

It was in the shrubbery that Denby's collie had met his mysterious death—that the thing seen by Miss Eltham had disappeared. What uncanny secret did it hold?

Caesar became silent.

As the stopping of a clock will sometimes awaken a sleeper, the abrupt cessation of that distant howling, to which I had grown accustomed, now recalled me from a world of gloomy imaginings.

I glanced at my watch in the moonlight. It was twelve minutes past midnight.

As I replaced it the dog suddenly burst out afresh, but now in a tone of sheer anger. He was alternately howling and snarling in a way that sounded now to me. The crashes, as he leapt to the end of his chain, shook the building in which he was confined. It was as I stood up to lean from the window and command a view of the corner of the house that he broke loose.

With a hoarse bay he took that decisive leap, and I heard his heavy body fall against the wooden wall. There followed a strange, guttural cry … and the growling of the dog died away at the rear of the house. He was out! But that guttural note had not come from the throat of a dog. Of what was he in pursuit?

At which point his mysterious quarry entered the shrubbery I do not know. I only know that I saw absolutely nothing until Caesar's lithe shape was streaked across the lawn, and the great creature went crashing into the undergrowth.

Then a faint sound above and to my right told me that I was not the only spectator of the scene. I leant further from the window.

"Is that you, Miss Eltham?" I asked.

"Oh, Dr. Petrie!" she said. "I am so glad you are awake. Can we do nothing to help? Caesar will be killed."

"Did you see what he went after?"

"No," she called back—and drew her breath sharply.

For a strange figure went racing across the grass. It was that of a man in a blue dressing-gown, who held a lantern high before him, and a revolver in his right hand. Coincident with my recognition of Mr. Eltham, he leapt, plunging into the shrubbery in the wake of the dog.

But the night held yet another surprise; for Nayland Smith's voice came:

"Come back! Come back, Eltham!"

I ran out into the passage and downstairs. The front door was open. A terrible conflict waged in the shrubbery, between the mastiff and something else. Passing around to the lawn, I met Smith fully dressed. He had just dropped from a first-floor window.

"The man is mad!" he snapped. "Heaven knows what lurks there! He should not have gone alone!"

Together we ran towards the dancing light of Eltham's lantern. The sounds of conflict ceased suddenly. Stumbling over stumps and lashed by low-sweeping branches, we struggled forward to where the clergyman knelt amongst the bushes. He glanced up with tears in his eyes, as was revealed by the dim light.

"Look!" he cried.

The body of the dog lay at his feet.

It was pitiable to think that the fearless brute should have met his death in such a fashion, and when I bent and examined him I was glad to find traces of life.

"Drag him out. He is not dead," I said.

"And hurry," rapped Smith, peering about him right and left.

So we three hurried from that haunted place, dragging the dog with us. We were not molested. No sound disturbed the now perfect stillness.

By the lawn edge we came upon Denby, half dressed; and almost immediately Edwards the gardener also appeared. The white faces of the house servants showed at one window, and Miss Eltham called to me from her room, "Is he dead?"

"No," I replied; "only stunned."

We carried the dog around to the yard, and I examined his head. It had been struck by some heavy blunt instrument, but the skull was not broken. It is hard to kill a mastiff.

"Will you attend to him, Doctor?" asked Eltham. "We must see that the villain does not escape."

His face was grim and set. This was a different man from the diffident clergyman we knew; this was "Parson Dan" again.

I accepted the care of the canine patient, and Eltham with the others went off for more lights to search the shrubbery. As I was washing a bad wound between the mastiff's ears, Miss Eltham joined me. It was the sound of her voice, I think, rather than my more scientific ministration, which recalled Caesar to life. For, as she entered, his tail wagged feebly, and a moment later he struggled to his feet—one of which was injured.

Having provided for his immediate needs, I left him in charge of his young mistress and joined the search-party. They had entered the shrubbery from four points and drawn blank.

"There is absolutely nothing there, and no one can possibly have left the grounds," said Eltham amazedly.

We stood on the lawn looking at one another, Nayland Smith, angry but thoughtful, tugging at the lobe of his left ear, as was his habit in moments of perplexity.

CHAPTER NINE

THE THIRD VICTIM

With the first coming of light, Eltham, Smith and I tested the electrical contrivances from every point. They were in perfect order. It became more and more incomprehensible how any one could have entered and quitted Redmoat during the night. The barbed-wire fencing was intact, and bore no signs of having been tampered with.

Smith and I undertook an exhaustive examination of the shrubbery.

At the spot where we had found the dog, some five paces to the west of the copper beech, the grass and weeds were trampled and the surrounding laurels and rhododendrons bore evidence of a struggle, but no human footprint could be found.

"The ground is dry," said Smith. "We cannot expect much."

"In my opinion," I said, "someone tried to get at Caesar; his presence is dangerous. And in his rage he broke loose."

"I think so too," agreed Smith. "But why did this person make for here? And how, having mastered the dog, get out of Redmoat? I am open to admit the possibility of some one's getting in during the day whilst the gates are open, and hiding until dusk. But how in the name of all that's wonderful does he *get out*? He must possess the attributes of a bird."

I thought of Greba Eltham's statements, reminding my friend of her description of the thing which she had seen passing into this strangely haunted shrubbery.

"That line of speculation soon takes us out of our depth, Petrie," he said. "Let us stick to what we can understand, and that may help us to a clearer idea of what, at present, is incomprehensible. My view of the case to date stands thus:

"(1) Eltham, having rashly decided to return to the interior of China, is warned by an official whose friendship he has won in some way to stay in England.

"(2) I know this official for one of the Yellow group represented in England by Dr. Fu-Manchu.

"(3) Several attempts, of which we know but little, to get at Eltham are frustrated, presumably by his curious 'defences'. An attempt in a train fails owing to Miss Eltham's distaste for refreshment-room coffee. An attempt here fails owing to her insomnia.

"(4) During Eltham's absence from Redmoat certain preparations are made for his return. These lead to:

"(*a*) The death of Denby's collie;

"(*b*) The things heard and seen by Miss Eltham;

"(*c*) The things heard and seen by us all last night.

"So that the clearing up of my fourth point—*id est*, the discovery of the nature of these preparations—becomes our immediate concern. The prime object of these preparations, Petrie, was to enable someone to gain access to Eltham's room. The other events are incidental. The dogs *had* to be got rid of, for instance; and there is no doubt that Miss Eltham's wakefulness saved her father a second time."

"But from what? For heaven's sake, from what?"

Smith glanced about into the light-patched shadows.

"From a visit by someone—perhaps by Fu-Manchu himself," he said, in a hushed voice. "The object of that visit I hope we may never learn; for that would mean that it had been achieved."

"Smith," I said, "I do not altogether understand you; but do you think he has some incredible creature hidden here somewhere? It would be like him."

"I begin to suspect the most formidable creature in the known world to be hidden here. I believe Fu-Manchu is somewhere inside Redmoat!"

Our conversation was interrupted at this point by Denby, who came to report that he had examined the moat, the roadside, and the bank of the stream, but found no footprints or clue of any kind.

"No one left the grounds of Redmoat last night, I think," he said. And his voice had awe in it.

That day dragged slowly on. A party of us scoured the neighbourhood for traces of strangers, examining every foot of the Roman ruin hard by; but vainly.

"May not your presence here induce Fu-Manchu to abandon his plans?" I asked Smith.

"I think not," he replied. "You see, unless we can prevail upon him, Eltham sails in a fortnight. So the Doctor has no time to waste. Furthermore, I have an idea that his arrangements are of such a character that they *must* go forward. He might turn aside, of course, to assassinate me, if opportunity arose! But we know, from experience, that he permits nothing to interfere with his schemes."

There are few states, I suppose, which exact so severe a toll from one's nervous system as the *anticipation* of calamity.

All anticipation is keener, be it of joy or pain, than the reality whereof it is a mental forecast; but that inactive waiting at Redmoat, for the blow which we knew full well to be pending, exceeded, in its nerve taxation, anything of the kind I hitherto had experienced.

I felt as one bound upon an Aztec altar, with the priest's obsidian knife raised above my breast!

Secret and malign forces throbbed about us; forces against which we had no armour. Dreadful as it was, I count it a mercy that the climax was reached so quickly. And it came suddenly enough; for there in that quiet Norfolk home we found ourselves at handgrips with one of the mysterious horrors which characterized the operations of Dr. Fu-Manchu. It was upon us before we realized it. There is no incidental music to the dramas of real life. As we sat on the little terrace in the creeping twilight, I remember thinking how the peace of the scene gave the lie to my fears that we bordered upon tragic things. Then Caesar, who had been a docile patient all day, began howling again; and I saw Greba Eltham's shudder.

I caught Smith's eye, and was about to propose our retirement indoors, when the party was broken up in more turbulent fashion. I suppose it was the presence of the girl which prompted Denby to the rash act, a desire personally to distinguish himself; but, as I recalled afterwards, his gaze had rarely left the shrubbery since dusk, save to seek her face, and now he leapt wildly to his feet, overturning his chair, and dashed across the grass to the trees.

"Did you see it?" he yelled. "Did you see it?"

He evidently carried a revolver, for from the edge of the shrubbery a shot sounded, and in the flash we saw Denby with the weapon raised.

"Greba, go in and fasten the windows," cried Eltham. "Mr. Smith, will you enter the bushes from the west. Dr. Petrie, east. Edwards, Edwards—" And he was off across the lawn with the nervous activity of a cat.

As I made off in an opposite direction, I heard the gardener's voice from the lower gate, and I saw Eltham's plan. It was to surround the shrubbery.

Two more shots and two flashes burst from the dense heart of greenwood; then a loud cry—I thought, from Denby—and a second muffled one.

Following—silence, only broken by the howling of the mastiff.

I sprinted through the rose garden, leapt heedlessly over a bed of geranium and heliotrope, and plunged in among the bushes and under the elms. Away on the left I heard Edwards shouting, and Eltham's answering voice.

"Denby!" I cried, and yet louder: "Denby!"

But the silence fell again.

Dusk was upon Redmoat now, but from sitting in the twilight my eyes had grown accustomed to gloom, and I could see fairly well what lay before me. Not daring to think what might lurk above, below, around me, I pressed on into the midst of the thicket.

"Vernon!" came Eltham's voice from one side.

"Bear more to the right, Edwards," I heard Nayland Smith cry directly ahead of me.

With an eerie and indescribable sensation of impending disaster upon me, I thrust my way through to a grey patch which marked a break in the elmen roof. At the foot of the copper beech I almost fell over Eltham. Then Smith plunged into view. Lastly, Edwards the gardener rounded a big rhododendron and completed the party.

We stood quite still for a moment.

A faint breeze whispered through the beech leaves.

"Where is he?"

I cannot remember who put it into words; I was too dazed with amazement to notice. Then Eltham began shouting:

"Vernon! Vernon! *Vernon!*"

His voice pitched higher upon each repetition. There was something horrible about that vain calling, under the whispering beech, with shrubs banked about us cloaking God alone could know what.

From the back of the house came Caesar's faint reply.

"Quick! Lights!" rapped Smith. "Every lamp you have!"

Off we went, dodging laurels and privets, and poured out on to the lawn, a disordered company. Eltham's face was deathly pale, and his jaw set hard. He met my eye.

"God forgive me!" he said. "I could do murder tonight!"

He was a man composed of strange perplexities.

It seemed an age before the lights were found. But at last we returned to the bushes, really after a very brief delay; and ten minutes sufficed us to explore the entire shrubbery, for it was not extensive. We found his revolver, but there was no one there—nothing.

When we all stood again on the lawn, I thought that I had never seen Smith so haggard.

"What in heaven's name can we do?" he muttered. "What does it mean?"

He expected no answer; for there was none to offer one.

"Search! Everywhere," said Eltham hoarsely.

He ran off into the rose garden, and began beating about among the flowers like a madman, muttering: "Vernon! Vernon!"

For close upon an hour we all searched. We searched every square yard, I think, within the wire fencing, and found no trace.

Miss Eltham slipped out in the confusion, and joined with the rest of us in that frantic hunt. Some of the servants assisted too.

It was a group terrified and awestricken which came together again on the terrace. One and then another would give up, until only Eltham and Smith were missing. Then they came back together from examining the steps to the lower gate.

Eltham dropped on to a rustic seat, and sank his head in his hands.

Nayland Smith paced up and down like a newly caged animal, snapping his teeth together and tugging at his ear.

Possessed by some sudden idea, or pressed to action by his tumultuous thoughts, he snatched up a lantern and strode silently off across the grass and to the shrubbery once more. I followed him, I think his idea was that he might surprise any one who lurked there. He surprised himself, and all of us.

For right at the margin he tripped and fell flat. I ran to him.

He had fallen over the body of Denby, which lay there!

Denby had not been there a few moments before, and how he came to be there now we dared not conjecture. Mr. Eltham joined us, uttered one short, dry sob, and dropped upon his knees. Then we were carrying Denby back to the house, with the mastiff howling a *marche funèbre*.

We laid him on the grass where it sloped down from the terrace. Nayland Smith's haggard face was terrible. But the stark horror of the thing inspired him to that which, conceived earlier, had saved Denby. Twisting suddenly to Eltham, he roared in a voice audible beyond the river:

"Heavens! we are fools! *Loose the dog!*"

"But the dog—" I began.

Smith clapped his hand over my mouth.

"I know he's crippled," he whispered. "But if anything human lurks there, the dog will lead us to it. If a *man* is there, he will fly! Why did we not think of it before. Fools, fools!" He raised his voice again. "Keep him on leash, Edwards. He will lead us."

The scheme succeeded.

Edwards barely had started on his errand when bells began ringing inside the house.

"Wait!" snapped Eltham, and rushed indoors.

A moment later he was out again, his eyes gleaming madly.

"Above the moat," he panted. And we were off *en masse* around the edge of the trees.

It was dark above the moat; but not so dark as to prevent our seeing a narrow ladder of thin bamboo joints and silken cord hanging by two hooks from the top of the twelve-foot wire fence. There was no sound.

"He's out!" screamed Eltham. "Down the steps!"

We all ran our best and swiftest. But Eltham outran us. Like a fury he tore at bolts and bars, and like a fury sprang out into the road. Straight and white it showed to the acclivity by the Roman ruin. But no living thing moved upon it. The distant baying of the dog was borne to our ears.

"Curse it! He's crippled," hissed Smith. "Without him, as well pursue a shadow!"

A few hours later the shrubbery yielded up its secret, a simple one enough: a big cask sunk in a pit, with a laurel shrub cunningly affixed to its movable lid, which was further disguised with tufts of grass. A slender bamboo-jointed rod lay near the fence. It had a hook on the top, and was evidently used for attaching the ladder.

"It was the end of this ladder which Miss Eltham saw," said Smith, "as he trailed it behind him into the shrubbery when she interrupted him in her father's room. He and whomever he had with him doubtless slipped in during the daytime—whilst Eltham was absent in London—bringing the prepared cask and all necessary implements with them. They concealed themselves somewhere—probably in the shrubbery—and during the night made the *cache*. The excavated earth would be disposed of on the flower-beds; the dummy bush they probably had ready. You see, the problem of getting *in* was never a big one. But owing to the "defences" it was impossible (whilst Eltham was in residence at any rate) to get *out* after dark. For Fu-Manchu's purposes, then, a working-base *inside* Redmoat was essential. His servant—for he needed assistance—must have been in hiding somewhere outside; heaven knows where! During the day they could come or go by the gates, as we have already noted "

"You think it was the Doctor himself?"

"It seems possible. Whom else has eyes like the eyes Miss Eltham saw from the window last night?"

Then remains to tell the nature of the outrage whereby Fu-Manchu had planned to prevent Eltham's leaving England for China. This we learnt from Denby. For Denby was not dead.

It was easy to divine that he had stumbled upon the fiendish visitor at the very entrance to his burrow; had been stunned (judging from the evidence, with a sand-bag), and dragged down into the *cache*—to which he must have lain in such dangerous proximity as to render detection of the dummy bush possible in removing him. The quickest expedient, then, had been to draw him beneath. When the search of the shrubbery was concluded, his body had been borne to the edge of the bushes and laid where we found it.

Why his life had been spared, I cannot conjecture but provision had been made against his recovering consciousness and revealing the secret of the shrubbery. The ruse of releasing the mastiff alone had terminated the visit of the unbidden guest within Redmoat.

Denby made a very slow recovery; and, even when convalescent, consciously added not one fact to those we already had collated; for the reason that his memory had completely deserted him!

This, in my opinion, as in those of the several specialists consulted, was due, not to the blow on the head, but to the presence, slightly below and to the right of the first cervical curve of the spine, of a minute puncture—undoubtedly caused by a hypodermic syringe. Then, unconsciously, poor Denby furnished the last link in the chain; for undoubtedly, by means of this operation, Fu-Manchu had designed to efface from Eltham's mind his plans of return to Ho-Nan.

The nature of the fluid which could produce such mental symptoms was a mystery—a mystery which defied Western science: one of the many strange secrets of Dr. Fu-Manchu.

CHAPTER TEN

SECRET CHINA

Since Nayland Smith's return from Burma I had rarely taken up a paper without coming upon evidences of that seething which had cast up Dr. Fu-Manchu. Whether, hitherto, such items had escaped my attention or had seemed to demand no particular notice, or whether they now became increasingly numerous, I was unable to determine.

One evening, some little time after our sojourn in Norfolk, in glancing through a number of papers which I had brought in with me, I chanced upon no fewer than four items of news bearing more or less directly upon the grim business which engaged my friend and myself.

No white man, I honestly believe, appreciates the unemotional cruelty of the Chinese. Throughout the time that Dr. Fu-Manchu remained in England, the Press preserved a uniform silence upon the subject of his existence. This was due to Nayland Smith. But, as a result, I feel assured that my account of the Chinaman's deeds will meet, in many quarters, with an incredulous reception.

I had been at work, earlier in the evening, upon the opening chapters of this chronicle, and I had realized how difficult it would be for my reader, amid secure and cosy surroundings, to credit any human being with a callous villainy great enough to conceive and to put into execution such a death plot as that directed against Sir Crichton Davey.

One would expect God's worst man to shrink from employing—against however vile an enemy—such an instrument as the Zayat Kiss. So thinking, my eye was caught by the following:

EXPRESS CORRESPONDENT　　　NEW YORK

Secret service men of the United States Government are searching the South Sea Islands for a certain Hawaiian from the island of Maui, who, it is believed, has been selling poisonous scorpions to Chinese in Honolulu anxious to get rid of their children.

Infanticide, by scorpion and otherwise among the Chinese, has increased so terribly that the authorities have started a searching inquiry, which has led to the hunt for the scorpion dealer of Maui.

Practically all the babies that die mysteriously are unwanted girls, and in nearly every case the parents promptly ascribe the death to the bite of a scorpion, and are ready to produce some more or less poisonous insect in support of the statement.

The authorities have no doubt that infanticide by scorpion bite is a growing practice, and orders have been given to hunt down the scorpion dealer at any cost.

Is it any matter for wonder that such a people had produced a Fu-Manchu? I pasted the cutting into a scrap-book, determined that, if I lived to publish my account of those days, I would quote it therein as casting a sidelight upon Chinese character.

A Reuter message to *The Globe* and a paragraph in *The Star* also furnished work for my scissors. Here were evidences of the deep-seated unrest, the secret turmoil, which manifested itself so far from its centre as peaceful England in the person of the sinister Doctor.

HONG KONG, *Friday*

Li Hon Hung, the Chinaman who fired at the Governor yesterday, was charged before the magistrate with shooting at him with intent to kill, which is equivalent to attempted murder. The prisoner, who was not defended, pleaded guilty. The Assistant Crown Solicitor, who prosecuted, asked for a remand until Monday, which was granted.

Snapshots taken by the spectators of the outrage yesterday disclosed the presence of an accomplice, also armed with a revolver. It is reported that this man, who was arrested last night, was in possession of incriminating documentary evidence.

Later

Examination of the documents found on Li Hon Hung's accomplice has disclosed the fact that both men were well financed by the Canton Triad Society, the directors of which had enjoined the assassination of Sir F. M. or Mr. C. S., the Colonial Secretary. In a report prepared by the accomplice for despatch to Canton, also found on his person, he expressed regret that the attempt had failed.—*Reuter.*

It is officially reported in St. Petersburg that a force of Chinese soldiers and villagers surrounded the house of a Russian subject named Said Effendi, near Khotan, in Chinese Turkestan.

They fired at the house and set it in flames. There were in the house about 100 Russians, many of whom were killed.

The Russian Government has instructed its Minister at Peking to make the most vigorous representations on the subject.—*Reuter.*

Finally, in a Personal Column, I found the following:
HO-NAN. Have abandoned visit.—ELTHAM.

I had just pasted it into my book when Nayland Smith came in and threw himself into an armchair, facing me across the table. I showed him the cutting.

"I am glad, for Eltham's sake—and for the girl's," was his comment. "But it marks another victory for Fu-Manchu! Just heaven! why is retribution delayed!"

Smith's darkly tanned face had grown leaner than ever since he had begun his fight with the most uncanny opponent, I suppose, against whom a man ever had pitted himself. He stood up and began restlessly to pace the room, furiously stuffing tobacco into his briar.

"I have seen Sir Lionel Barton," he said abruptly; "and, to put the whole thing in a nutshell, he has laughed at me! During the months that I have been wondering where he had gone to he has been somewhere in Egypt. He certainly bears a charmed life, for on the evidence of his letter to *The Times* he has seen things in Tibet which Fu-Manchu would have the West blind to; in fact, I think he has found a new keyhole to the gate of the Indian Empire!"

Long ago we had placed the name of Sir Lionel Barton upon the list of those whose lives stood between Fu-Manchu and the attainment of his end. Orientalist and explorer, the fearless traveller who first had penetrated to Lhassa, who thrice, as a pilgrim, had entered into forbidden Mecca, he now had turned his attention again to Tibet—thereby signing his own death-warrant.

"That he has reached England alive is a hopeful sign?" I suggested.

Smith shook his head, and lighted the blackened briar.

"England at present is the web," he replied. "The spider will be waiting. Petrie, I sometimes despair. Sir Lionel is an impossible man to shepherd. You ought to see his house at Finchley. A low, squat place completely hemmed in by trees. Damp as a swamp; smells like a jungle. Everything topsy-turvy. He only arrived today, and he is working and eating (and sleeping, I expect) in a study that looks like an earthquake at Sotheby's auction-rooms. The rest of the house is half a menagerie and half a circus. He has a Bedouin groom, a Chinese body-servant, and heaven only knows what other strange people!"

"Chinese!"

"Yes, I saw him; a squinting Cantonese he calls Kwee. I don't like him. Also, there is a secretary known as Strozza, who has an unpleasant face. He is a fine linguist, I understand, and is engaged upon the Spanish notes for Barton's forthcoming book on the Mayapan temples. By the way, all Sir Lionel's baggage disappeared from the landing-stage—including his Tibetan notes."

"Significant!"

"Of course. But he argues that he has crossed Tibet from the Keun-Lun to the Himalayas without being assassinated, and therefore that it is unlikely he will meet with that fate in London. I left him dictating the book from memory, at the rate of about two hundred words a minute."

"He is wasting no time."

"Wasting time! In addition to the Yucatan book and the work on Tibet, he has to read a paper at the Institute next week about some tomb he has unearthed in Egypt. As I came away, a van drove up from the docks and a couple of fellows delivered a sarcophagus as big as a boat. It is unique, according to Sir Lionel, and will go to the British Museum after he has examined it. The man crams six months' work into six weeks; then he is off again."

"What do you propose to do?"

"What *can* I do? I know that Fu-Manchu will make an attempt upon him. I cannot doubt it. Ugh! That house gave me the shudders. No sunlight, I'll swear, Petrie, can ever penetrate to the rooms, and when I arrived this afternoon clouds of gnats floated like motes wherever a stray beam filtered through the trees of the avenue. There's a steamy smell about the place that is almost malarious, and the whole of the west front is covered with a sort of monkey-creeper, which he has imported at some time or other. It has a close, exotic perfume that is quite in the picture. I tell you, the place was made for murder."

"Have you taken any precautions?"

"I called at Scotland Yard and sent a man down to watch the house, but—"

He shrugged his shoulders helplessly.

"What is Sir Lionel like?"

"A madman, Petrie. A tall, massive man, wearing a dirty dressing-gown of neutral colour; a man with untidy grey hair and a bristling moustache, keen blue eyes, and a brown skin; who wears a short beard or rarely shaves—I don't know which. I left him striding about among the thousand and one curiosities of that incredible room, picking his way through his antique furniture, works of reference, manuscripts, mummies, spears, pottery, and what not—sometimes kicking a book from his course, or stumbling over a stuffed crocodile or a Mexican mask—alternately dictating and conversing. Phew!"

For some time we were silent.

"Smith," I said, "we are making no headway in this business. With all the forces arrayed against him, Fu-Manchu still eludes us, still pursues his devilish, inscrutable way."

Nayland Smith nodded.

"And we don't know all," he said. "We mark such and such a man as one alive to the Yellow Peril, and we warn him—if we have time. Perhaps he escapes; perhaps he does not. But what do we know, Petrie, of those others who may die every week by his murderous agency? We cannot know *every one* who has read the riddle of China. I never see a report of someone found drowned, of an apparent suicide, of a sudden, though seemingly natural, death, without wondering. I tell you, Fu-Manchu is omnipresent; his tentacles embrace everything. I said that Sir Lionel must bear a charmed life. The fact that *we* are alive is a miracle."

He glanced at his watch.

"Nearly eleven," he said. "But sleep seems a waste of time—apart from its danger.

We heard a bell ring. A few moments later followed a knock at the room door.

"Come in!" I cried.

A girl entered with a telegram, addressed to Smith. His jaw looked very square in the lamplight, and his eyes shone like steel as he took it from her and opened the envelope. He glanced at the form, stood up and passed it to me, reaching for his hat, which lay upon my writing-table.

"God help us, Petrie!" he said.

This was the message:

"Sir Lionel Barton murdered. Meet me at his house at once.—WEYMOUTH, INSPECTOR."

CHAPTER ELEVEN

THE GREEN MIST

Although we avoided all unnecessary delay, it was close upon midnight when our cab swung around into a darkly shadowed avenue at the further end of which, as seen through a tunnel, the moonlight glittered upon the windows of Rowan House, Sir Lionel Barton's home.

Stepping out before the porch of the long, squat building, I saw that it was banked in, as Smith had said, by trees and shrubs. The façade showed mantled in the strange exotic creeper which he had mentioned, and the air was pungent with an odour of decaying vegetation, with which mingled the heavy perfume of the little nocturnal red flowers which bloomed luxuriantly upon the creeper.

The place looked a veritable wilderness, and when we were admitted to the hall by Inspector Weymouth I saw that the interior was in keeping with the exterior, for the hall was constructed from the model of some apartment in an Assyrian temple, and the squat columns, the low seats, the hangings, all were eloquent of neglect, being thickly dust-coated. The musty smell, too, was almost as pronounced here as outside beneath the trees.

To a library, whose contents overflowed in many literary torrents upon the floor, the detective conducted us.

"Good heavens!" I cried, "what's that?"

Something leapt from the top of the bookcase, ambled silently across the littered carpet, and passed from the library like a golden streak. I stood looking after it with startled eyes. Inspector Weymouth laughed dryly.

"It's a young puma, or civet-cat, or something, Doctor," he said. "This house is full of surprises—and mysteries."

His voice was not quite steady, I thought, and he carefully closed the door ere proceeding further.

"Where is he?" asked Nayland Smith harshly. "How was it done?"

Weymouth sat down and lighted a cigar which I offered him.

"I thought you would like to hear what led up to it—so far as we know—before seeing him?"

Smith nodded.

"Well," continued the inspector, "the man you arranged to send down from the Yard got here all right and took up a post in the road outside, where he could command a good view of the gates. He saw and heard nothing, until going on for half-past ten, when a young lady turned up and went in."

"A young lady?"

"Miss Edmonds, Sir Lionel's shorthand typist. She had found, after getting home, that her bag, with her purse in, was missing, and she came back to see if she had left it here. She gave the alarm. My man heard the row from the road and came in. Then he ran out and rang us up. I came, and immediately wired for you."

"He heard the row, you say. What row?"

"Miss Edmonds went into violent hysterics!"

Smith was pacing the room now in tense excitement.

"Describe what he saw when he came in."

"He saw a negro footman—there isn't an Englishman in the house—trying to pacify the girl out in the hall yonder, and a Malay and another coloured man beating their foreheads and howling. There was no sense to be got out of any of them, so he started to investigate for himself. He had taken the bearings of the place earlier in the evening, and from the light in a window on the ground floor had located the study; so he set out to look for the door. When he found it, it was locked from the inside."

"Well?"

"He went out and round to the window. There's no blind, and from the shrubbery you can see into the lumber-room known as the study. He looked in, as apparently Miss Edmonds had done before him. What he saw accounted for her hysterics."

Both Smith and I were hanging upon his words.

"All amongst the rubbish on the floor, a big Egyptian mummy-case was lying on its side, and face downwards, with his arms thrown across it, lay Sir Lionel Barton."

"My God! Yes. Go on."

"There was only a shaded reading-lamp alight, and it stood on a chair, shining right down on him; it made a patch of light on the floor, you understand." The inspector indicated its extent with his hands. "Well, as the man smashed the glass and got the window open, and was just climbing in, he saw something else, so he says."

He paused.

"What did he see?" demanded Smith shortly.

"A sort of *green mist*, sir. He says it seemed to be alive. It moved over the floor, about a foot from the ground, going away from him and towards a curtain at the other end of the study."

Nayland Smith fixed his eyes upon the speaker.

"Where did he first see this green mist?"

"He says, Mr. Smith, that he thinks it came from the mummy-case."

"Yes; go on."

"It is to his credit that he climbed into the room after seeing a thing like that. He did. He turned the body over, and Sir Lionel looked horrible. He was quite dead. Then Croxted—that's the man's name—went over to this curtain. There was a glass door—shut. He opened it, and it gave on a conservatory—a place stacked from the tiled floor to the glass roof with more rubbish. It was dark inside, but enough light came from the study—it's really a drawing-room, by the way—as he'd turned all the lamps on, to give him another glimpse of this green, crawling mist. There are three steps to go down. On the steps lay a dead Chinaman."

"A dead Chinaman!"

"A dead Chinaman."

"Doctor seen them?" rapped Smith.

"Yes; a local man. He was out of his depth, I could see. Contradicted himself three times. But there's no need for another opinion—until we get the coroner's."

"And Croxted?"

"Croxted was taken ill, Mr. Smith, and had to be sent home in a cab."

"What ails him?"

Detective-Inspector Weymouth raised his eyebrows and carefully knocked the ash from his cigar.

"He held out until I came, gave me the story, and then fainted right away. He said that something in the conservatory seemed to get him by the throat."

"Did he mean that literally?"

"I couldn't say. We had to send the girl home, too, of course."

Nayland Smith was pulling thoughtfully at the lobe of his left ear.

"Got any theory?" he jerked.

Weymouth shrugged his shoulders.

"Not one that includes the green mist," he said. "Shall we go in now?"

We crossed the Assyrian hall, where the members of that strange household were gathered in a panic-stricken group. They numbered four. Two of them were negroes, and two Easterns of some kind. I missed the Chinaman, Kwee, of whom Smith had spoken, and the Italian secretary; and from the way in which my friend peered about into the shadows of the hall I divined that he, too, wondered at their absence. We entered Sir Lionel's study—an apartment which I despair of describing.

Nayland Smith's words, "an earthquake at Sotheby's auction-rooms", leapt to my mind at once; for the place was simply stacked with curious litter—loot of Africa, Mexico and Persia. In a clearing by the hearth a gas stove stood upon a packing-case, and about it lay a number of utensils for camp cookery. The odour of rotting vegetation, mingled with the insistent perfume of the strange night-blooming flowers, was borne in through the open window.

In the centre of the floor, beside an overturned sarcophagus, lay a figure in a neutral-coloured dressing-gown, face downwards, and arms thrust forward and over the side of the ancient Egyptian mummy-case.

My friend advanced and knelt beside the dead man.

"Good God!"

Smith sprang upright and turned with an extraordinary expression to Inspector Weymouth.

"You do not know Sir Lionel Barton by sight?" he rapped.

"No," began Weymouth, "but—"

"This is not Sir Lionel. This is Strozza, the secretary."

"What!" shouted Weymouth.

"Where is the other—the Chinaman—quick!" cried Smith.

"I have had him left where he was found—on the conservatory steps," said the inspector.

Smith ran across the room to where, beyond the open door, a glimpse might be obtained of stacked-up curiosities. Holding back the curtain to allow more light to penetrate, he bent forward over a crumpled-up figure which lay upon the steps below.

"It is!" he cried aloud. "It is Sir Lionel's servant, Kwee!"

Weymouth and I looked at one another across the body of the Italian; then our eyes turned together to where my friend, grim-faced, stood over the dead Chinaman. A breeze whispered through the leaves; a great wave of exotic perfume swept from the open window towards the curtained doorway.

It was a breath of the East—that stretched out a yellow hand to the West. It was symbolic of the subtle, intangible power manifested in Dr. Fu-Manchu, as Nayland Smith—lean, agile, bronzed with the suns of Burma—was symbolic of the clean British efficiency which sought to combat the insidious enemy.

"One thing is evident," said Smith: "no one in the house, Strozza excepted, knew that Sir Lionel was absent."

"How do you arrive at that?" asked Weymouth.

"The servants in the hall are bewailing him as dead. If they had seen him go out they would know that it must be someone else who lies here."

"What about the Chinaman?"

"Since there is no other means of entrance to the conservatory save through the study, Kwee must have hidden himself there at some time when his master was absent from the room."

"Croxted found the communicating door closed. What killed the Chinaman?"

"Both Miss Edmonds and Croxted found the study door locked from the inside. What killed Strozza?" retorted Smith.

"You will have noted," continued the inspector, "that the secretary is wearing Sir Lionel's dressing-gown. It was seeing him in that, as she looked in at the window, which led Miss Edmonds to mistake him for her employer—and consequently to put us on the wrong scent."

"He wore it in order that anybody looking in at the window would be sure to make that mistake," rapped Smith.

"Why?" I asked.

"Because he came here for a felonious purpose. See." Smith stopped and took up several tools from the litter on the floor. "There lies the lid. He came to open the sarcophagus. It contained the mummy of some notable person who flourished under Meneptah II; and Sir Lionel told me that a number of valuable ornaments and jewels probably were secreted amongst the wrappings. He proposed to open the thing and to submit the entire contents to examination tonight. He evidently changed his mind—fortunately for himself."

I ran my fingers through my hair in perplexity.

"Then what has become of the mummy?"

Nayland Smith laughed dryly.

"It has vanished in the form of a green vapour, apparently," he said. "Look at Strozza's face."

He turned the body over, and, used as I was to such spectacles, the contorted features of the Italian filled me with horror, so suggestive were they of a death more than ordinarily violent. I pulled aside the dressing-gown and searched the body for marks, but failed to find any. Nayland Smith crossed the room, and, assisted by the detective, carried Kwee, the Chinaman, into the study and laid him fully in the light. His puckered yellow face presented a sight even more awful than the other, and his blue lips were drawn back, exposing both upper and lower teeth. There were no marks of violence, but his limbs, like Strozza's, had been tortured during his mortal struggles into unnatural postures.

The breeze was growing higher, and pungent odour-waves from the damp shrubbery, bearing, too, the oppressive sweetness of the creeping plant, swept constantly through the open window. Inspector Weymouth carefully relighted his cigar.

"I'm with you this far, Mr. Smith," he said. "Strozza, knowing Sir Lionel to be absent, locked himself in here to rifle the mummy-case; for Croxted, entering by way of the window, found the key on the inside. Strozza didn't know that the Chinaman was hidden in the conservatory—"

"And Kwee did not dare to show himself, because he too was there for some mysterious reason of his own," interrupted Smith.

"Having got the lid off, something—somebody—"

"Suppose we say the mummy?"

Weymouth laughed uneasily.

"Well, sir, something that vanished from a locked room without opening the door or the window, killed Strozza."

"And something which, having killed Strozza, next killed the Chinaman, apparently without troubling to open the door behind which he lay concealed," Smith continued. "For once in a way, Inspector, Dr. Fu-Manchu has employed an ally which even his giant will was incapable entirely to subjugate. What blind force—what terrific agent of death—had he confined in that sarcophagus!"

"You think this is the work of Fu-Manchu?" I said. "If you are correct, his power indeed is more than human."

Something in my voice, I suppose, brought Smith right about. He surveyed me curiously.

"Can you doubt it? The presence of a concealed Chinaman surely is sufficient. Kwee, I feel assured, was one of the murder group, though probably he had only recently entered that mysterious service. He is unarmed, or I should feel disposed to think that his part was to assassinate Sir Lionel whilst, unsuspecting the presence of a hidden enemy, he was at work here. Strozza's opening the sarcophagus clearly spoiled the scheme."

"And led to the death—"

"Of a servant of Fu-Manchu. Yes. I am at a loss to account for that."

"Do you think that the sarcophagus entered into the scheme?"

My friend looked at me in evident perplexity.

"You mean that its arrival at the time when a creature of the Doctor—Kwee—was concealed here, may have been a coincidence?"

I nodded; and Smith bent over the sarcophagus, curiously examining the garish paintings with which it was decorated inside and out. It lay sideways upon the floor, and seizing it by its edge he turned it over.

"Heavy," he muttered; "but Strozza must have capsized it as he fell. He would not have laid it on its side to remove the lid. Hallo!"

He bent further fowards, catching at a piece of twine, and out of the mummy-case pulled a rubber stopper or "cork".

"This was stuck in a hole level with the floor of the thing," he said. "Ugh! it has a disgusting smell."

I took it from his hands, and was about to examine it, when a loud voice sounded outside in the hall. The door was thrown open, and a big man, who, despite the warmth of the weather, wore a fur-lined overcoat, rushed impetuously into the room.

"Sir Lionel!" cried Smith eagerly. "I warned you! And see, you have had a very narrow escape."

Sir Lionel Barton glanced at what lay upon the floor, then from Smith to myself, and from me to Inspector Weymouth. He dropped into one of the few chairs unstacked with books.

"Mr. Smith," he said, with emotion, "what does this mean? Tell me—quickly."

In brief terms Smith detailed the happenings of the night—or so much as he knew of them. Sir Lionel Barton listened, sitting quite still the while—an unusual repose in a man of such evidently tremendous nervous activity.

"He came for the jewels," he said slowly, when Smith was finished; and his eyes turned to the body of the dead Italian. "I was wrong to submit him to the temptation. God knows what Kwee was doing in hiding. Perhaps he had come to murder me, as you surmise, Mr. Smith, though I find it hard to believe. But—I don't think this is the handiwork of your Chinese doctor." He fixed his gaze upon the sarcophagus.

Smith stared at him in surprise. "What do you mean, Sir Lionel?"

The famous traveller continued to look towards the sarcophagus with something in his blue eyes that might have been dread.

"I received a wire from Professor Rembold tonight," he continued. "You were correct in supposing that no one but Strozza knew of my absence. I dressed hurriedly and met the professor at the Travellers'. He knew that I was to read a paper next week upon"—again he looked toward the mummy-case—"the tomb of Mekara; and he knew that the sarcophagus had been brought, untouched, to England. He begged me not to open it."

Nayland Smith was studying the speaker's face.

"What reason did he give for so extraordinary a request?" he asked.

Sir Lionel Barton hesitated.

"One," he replied at last, "which amused me—at the time. I must inform you that Mekara—whose tomb my agent had discovered during my absence in Tibet, and to enter which I broke my return journey at Alexandria—was a high priest and first prophet of Amen—under the Pharaoh of the Exodus; in short, one of the magicians who contested in magic arts with Moses. I thought the discovery unique, until Professor Rembold furnished me with some curious particulars respecting the death of M. Page le Roi, the French Egyptologist—particulars new to me."

We listened in growing surprise, scarcely knowing to what this tended.

"M. le Roi," continued Barton, "discovered, but kept secret, the tomb of Amenti—another of this particular brotherhood. It appears that he opened the mummy-case on the spot—these priests were of royal line, and are buried in the valley of Bibân-el-Molûk. His fellah and Arab servants deserted him for some reason—on seeing the mummy-case—and he was found dead, apparently strangled, beside it. The matter was hushed up by the Egyptian Government. Rembold could not explain why, but he begged of me not to open the sarcophagus of Mekara."

A silence fell.

The true facts regarding the sudden death of Page le Roi, which I now heard for the first time, had impressed me unpleasantly, coming from a man of Sir Lionel Barton's experience and reputation.

"How long had it lain in the docks?" jerked Smith.

"For two days, I believe. I am not a superstitious man, Mr. Smith, but neither is Professor Rembold, and now that I know the facts respecting Page le Roi, I can find it in my heart to thank God that I did not see ... whatever came out of that sarcophagus."

Nayland Smith stared him hard in the face.

"I am glad you did not, Sir Lionel," he said, "for whatever the priest, Mekara, has to do with the matter, by means of his sarcophagus, Dr. Fu-Manchu has made his first attempt upon your life. He has failed, but I hope you will accompany me from here to a hotel. He will not fail twice."

CHAPTER TWELVE

THE SLAVE

It was the night following that of the double tragedy at Rowan House. Nayland Smith, with Inspector Weymouth, was engaged in some mysterious inquiry at the docks, and I had remained at home to resume my strange chronicle. And—why should I not confess it?—my memories had frightened me.

I was arranging my notes respecting the case of Sir Lionel Barton. They were hopelessly incomplete. For instance, I had jotted down the following queries:—(1) Did any true parallel exist between the death of M. Page le Roi and the death of Kwee, the Chinaman, and of Strozza? (2) What had become of the mummy of Mekara? (3) How had the murderer escaped from a locked room? (4) What was the purpose of the rubber stopper? (5) Why was Kwee hiding in the conservatory? (6) Was the green mist a mere subjective hallucination—a figment of Croxted's imagination—or had he actually seen it?

Until these questions were satisfactorily answered, further progress was impossible. Nayland Smith frankly admitted that he was out of his depth. "It looks, on the face of it, more like a case for the Psychical Research people than for a plain Civil Servant, lately of Mandalay," he had said only that morning.

"Sir Lionel Barton really believes that supernatural agencies were brought into operation by the opening of the high priest's coffin. For my part, even if I believed the same, I should still maintain that Dr. Fu-Manchu controlled those agencies. But reason it out for yourself and see if we arrive at any common centre. Don't work so much upon the datum of the green mist, but keep to the *facts* which are established."

I commenced to knock out my pipe in the ash-tray; then paused, pipe in hand. The house was quite still, for my landlady and all the small household were out.

Above the noise of a passing tramcar I thought I had heard the hall door open. In the ensuring silence I sat and listened.

Not a sound could I detect. Stay! I slipped my hand into the table drawer, took out my revolver, and stood up.

There *was* a sound. Someone or something was creeping upstairs in the dark!

Familiar with the ghastly media employed by the Chinaman, I was seized with an impulse to leap to the door, shut and lock it. But the rustling sound proceeded, now, from immediately outside my partially open door. I had not the time to close it; knowing somewhat of the horrors at the command of Fu-Manchu, I had not the courage to open it. My heart leaping wildly, and my eyes upon that bar of darkness with its gruesome potentialities, I waited—waited for whatever was to come. Perhaps twelve seconds passed in silence.

"Who's there?" I cried. "Answer, or I fire!"

"Ah! no," came a soft voice, thrillingly musical. "Put it down— that pistol. Quick! I must speak to you."

The door was pushed open, and there entered a slim figure wrapped in a hooded cloak. My hand fell, and I stood, stricken to silence, looking into the beautiful dark eyes of Dr. Fu-Manchu's messenger—if her own statement could be credited, slave. On two occasions this girl, whose association with the Doctor was one of the most profound mysteries of the case, had risked—I cannot say what; unnameable punishment, perhaps—to save me from death; in both cases from a terrible death. For what was she come now?

Her lips slightly parted, she stood, holding her cloak about her, and watching me with great passionate eyes.

"How—" I began.

But she shook her head impatiently.

"*He* has a duplicate key of the house door," was her amazing statement. "I have never betrayed a secret of my master before, but you must arrange to replace the lock."

She came forward and rested her slim hands confidently upon my shoulders. "I have come again to ask you to take me away from him," she said simply.

And she lifted her face to me.

Her words struck a chord in my heart which sang with strange music, with music so barbaric that, frankly, I blushed to find it harmony. Have I said that she was beautiful? It can convey no faint conception of her. With her pure, fair skin, eyes like the velvet darkness of the East, and red lips so tremulously near to mine, she was the most seductively lovely creature I ever had looked upon. In that electric moment my heart went out in sympathy to every man who had bartered honour, country, all—for a woman's kiss.

"I will see that you are placed under proper protection," I said firmly, but my voice was not quite my own. "It is quite absurd to talk of slavery here in England. You are a free agent, or you could not be here now. Dr. Fu-Manchu cannot control your actions."

"Ah!" she cried, casting back her head scornfully, and releasing a cloud of hair, through whose softness gleamed a jewelled headdress. "No? He cannot? Do you know what it means to have been a slave? Here, in your free England, do you know what it means—the *razzia*, the desert journey, the whips of the drivers, the house of the dealer, the shame. Bah!"

How beautiful she was in her indignation!

"Slavery is put down, you imagine, perhaps? You do not believe that today—*today*—twenty-five English sovereigns will buy a Galla girl, who is brown, and"—whisper—"two hundred and fifty a Circassian, who is white. No, there is no slavery! So! Then what am I?"

She threw open her cloak, and it is a literal fact that I rubbed my eyes, half believing that I dreamed. For beneath she was arrayed in gossamer silk which more than indicated the perfect lines of her slim shape; wore a jewelled girdle and barbaric ornaments; was a figure fit for the walled garden of Stamboul—a figure amazing, incomprehensible, in the prosaic setting of my rooms.

"Tonight I had no time to make myself an English miss," she said, wrapping her cloak quickly about her. "You see me as I am."

Her garments exhaled a faint perfume, and it reminded me of another meeting I had had with her. I looked into the challenging eyes.

"Your request is but a pretence," I said. "Why do you keep the secrets of that man, when they mean death to so many?"

"Death! I have seen my own sister die of fever in the desert—seen her thrown like carrion into a hole in the sand. I have seen men flogged until they prayed for death as a boon. I have known the lash myself. Death! What does it matter?"

She shocked me inexpressibly. Enveloped in her cloak again, and with only her slight accent to betray her, it was dreadful to hear such words from a girl who, save for her singular type of beauty, might have been a cultured European.

"Prove, then, that you really wish to leave this man's service. Tell me what killed Strozza and the Chinaman," I said.

She shrugged her shoulders.

"I do not know that. But if you will carry me off"—she clutched me nervously—"so that I am helpless, lock me up so that I cannot escape, beat me, if you like, I will tell you all I do know. While he is my master I will never betray him. Tear me from him—by force, do you understand, *by force*, and my lips will be sealed no longer. Ah! but you do not understand, with your 'proper authorities'—your police. Police! Ah, I have said enough."

A clock across the common began to strike. The girl started and laid her hands upon my shoulders again. There were tears glittering among the curved black lashes.

"You do not understand," she whispered. "Oh, will you never understand and release me from him! I must go. Already I have remained too long. Listen. Go out without delay. Remain out—at a hotel, where you will, but do not stay here."

"And Nayland Smith?"

"What is he to me, this Nayland Smith? Ah, why will you not unseal my lips? You are in danger—you hear me, in danger! Go away from here tonight."

She dropped her hands and ran from the room. In the open doorway she turned, stamping her foot passionately.

"You have hands and arms," she cried, "and you let me go! Be warned, then; fly from here—" She broke off with something that sounded like a sob.

I made no move to stay her—this beautiful accomplice of the arch-murderer, Fu-Manchu. I heard her light footsteps pattering down the stairs, I heard her open and close the door—the door which was no barrier to Dr. Fu-Manchu. Still I stood where she had parted from me, and was so standing when a key grated in the lock and Nayland Smith came running up.

"Did you see her?" I began.

But his face showed that he had not done so, and rapidly I told him of my strange visitor, of her words, of her warning.

"How can she have passed through London in that costume?" I cried in bewilderment. "Where can she have come from?"

Smith shrugged his shoulders and began to stuff broad-cut mixture into the cracked briar.

"She might have travelled in a car or in a cab," he said, "and undoubtedly she came direct from the house of Dr. Fu-Manchu. You should have detained her, Petrie. It is the third time we have had that woman in our power, the third time we have let her go free."

"Smith," I replied, "I couldn't. She came of her own free will to give me a warning. She disarms me."

"Because you can see she is in love with you?" he suggested, and burst into one of his rare laughs when the angry flush rose to my cheek. "She is, Petrie—why pretend to be blind to it? You don't know the Oriental mind as I do; but I quite understand the girl's position. She fears the English authorities, but would submit to capture by you! If you would only seize her by the hair, drag her to some cellar, hurl her down, and stand over her with a whip, she would tell you everything she knows, and salve her strange Eastern conscience with the reflection that speech was forced from her. I am not joking; it is so, I assure you. And she would adore you for your savagery, deeming you forceful and strong!"

"Smith," I said, "be serious. You know what her warning meant before."

"I can guess what it means now," he rapped. "Hallo!"

Someone was furiously ringing the bell.

"No one at home?" said my friend. "I will go. I think I know what it is."

A few minutes later he returned, carrying a large square package.

"From Weymouth," he explained, "by district messenger. I left him behind at the docks, and he arranged to forward any evidence which subsequently he found. This will be fragments of the mummy."

"What! You think the mummy was abstracted?"

"Yes, at the docks. I am sure of it; and somebody else was in the sarcophagus when it reached Rowan House. A sarcophagus, I find, is practically air-tight, so that the use of the rubber stopper becomes evident—ventilation. How this person killed Strozza I have yet to learn."

"Also, how he escaped from a locked room. And what about the green mist?"

Nayland Smith spread his hands in a characteristic gesture.

"The green mist, Petrie, can be explained in several ways. Remember, we have only one man's word that it existed. It is at best a confusing datum, to which we must not attach a fictitious importance."

He threw the wrappings on the floor and tugged at a twine loop in the lid of the square box, which now stood upon the table. Suddenly the lid came away, bringing with it a lead lining, such as is usual in tea-chests. This lining was partially attached to one side of the box, so that the action of removing the lid at once raised and tilted it.

Then happened a singular thing. Out over the table billowed a sort of yellowish-green cloud—an oily vapour; and an inspiration, it was nothing less, born of a memory and of some words of my beautiful visitor, came to me.

"*Run, Smith!*" I screamed. "The door! the door, for your life! Fu-Manchu sent that box!"

I threw my arms around him. As he bent forward the moving vapour rose almost to his nostrils. I dragged him back and all but pitched him out on to the landing. We entered my bedroom, and there, as I turned on the light, I saw that Smith's tanned face was unusually drawn, and touched with pallor.

"It is a poisonous gas!" I said hoarsely, "in many respects identical with *chlorine*, but having unique properties which prove it to be something else—God, and Fu-Manchu, alone know what! It is the fumes of chlorine that kill the men in the bleaching-powder works. We have been blind—I particularly. Don't you see? There was no one in the sarcophagus, Smith, but there was enough of that fearful stuff to have suffocated a regiment!"

Smith clenched his fists convulsively.

"My God!" he said, "how can I hope to deal with the author of such a scheme? I see the whole plan. He did not reckon on the mummy-case being overturned, and Kwee's part was to remove the plug with the aid of the string—after Sir Lionel had been suffocated. The gas, I take it, is heavier than air."

"Chlorine gas has a specific gravity of 2.470," I said, "two and a half times heavier than air. You can pour it from jar to jar like a liquid—if you are wearing a chemist's mask. In these respects this stuff appears to be similar; the points of difference would not interest you. The sarcophagus would have emptied through the vent, and the gas have dispersed, with no clue remaining—except the smell."

"I did smell it, Petrie, on the stopper, but, of course, was unfamiliar with it. You may remember that you were prevented from doing so by the arrival of Sir Lionel? The scent of those infernal flowers must partially have drowned it, too. Poor, misguided Strozza inhaled the stuff, capsized the case in his fall, and all the gas—"

"Went pouring under the conservatory door, and down the steps, where Kwee was crouching. Croxted's breaking the window created sufficient draught to disperse what little remained. It will have settled on the floor now. I will go and open both windows."

Smith raised his haggard face.

"He evidently made more than was necessary to despatch Sir Lionel Barton," he said, "and contemptuously—you note the attitude, Petrie?—contemptuously devoted the surplus to me. His contempt is justified. I am a child striving to cope with a mental giant. It is by no wit of mine that Dr. Fu-Manchu scores a double failure."

CHAPTER THIRTEEN

I DREAM—AND AWAKEN

I will tell you, now, of a strange dream which I dreamed, and of the stranger things to which I awakened. Since, out of a blank—a void—this vision burst in upon my mind, I cannot do better than relate it without preamble. It was thus:

I dreamed that I lay writhing on the floor in agony indescribable. My veins were filled with liquid fire, and but that Stygian darkness was about me, I told myself that I must have seen the smoke arising from my burning body.

This, I thought, was death.

Then, a cooling shower descended upon me, soaked through skin and tissue to the tortured arteries and quenched the fire within. Panting, but free from pain, I lay—exhausted.

Strength gradually returning to me, I tried to rise; but the carpet felt so singularly soft that it offered me no foothold. I waded and plunged like a swimmer treading water; and all about me rose impenetrable walls of darkness, darkness all but palpable.

I wondered why I could not see the windows. The horrible idea flashed to my mind that I was become blind!

Somehow I got upon my feet, and stood swaying dizzily. I became aware of a heavy perfume, and knew it for some kind of incense.

Then—a dim light was born, at an immeasurable distance away. It grew steadily in brilliance. It spread like a bluish-red stain—like a liquid. It lapped up the darkness and spread throughout the room.

But this was not my room! Nor was it any room known to me.

It was an apartment of such size that its dimensions filled me with a kind of awe such as I never had known; the awe of walled vastness. Its immense extent produced a sensation of sound. Its hugeness had a distinct *note*.

Tapestries covered the four walls. There was no door visible. These tapestries were magnificently figured with golden dragons; and as the serpentine bodies gleamed and shimmered in the increasing radiance, each dragon, I thought, intertwined its glittering coils more closely with those of another. The carpet was of such richness that I stood knee-deep in its pile. And this, too, was fashioned all over with golden dragons; and they seemed to glide about amid the shadows of the design—stealthily.

At the further end of the hall—for hall it was—a huge table with dragon's legs stood solitary amid the luxuriance of the carpet. It bore scintillating globes, and tubes that held living organisms, and books of a size and in such bindings as I never had imagined, with instruments of a type unknown to Western science—a heterogeneous litter quite indescribable, which overflowed on to the floor, forming an amazing oasis in a dragon-haunted desert of carpet. A lamp hung above this table suspended by golden chains from the ceiling—which was so lofty that, following, the chains upward, my gaze lost itself in the purple shadows above.

In a chair piled high with dragon-covered cushions a man sat behind this table. The light from the swinging lamp fell fully upon one side of his face, as he leaned forward amid the jumble of weird objects, and left the other side in purplish shadow. From a plain brass bowl upon the corner of the huge table smoke writhed aloft and at times partially obscured that dreadful face.

From the moment that I looked toward the table and to the man who sat there, neither the incredible extent of the room, nor the nightmare fashion of its mural decorations, could reclaim my attention. I had eyes only for him.

For it was Dr. Fu-Manchu!

Something of the delirium which had seemed to fill my veins with fire, to people the walls with dragons, and to plunge me knee-deep in the carpet, left me. Those dreadful, filmed green eyes acted somewhat like a cold douche. I knew, without removing my gaze from the still face, that the walls no longer lived, but were merely draped in exquisite Chinese dragon tapestry. The rich carpet beneath my feet ceased to be as a jungle and became a normal carpet—extraordinarily rich, but merely a carpet. But the sense of vastness nevertheless remained, with the uncomfortable knowledge that the things upon the table and overflowing about it were all, or nearly all, of a fashion strange to me.

Then, and almost instantaneously, the comparative sanity which I had temporarily experienced began to slip from me again; for the smoke faintly pencilled through the air— from the burning perfume on the table—grew in volume, thickened, and wafted toward me in a cloud of grey horror. It enveloped me, clammily. Dimly, through its oily wreaths, I saw the immobile yellow face of Fu-Manchu. And my stupefied brain acclaimed him a sorcerer, against whom unavailingly we had pitted our poor human wits. The green eyes showed filmy through the fog. An intense pain shot through my lower limbs, and catching my breath, I looked down. As I did so, the points of the red slippers which I dreamed that I wore increased in length, curled sinuously upward, twined about my throat and choked the breath from my body!

Came an interval, and then a dawning like consciousness; but it was a false consciousness, since it brought with it the idea that my head lay softly pillowed and that a woman's hand caressed my throbbing forehead. Confusedly, as though in the remote past, I recalled a kiss—and the recollection thrilled me strangely. Dreamily content I lay, and a voice stole to my ears:

"They are killing him! They are killing him! Oh! do you not understand?"

In my dazed condition, I thought that it was I who had died, and that this musical girl-voice was communicating to me the fact of my own dissolution.

But I was conscious of no interest in the matter.

For hours and hours, I thought, that soothing hand caressed me. I never once raised my heavy lids, until there came a resounding crash that seemed to set my very bones vibrating—a metallic, jangling crash, as the fall of heavy chains. I thought that, then, I half opened my eyes, and that in the dimness I had a fleeting glimpse of a figure clad in gossamer silk, with arms covered in barbaric bangles and slim ankles surrounded by gold bands. The girl was gone, even as I told myself that she was an houri, and that I, though a Christian, had been consigned by some error to the paradise of Mohammed.

Then—a complete blank.

My head throbbed madly; my brain seemed to be clogged—inert; and though my first, feeble movement was followed by the rattle of a chain, some moments more elapsed ere I realized that the chain was fastened to a steel collar—that the steel collar was clasped about my neck.

I moaned weakly.

"Smith!" I muttered, "where are you? Smith!"

On to my knees I struggled, and the pain on the top of my skull grew all but insupportable. It was coming back to me now: how Nayland Smith and I had started for the hotel to warn Graham Guthrie; how, as we passed up the steps from the Embankment and into Essex Street, we saw the big motor standing before the door of one of the offices. I could recall coming up level with the car— a modern limousine; but my mind retained no impression of our having passed it—only a vague memory of a rush of footsteps—a blow. Then, my vision of the hall of dragons, and now this real awakening to a worse reality.

Groping in the darkness, my hands touched a body that lay close beside me. My fingers sought and found the throat, sought and found the steel collar about it.

"Smith," I groaned; and I shook the still form. "Smith, old man —speak to me! Smith!"

Could he be dead? Was this the end of his gallant fight with Dr. Fu-Manchu and the murder group? If so, what did the future hold for me—what had I to face?

He stirred beneath my trembling hands.

"Thank God!" I muttered, and I cannot deny that my joy was tainted with selfishness. For, waking in that impenetrable darkness, and yet obsessed with the dream I had dreamed, I had known what fear meant, at the realization that alone, chained, I must face the dreadful Chinese doctor in the flesh.

Smith began incoherent mutterings.

"Sand-bagged! ... Look out, Petrie! ... He has us at last! ... Oh, heavens! ... He struggled on to his knees, clutching at my hand.

"All right, old man," I said. "We are both alive, so let's be thankful."

A moment's silence, a groan, then:

"Petrie, I have dragged you into this. God forgive me—"

"Dry up, Smith," I said slowly. "I'm not a child. There is no question of being dragged into the matter. I'm here; and if I can be of any use, I'm glad I am here!"

He grasped my hand.

"There were two Chinese, in European clothes—lord, how my head throbs!—in that office door. They sandbagged us, Petrie—think of it!—in broad daylight, within hail of the Strand! We were rushed into the car—and it was all over before—" His voice grew faint. "God! they gave me an awful knock!"

"Why have we been spared, Smith? Do you think he is saving us for—"

"Don't, Petrie! If you had been in China, if you had seen what I have seen—"

Footsteps sounded on the flagged passage. A blade of light crept across the floor towards us. My brain was growing clearer. The place had a damp, earthen smell. It was slimy—some noisome cellar. A door was thrown open and a man entered, carrying a lantern. Its light showed my surmise to be accurate, showed the slime-coated walls of a dungeon some fifteen feet square—shone upon the long yellow robe of the man who stood watching us, upon the malignant, intellectual countenance.

It was Dr. Fu-Manchu.

At last they truly were face to face—the head of the great Yellow movement, and the man who fought on behalf of the entire white race. How can I paint the individual whom now I had leisure to study—perhaps the greatest genius of modern times? Of him it has been fitly said that he had a brow like Shakespeare and a face like Satan. Something serpentine, hypnotic, was in his very presence. Smith drew one sharp breath, and was silent.

Together, chained to the wall, two medieval captives, living mockeries of our boasted modern security, we crouched before Dr. Fu-Manchu.

He came forward with an indescribable gait, catlike yet awkward, carrying his high shoulders almost hunched. He placed the lantern in a niche in the wall, never turning away the reptilian gaze of those eyes which must haunt my dreams for ever. They possessed a viridescence which hitherto I had only supposed possible in the eye of the cat—and the film intermittently clouded their brightness—but I can speak of them no more.

I had never supposed, prior to meeting Dr. Fu-Manchu, that so intense a force of malignancy could radiate—from any human being. He spoke. His English was perfect, though at times his words were oddly chosen; his delivery alternately was guttural and sibilant.

"Mr. Smith and Dr. Petrie, your interference with my plans has gone too far. I have seriously turned my attention to you."

He displayed his teeth, small and evenly separated, but discoloured in a way that was familiar to me. I studied his eyes with a new, professional interest, which even the extremity of our danger could not wholly banish. Their greenness seemed to be of the iris; the pupil was oddly contracted—a pin-point.

Smith leaned his back against the wall with assumed indifference.

"You have presumed," continued Fu-Manchu, "to meddle with a world-change. Poor spiders—caught in the wheels of the inevitable! You have linked my name with the futility of the Young China movement—the name of Fu-Manchu! Mr. Smith, you are an incompetent meddler—I despise you! Dr. Petrie, you are a fool—I am sorry for you!"

He rested one bony hand on his hip, narrowing the long eyes as he looked down on us. The purposeful cruelty of the man was inherent; it was entirely untheatrical. Still Smith remained silent.

"So I am determined to remove you from the scene of your blunders!" added Fu-Manchu.

"Opium will very shortly do the same for you!" I rapped at him savagely.

Without emotion he turned the narrowed eyes upon me.

"That is a matter of opinion, Doctor," he said. "You may have lacked the opportunities which have been mine for studying that subject—and in any event I shall not be privileged to enjoy your advice in the future."

"You will not long outlive me," I replied. "And our deaths will not profit you, incidentally; because—" Smith's foot touched mine.

"Because?" enquired Fu-Manchu softly. "Ah! Mr. Smith is so prudent! He is thinking that I have *files*!" He pronounced the word in a way that made me shudder. "Mr. Smith has seen a *wire jacket*! Have you ever seen a wire jacket? As a surgeon, its functions would interest you!"

I stifled a cry that rose to my lips; for, with a shrill whistling sound, a small shape came bounding into the dimly lit vault, then shot upward. A marmoset landed on the shoulder of Dr. Fu-Manchu and peered grotesquely into the dreadful yellow face. The Doctor raised his bony hand and fondled the little creature, crooning to it.

"One of my pets, Mr. Smith," he said, suddenly opening his eyes fully so that they blazed like green lamps. "I have others, equally useful. My scorpions—have you met my scorpions? No? My pythons and hamadryads? Then there are my fungi and my tiny allies, the bacilli. I have a collection in my laboratory quite unique. Have you ever visited Molokai, the leper island, Doctor? No? But Mr. Nayland Smith will be familiar with the asylum at Rangoon! And we most not forget my black spiders, with their diamond eyes—my spiders, that sit in the dark and watch—then leap!"

He raised his lean hands, so that the sleeve of the robe fell back to the elbow, and the ape dropped, chattering, to the floor and ran from the cellar.

"O God of Cathay!" he cried, "by what death shall these die— these miserable ones who would bind thine Empire, which is boundless!"

Like some priest of Tezcat he stood, his eyes upraised to the roof, his lean body quivering—a sight to shock the most unimpressionable mind.

"He is mad!" I whispered to Smith. "God help us, the man is a dangerous homicidal maniac!"

Nayland Smith's face was very drawn, but he shook his head grimly.

"Dangerous, yes, I agree," he muttered, "his existence is a danger to the entire white race which, now, we are powerless to avert."

Dr. Fu Manchu recovered himself, took up the lantern and, turning abruptly, walked to the door, with his awkward yet feline gait. At the threshold he looked back.

"You would have warned Mr. Graham Guthrie?" he said, in a soft voice. "Tonight, at half-past twelve, Mr Graham Guthrie dies!"

Smith sat silent and motionless, his eyes fixed upon the speaker.

"You were in Rangoon in 1908?" continued Dr. Fu-Manchu. "You remember the Call?"

From somewhere above us—I could not determine the exact direction—came a low, wailing cry, an uncanny thing of falling cadences, which, in that dismal vault, with the sinister yellow-robed figure at the door, seemed to pour ice into my veins. Its effect upon Smith was truly extraordinary. His face showed greyly in the faint light, and I heard him draw a hissing breath through clenched teeth.

"It calls for you!" said Fu-Manchu. "At half-past twelve it calls for Graham Guthrie!"

The door closed, and darkness mantled us again.

"Smith," I said, "what was that?" The horrors about us were playing havoc with my nerves.

"It was the Call of Siva!" replied Smith hoarsely.

"What is it? Who uttered it? What does it mean?"

"I don't know what it is, Petrie, nor who utters it. But it means death!"

CHAPTER FOURTEEN

I AWAKEN—AND DREAM

There may be some who could have lain, chained in that noisome cell, and felt no fear—no dread of what the blackness might hold. I confess that I am not one of these. I knew that Nayland Smith and I stood in the path of the most stupendous genius who in the world's history had devoted his intellect to crime. I knew that the enormous wealth of the political group backing Dr. Fu-Manchu rendered him a menace to Europe and to America greater than that of the plague. He was a scientist trained at a great university—an explorer of nature's secrets, who had gone further into the unknown, I suppose, than any living man. His mission was to remove all obstacles—human obstacles—from the path of that secret movement which was progressing in the Far East. Smith and I were two such obstacles; and of all the horrible devices at his command, I wondered, and my tortured brain refused to leave the subject, by which of them we were doomed to be despatched.

Even at that very moment some venomous centipede might be wriggling towards us over the slime of the stones, some poisonous spider be preparing to drop from the roof! Fu-Manchu might have released a serpent in the cellar, or the air be alive with microbes of a loathsome disease!

"Smith," I said, scarcely recognizing my own voice, "I can't bear this suspense. He intends to kill us, that is certain, but—"

"Don't worry," came the reply: "he intends to learn our plans first."

"You mean—?"

"You heard him speak of his files and of his wire jacket?"

"Oh, my God!" I groaned, "can this be England?"

Smith laughed dryly, and I heard him fumbling with the steel collar about his neck.

"I have one great hope," he said, "since you share my captivity, but we must neglect no minor chance. Try with your pocket-knife if you can force the lock. I am trying to break this one."

Truth to tell, the idea had not entered my half-dazed mind, but I immediately acted upon my friend's suggestion, setting to work with the small blade of my knife. I was so engaged, and, having snapped one blade, was about to open another, when a sound arrested me. It came from beneath my feet.

"Smith", I whispered, "listen!"

The scraping and clicking which told of Smith's efforts ceased. Motionless, we sat in that humid darkness and listened.

Something was moving beneath the stones of the cellar. I held my breath; every nerve in my body was strung up.

A line of light showed a few feet from where we lay. It widened— became an oblong. A trap was lifted, and, within a yard of me, there rose a dimly seen head. Horror I had expected—and death, or worse. Instead, I saw a lovely face, crowned with a disordered mass of curling hair; I saw a white arm upholding the stone slab, a shapely arm clasped above the elbow by a broad gold bangle.

The girl climbed into the cellar and placed the lantern on the stone floor. In the dim light she was unreal—a figure from an opium vision, with her clinging silk draperies and garish jewellery, with her feet encased in little red slippers. In short, this was the houri of my vision, materialized. It was difficult to believe that we were in modern, up-to-date England; easy to dream that we were the captives of a caliph, in a dungeon in old Baghdad.

"My prayers are answered," said Smith softly. "She has come to save *you*!"

"S-sh!" warned the girl, and her wonderful eyes opened widely, fearfully. "A sound and he will kill us all."

She bent over me; a key jarred in the lock which had broken my penknife—and the collar was off. As I rose to my feet the girl turned and released Smith. She raised the lantern above the trap, and signed to us to descend the wooden steps which its light revealed.

"Your knife," she whispered to me. "Leave it on the floor. He will think you forced the locks. Down! Quickly!"

Nayland Smith, stepping gingerly, disappeared into the darkness. I followed rapidly. Last of all came our mysterious friend, a gold band about one of her ankles gleaming in the rays of the lantern which she carried. We stood in a low-arched passage.

"Tie your handkerchiefs over your eyes and do exactly as I tell you," she ordered.

Neither of us hesitated to obey her. Blindfolded, I allowed her to lead me, and Smith rested his hand upon my shoulder. In that order we proceeded, and came to stone steps, which we ascended.

"Keep to the wall on the left," came a whisper. "There is danger on the right."

With my free hand I felt for and found the wall, and we pressed forward. The atmosphere of the place through which we were passing was steamy, and loaded with an odour like that of exotic plant life. But a faint animal scent crept to my nostrils, too, and there was a subdued stir about me infinitely suggestive—mysterious.

Now my feet sank in a soft carpet, and a curtain brushed my shoulder. A gong sounded. We stopped.

The din of distant drumming came to my ears.

"Where in heaven's name are we?" hissed Smith in my ear, "that is a tom-tom!"

"S-sh! S-sh!"

The little hand grasping mine quivered nervously. We were near a door or a window, for a breath of perfume was wafted through the air; and it reminded me of my other meetings with the beautiful woman who was now leading us from the house of Fu-Manchu; who, with her own lips, had told me that she was his slave. Through the horrible phantasmagoria she flitted—a seductive vision, her piquant loveliness standing out richly in its black setting of murder and devilry. Not once, but a thousand times, I had tried to reason out the nature of the tie which bound her to the sinister Doctor.

Silence fell.

"Quick! This way!"

Down a thickly carpeted stair we went. Our guide opened a door, and led us along a passage. Another door was opened; and we were in the open air. But the girl never tarried, pulling me along a gravelled path, with a fresh breeze blowing in my face, and along until, unmistakably, I stood upon the river bank. Now, planking creaked to our tread; and, looking downward beneath the handkerchief, I saw the gleam of water beneath my feet.

"Be careful!" I was warned, and found myself stepping into a narrow boat—a punt.

Nayland Smith followed, and the girl pushed the punt off and poled out into the stream.

"Don't speak!" she directed.

My brain was fevered; I scarce knew if I dreamed and was waking, or if the reality ended with my imprisonment in the clammy cellar, and this silent escape, blindfolded, upon the river, with a girl for our guide, who might have stepped out of the pages of *The Arabian Nights,* were fantasy—the mockery of sleep.

Indeed, I began seriously to doubt if this stream whereon we floated, whose waters splashed and tinkled about us, were the Thames, the Tigris, or the Styx.

The punt touched a bank.

"You will hear a clock strike in a few minutes," said the girl, with her soft, charming accent, "but I rely upon your honour not to remove the handkerchiefs until then. You owe me this."

"We do!" said Smith fervently.

I heard him scrambling to the bank, and a moment later a soft hand was placed in mine, and I too was guided on to terra firma. Arrived on the bank, I still held the girl's hand, drawing her toward me.

"You must not go back," I whispered. "We will take care of you. You must not return to that place."

"Let me go!" she said. "When, once, I asked you to take me from him, you spoke of police protection; that was your answer, police protection! You would let them lock me up—imprison me—and make me betray him! For what? For what?" She wrenched herself free. "How little you understand me. Never mind. Perhaps one day you will know! Until the clock strikes!"

She was gone. I heard the creak of the punt, the drip of the water from the pole. Fainter it grew, and fainter.

"What is her secret?" muttered Smith, beside me. "Why does she cling to that monster?"

The distant sound died away entirely. A clock began to strike; it struck the half-hour. In an instant my handkerchief was off, and so was Smith's. We stood upon a towing-path. Away to the left the moon shone upon the towers and battlements of an ancient fortress.

It was Windsor Castle.

"Half-past ten," cried Smith. "Two hours to save Graham Guthrie!"

We had exactly fourteen minutes in which to catch the last train to Waterloo; and we caught it. But I sank into a corner of the compartment in a state bordering upon collapse. Neither of us, I think, could have managed another twenty yards. With a lesser stake than a human life at issue, I doubt if we should have attempted that dash to Windsor Station.

"Due at Waterloo at eleven fifty-one," panted Smith. "That gives us thirty-nine minutes to get to the other side of the river and reach his hotel."

"Where in heaven's name is that house situated? Did we come up or down stream?"

"I couldn't determine. But at any rate, it stands close to the riverside. It should be merely a question of time to identify it. I shall set Scotland Yard to work immediately; but I am hoping for nothing. Our escape will warn him."

I said no more for a time, sitting wiping the perspiration from my forehead and watching my friend load his cracked briar with the broad-cut Latakia mixture.

"Smith," I said at last, "what was that horrible wailing we heard, and what did Fu-Manchu mean when he referred to Rangoon? I noticed how it affected you."

My friend nodded and lighted his pipe.

"There was a ghastly business there in 1908 or early in 1909," he replied. "An utterly mysterious epidemic. And this beastly wailing was associated with it."

"In what way? And what do you mean by an epidemic?"

"It began, I believe, at the Palace Mansions Hotel, in the cantonments. A young American, whose name I cannot recall, was staying there on business connected with some new iron buildings. One night he went to his room, locked the door, and jumped out of the window into the courtyard. Broke his neck, of course."

"Suicide?"

"Apparently. But there was singular features in the case. For instance, his revolver lay beside him, fully loaded!"

"In the courtyard?"

"In the courtyard!"

"Was it murder by any chance?"

Smith shrugged his shoulders.

"His door was found locked from the inside; had to be broken in."

"But the wailing business?"

"That began later, or was only noticed later. A French doctor, named Lafitte, died in exactly the same way."

"At the same place?"

"At the same hotel; but he occupied a different room. Here is the extraordinary part of the affair: a friend shared the room with him, and actually saw him go!"

"Saw him leap from the window?"

"Yes. The friend—an Englishman—was aroused by the uncanny wailing. I was in Rangoon at the time, so that I know more of the case of Lafitte than of that of the American. I spoke to the man about it personally. He was an electrical engineer, Edward Martin, and he told me that the cry seemed to come from above him."

"It seemed to come from above when we heard it at Fu-Manchu's house."

"Martin sat up in bed; it was a clear, moonlit night—the sort of moonlight you get in Burma. Lafitte, for some reason, had just gone to the window. His friend saw him look out. The next moment, with a dreadful scream, he threw himself forward—and crashed down into the courtyard!"

"What then?"

"Martin ran to the window and looked down. Lafitte's scream had aroused the place, of course, but there was absolutely nothing to account for the occurrence. There was no balcony, no ledge, by means of which anyone could reach the window."

"But how did you come to recognize the cry?"

"I stopped at the Palace Mansions for some time; and one night this uncanny howling aroused me. I heard it quite distinctly, and am never likely to forget it. It was followed by a hoarse yell. The man in the next room, an orchid hunter, had gone the same way as the others!"

"Did you change your quarters?"

"No. Fortunately for the reputation of the hotel—a first-class establishment—several similar cases occurred elsewhere, both in Rangoon, in Prome and in Moulmein. A story got about the native quarter, and was fostered by some mad fakir, that the god Siva was reborn and that the cry was his call for victims; a ghastly story, which led to an outbreak of dacoity and gave the District Superintendent no end of trouble."

"Was there anything unusual about the bodies?"

"They all developed marks after death, as though they had been strangled! The marks were said all to possess a peculiar form, though it was not appreciable to my eye; and this, again, was declared to be the five heads of Siva."

"Were the deaths confined to Europeans?"

"Oh no. Several Burmans and others died in the same way. At first there was a theory that the victims had contracted leprosy and committed suicide as a result; but the medical evidence disproved that. The Call of Siva became a perfect nightmare throughout Burma."

"Did you ever hear it again, before this evening?"

"Yes. I heard it on the Upper Irrawaddy one clear, moonlit night, and a Collasie—a deck-hand—leapt from the top deck of the steamer aboard which I was travelling! My God! to think that the fiend Fu-Manchu has brought *that* to England!"

"But brought what, Smith?" I cried, in perplexity. "What has he brought? An evil spirit? A mental disease? What is it? What *can* it be?"

"A new agent of death, Petrie! Something born in a plague-spot of Burma—the home of much that is unclean and much that is inexplicable. Heaven grant that we be in time, and are able to save Guthrie."

CHAPTER FIFTEEN

THE CALL OF SIVA

The train was late, and as our cab turned out of Waterloo Station and began to ascend to the bridge, from a hundred steeples rang out the gongs of midnight, the bell of St. Paul's raised above them all to vie with the deep voice of Big Ben.

I looked out from the cab window across the river to where, towering above the Embankment, that place of a thousand tragedies, the lights of some of London's greatest caravanserais formed a sort of minor constellation. From the subdued blaze that showed the public supper-rooms I looked up to the hundreds of starry points marking the private apartments of those giant inns.

I thought how each twinkling window denoted the presence of some bird of passage, some wanderer temporarily abiding in our midst. There, floor piled upon floor above the chattering throngs, were these less gregarious units, each something of a mystery to his fellow-guests, each in his separate cell; and each as remote from real human companionship as if that cell were fashioned, not in the bricks of London, but in the rocks of Hindustan!

In one of those rooms Graham Guthrie might at that moment be sleeping, all unaware that he would awake to the Call of Siva, to the summons of death. As we neared the Strand, Smith stopped the cab, discharging the man outside Sotheby's auction-rooms.

"One of the Doctor's watch-dogs may be in the foyer," he said thoughtfully, "and it might spoil everything if we were seen to go to Guthrie's rooms. There must be a back entrance to the kitchens, and so on?"

'There is," I replied quickly. "I have seen the vans delivering there. But have we time?"

"Yes. Lead on."

We walked up the Strand and hurried westward. Into that narrow court, with its iron posts and descending steps, upon which opens a well-known wine-cellar, we turned. Then, going parallel with the Strand, but on the Embankment level, we ran around the back of the great hotel, and came to double doors which were open. An arc lamp illuminated the interior and a number of men were at work among the casks, crates, and packages stacked about the place. We entered.

"Hallo!" cried a man in a white overall, "where d'you think you're going?"

Smith grasped him by the arm.

"I want to get to the public part of the hotel without being seen from the entrance hall," he said. "Will you please lead the way?"

"Here—" began the other, staring.

"Don't waste time!" snapped my friend, in that tone of authority which he knew so well how to assume. "It's a matter of life and death. Lead the way, I say!"

"Police, sir?" asked the man civilly.

"Yes," said Smith, "hurry!"

Off went our guide without further demur. Skirting sculleries, kitchens, laundries and engine-rooms, he led us through those mysterious labyrinths which have no existence for the guest above, but which contain the machinery that renders these modern *khans* the Aladdin's palaces they are. On a second-floor landing we met a man in a tweed suit, to whom our cicerone presented us.

"Glad I met you, sir. Two gentlemen from the police."

The man regarded us with a suspicious smile.

"Who are you?" he asked. "You're not from Scotland Yard, at any rate!"

Smith pulled out a card and thrust it into the speaker's hand.

"If you are the hotel detective," he said, "take us without delay to Mr. Graham Guthrie."

A marked change took place in the other's demeanour on glancing at the card in his hand.

"Excuse me, sir," he said deferentially, "but, of course, I didn't know who I was speaking to. We all have instructions to give you every assistance."

"Is Mr. Guthrie in his room?"

"He's been in his room for some time, sir. You will want to get there without being seen? This way. We can join the lift on the third floor."

Off we went again, with our new guide. In the lift:

"Have you noticed anything suspicious about the place tonight?" asked Smith.

"I have!" was the startling reply. That accounts for you finding me where you did. My usual post is in the lobby. But about eleven o'clock, when the theatre people began to come in, I had a hazy sort of impression that some one or something slipped past in the crowd—something that had no business in the hotel."

We got out of the lift.

"I don't quite follow you," said Smith. "If you thought you saw something entering, you must have formed a more or less definite impression regarding it."

"That's the funny part of the business," answered the man doggedly. "I didn't! But as I stood at the top of the stairs I could have sworn that there was something crawling up behind a party—two ladies and two gentlemen."

"A dog, for instance?"

"It didn't strike me as being a dog, sir. Anyway, when the party passed me, there was nothing there. Mind you, whatever it was, it hadn't come in by the front. I have made inquiries everywhere, but without result." He stopped abruptly. "No. 189—Mr. Guthrie's door, sir."

Smith knocked.

"Hallo!" came a muffled voice, "what do you want?"

"Open the door! Don't delay; it is important."

He turned to the hotel detective.

"Stay right there where you can watch the stairs and the lift," he instructed, "and note everyone and everything that passes this door. But whatever you see or hear, do nothing without my orders."

The man moved off, and the door was opened. Smith whispered in my ear:

"Some creature of Dr. Fu-Manchu is in the hotel!"

Mr. Graham Guthrie, British Resident in North Bhutan, was a big, thick-set man—grey-haired and florid, with widely opened eyes of the true fighting blue, a bristling moustache, and prominent shaggy brows. Nayland Smith introduced himself tersely, proffering his card and an open letter.

"Those are my credentials, Mr. Guthrie," he said; "so no doubt you will realize that the business which brings me and my friend, Dr. Petrie, here at such an hour is of the first importance."

He switched off the light.

"There is no time for ceremony," he explained. "It is now twenty-five minutes past twelve. At half-past an attempt will be made upon your life!"

"Mr. Smith," said the other, who, arrayed in his pyjamas, was seated on the edge of the bed, "you alarm me very greatly. I may mention that I was advised of your presence in England this morning."

"Do you know anything respecting the person called Fu-Manchu—Dr. Fu-Manchu?"

"Only what I was told today—that he is the agent of an advanced political group."

"It is opposed to his interests that you should return to Bhutan. A more gullible agent would be preferable. Therefore, unless you implicitly obey my instructions, you will never leave England!"

Graham Guthrie breathed quickly. I was growing more used to the gloom, and I could dimly discern him, his face turned toward Nayland Smith, whilst with his hand he clutched the bed-rail. Such a visit as ours, I think, must have shaken the nerve of any man.

"But, Mr. Smith," he said, "surely I am safe enough here! The place is full of American visitors at present, and I have had to be content with a room right at the top; so that the only danger I apprehend is that of fire."

"There is another danger," replied Smith. "The fact that you are at the top of the building enhances that danger. Do you recall anything of the mysterious epidemic which broke out in Rangoon in 1908—the deaths due to the Call of Siva?"

"I read of it in the Indian papers," said Guthrie uneasily. "Suicides, were they not?"

"No!" snapped Smith. "Murders!"

There was a brief silence.

"From what I recall of the cases," said Guthrie, "that seems impossible. In several instances the victims threw themselves from the windows of locked rooms—and the windows were quite inaccessible."

"Exactly," replied Smith; and in the dim light his revolver gleamed dully, as he placed it on the small table beside the bed. "Except that your door is unlocked, the conditions tonight are identical. Silence, please; I hear a clock striking."

It was Big Ben. It struck the half-hour, leaving the stillness complete. In that room, high above the activity which yet prevailed below, high above the supping crowds in the hotel, high above the starving crowds on the Embankment, a curious chill of isolation swept about me. Again I realized how, in the very heart of the great metropolis, a man may be as far from aid as in the heart of a desert. I was glad that I was not alone in that room—marked with the death-mark of Fu-Manchu; and I am certain that Graham Guthrie welcomed his unexpected company.

I may have mentioned the fact before, but on this occasion it became so peculiarly evident to me that I am constrained to record it here—I refer to the sense of impending danger which invariably preceded a visitor from Fu-Manchu. Even had I not known that an attempt was to be made that night, I should have realized it, as, strung to high tension, I waited in the darkness. Some invisible herald went ahead of the dreadful Chinaman, proclaiming his coming to every nerve in one's body. It was like a breath of astral incense, announcing the presence of the priests of death.

A wail, low but singularly penetrating, falling in minor cadences to a new silence, came from somewhere close at hand.

"My God!" hissed Guthrie, "what was that?"

"The Call of Siva," whispered Smith. "Don't stir, for your life!"

Guthrie was breathing hard.

I knew that we were three; that the hotel detective was within hail; that there was a telephone in the room; that the traffic of the Embankment moved almost beneath us; but I knew, and am not ashamed to confess, that Fear had icy fingers about my heart. It was awful—that tense waiting—for—what?

Three taps sounded very distinctly upon the window.

Graham Guthrie started so as to shake the bed. "It's supernatural!" he muttered—all that was Celtic in his blood recoiling from the omen. "Nothing human can reach that window!"

"S-sh!" from Smith. "Don't stir."

The tapping was repeated.

Smith softly crossed the room. My heart was beating painfully. He threw open the window. Further inaction was impossible. I joined him; and we looked out into the empty air.

"Don't come too near, Petrie!" he warned over his shoulder.

One on either side of the open window, we stood and looked down at the moving Embankment lights, at the glitter of the Thames, at the silhouetted buildings on the further bank, with the Shot Tower starting above them all.

Three taps sounded on the panes above us.

In all my dealings with Dr. Fu-Manchu I had had to face nothing so uncanny as this. What Burmese ghoul had he loosed? Was it outside, in the air? Was it actually in the room?

"Don't let me go, Petrie!" whispered Smith suddenly. "Get a tight hold on me!"

That was the last straw; for I thought that some dreadful fascination was impelling my friend to hurl himself out! Wildly I threw my arms about him, and Guthrie leapt forward to help.

Smith leaned from the window and looked up.

One choking cry he gave— smothered, inarticulate—and I found him slipping from my grip—being drawn out of the window—drawn to his death!

"Hold him, Guthrie!" I gasped hoarsely. "My God, he's going! Hold him!"

My friend writhed in our grasp, and I saw him stretch his arm upward. The crack of his revolver came, and he collapsed on to the floor, carrying me with him.

But as I fell I heard a scream above. Smith's revolver went hurtling through the air, and, hard upon it, went a black shape—flashing past the open window into the gulf of the night.

"The light! The light!" I cried.

Guthrie ran and turned on the light. Nayland Smith, his eyes starting from his head, his face swollen, lay plucking at a silken cord which showed tight about his throat.

"It was a *Thug*!" screamed Guthrie. "Get the rope off! He's choking!"

My hand a-twitch, I seized the strangling cord.

"A knife! Quick!" I cried. "I have lost mine!"

Guthrie ran to the dressing-table and passed me an open penknife. I somehow forced the blade between the rope and Smith's swollen neck, and severed the deadly silken thing.

Smith made a choking noise, and fell back, swooning in my arms. When, later, we stood looking down upon the mutilated thing which had been brought in from where it fell, Smith showed me a mark on the brow—close beside the wound where his bullet had entered.

"The mark of Káli," he said. The man was a *phansigar*—a religious strangler. Since Fu-Manchu has dacoits in his service I might have expected that he would have Thugs. A group of these fiends would seem to have fled into Burma; so that the mysterious epidemic in Rangoon was really an outbreak of thuggee—on slightly improved lines! I had suspected something of the kind, but, naturally, I had not looked for Thugs near Rangoon. My unexpected resistance led the strangler to bungle the rope. You have seen how it was fastened about my throat? That was unscientific. The true method, as practised by the group operating in Burma, was to throw the line about the victim's neck and jerk him from the window. A man leaning from an open window is very nicely poised: it requires only a slight jerk to pitch him forward. No loop was used, but a running line, which, as the victim fell, remained in the hand of the murderer. No clue! Therefore we see at once what commended the system to Fu-Manchu."

Graham Guthrie, very pale, stood looking down at the dead strangler.

"I owe you my life, Mr. Smith," he said. "If you had come five minutes later—"

He grasped Smith's hand.

"You see," Guthrie continued, "no one thought of looking for a Thug in Burma! And no one thought of the *roof*! These fellows are as active as monkeys, and where an ordinary man would infallibly break his neck, they are entirely at home. I might have chosen my room specially for the business!"

"He slipped in late this evening," said Smith. "The hotel detective saw him, but these stranglers are as elusive as shadows, otherwise, despite their having changed the scene of their operations, not one could have survived."

"Didn't you mention a case of this kind on the Irrawaddy?" I asked.

"Yes," was the reply, "and I know of what you are thinking. The steamers of the Irrawaddy Flotilla have a corrugated-iron roof over the top deck. The Thug must have been lying up there as the Colassie passed on the deck below."

"But, Smith, what is the motive of the Call?" I continued.

"Partly religious," he explained, "and partly to wake the victims! You are perhaps going to ask me how Dr. Fu-Manchu has obtained power over such people as *phansigars?* I can only reply that Dr. Fu-Manchu has secret knowledge of which, so far, we know absolutely nothing; but, despite all, at last I begin to score."

"You do," I agreed, "but your victory took you near to death."

"I owe my life to you, Petrie," he said. "Once to your strength of arm, and once to—"

"Don't speak of her, Smith," I interrupted. "Dr. Fu-Manchu may have discovered the part she played! In which event—"

"God help her!"

CHAPTER SIXTEEN

KÂRAMANÈH

Upon the following day we were afoot again, and shortly at handgrips with the enemy. In retrospect, that restless time offers a chaotic prospect, with few peaceful spots amid its turmoils.

All that was resposeful in nature seemed to have become an irony and a mockery to us—who knew how an evil demigod had his sacrificial altars amid our sweetest groves. This idea ruled strongly in my mind upon that soft autumnal day.

"The net is closing in," said Nayland Smith.

"Let us hope upon a big catch," I replied, with a laugh.

Beyond where the Thames tided slumberously seaward peeped the roofs of Royal Windsor, the castle towers showing through the autumn haze. The peace of beautiful Thames-side was about us.

This was one of the few tangible clues upon which thus far we had chanced; but at last it seemed indeed that we were narrowing the resources of that enemy of the white race who was writing his name over England in characters of blood. To capture Dr. Fu-Manchu we did not hope; but at least there was every promise of destroying one of the enemy's strongholds.

We had circled upon the map a tract of country cut by the Thames, with Windsor for its centre. Within that circle was the house from which miraculously we had escaped—a house used by the most highly organized group in the history of criminology. So much we knew. Even if we found the house, and this was likely enough, to find it vacated by Fu-Manchu and his mysterious servants we were prepared. But is would be a base destroyed.

We were working upon a methodical plan, and although our co-operators were invisible, these numbered no fewer than twelve—all of them experienced men. Thus far we had drawn blank, but the place for which Smith and I were making now came clearly into view: an old mansion situated in extensive walled grounds. Leaving the river behind us, we turned sharply to the right along a lane flanked by a high wall. On an open patch of ground, as we passed, I noted a gipsy caravan. An old woman was seated on the steps, her wrinkled face bent, her chin resting in the palm of her hand.

I scarcely glanced at her, but pressed on; nor did I notice that my friend no longer was beside me. I was all anxiety to come to some point from whence I might obtain a view of the house; all anxiety to know if this was the abode of our mysterious enemy—the place where he worked amid his weird company, where he bred his deadly scorpions and his bacilli, reared his poisonous fungi, from whence he despatched his murder ministers. Above all, perhaps, I wondered if this would prove to be the hiding-place of the beautiful slave girl who was such a potent factor in the Doctor's plans, but a two-edged sword which yet we hoped to turn upon Fu-Manchu. Even in the hands of a master, a woman's beauty is a dangerous weapon.

A cry rang out behind me. I turned quickly, and a singular sight met my gaze.

Nayland Smith was engaged in a furious struggle with the old gipsy woman! His long arms clasped about her, he was roughly dragging her out into the roadway, she fighting like a wild thing— silently, fiercely.

Smith often surprised me, but at that sight, frankly, I thought that he was become bereft of reason. I ran back; and I had almost reached the scene of this incredible contest, and Smith now was evidently hard put it to hold his own, when a man, swarthy, with big rings in his ears, leapt from the caravan.

One quick glance he threw in our direction, and made it off towards the river.

Smith twisted around upon me, never releasing his hold of the woman.

"After him, Petrie!" he cried. "After him. Don't let him escape. It's a dacoit!"

My brain in a confused whirl, my mind yet disposed to a belief that my friend had lost his senses, the word "dacoit" was sufficient.

I started down the road after the fleetly running man. Never once did he glance behind him, so that he evidently had occasion to fear pursuit. The dusty road rang beneath my flying footsteps. That sense of fantasy, which claimed me often enough in those days of our struggle with the titanic genius whose victory meant the victory of the yellow races over the white, now had me fast in its grip again. I was an actor in one of those dream-scenes of the grim Fu-Manchu drama.

Out over the grass and down to the river's brink ran the gipsy who was no gipsy, but one of that far more sinister brotherhood, the dacoits. I was close upon his heels. But I was not prepared for him to leap in amongst the rushes at the margin of the stream; and seeing him do this I pulled up quickly. Straight into the water he plunged; and I saw that he held some object in his hand. He waded out; he dived; and as I gained the bank and looked to right and left he had vanished completely. Only ever-widening rings showed where he had been.

I had him!

For directly he rose to the surface he would be visible from either bank, and, with the police whistle which I carried, I could, if necessary, summon one of the men in hiding across the stream. I waited. A wildfowl floated serenely past, untroubled by this strange invasion of his precincts. A full minute I waited. From the lane behind me came Smith's voice:

"Don't let him escape, Petrie!"

Never lifting my eyes from the water, I waved my hand reassuringly. But still the dacoit did not rise. I searched the surface in all directions as far as my eyes could reach; but no swimmer showed above it. Then it was that I concluded he had dived too deeply, become entangled in the weeds and was drowned. With a final glance to right and left, and some feeling of awe at this sudden tragedy—this grim going out of a life at glorious noonday—I turned away. Smith had the woman securely; but I had not taken five steps toward him when a faint splash behind warned me. Instinctively I ducked. From whence that saving instinct arose I cannot surmise, but to it I owed my life. For as I rapidly lowered my head, something hummed past me, something that flew out over the grass bank, and fell with a jangle upon the dusty roadside: a knife!

I turned and bounded back to the river's brink. I heard a faint cry behind me, which could only have come from the gipsy woman. Nothing disturbed the calm surface of the water. The reach was lonely of rowers. Out by the further bank a girl was poling a punt along, and her white-clad figure was the only living thing that moved upon the river within the range of the most expert knife-thrower.

To say that I was nonplussed is to say less than the truth; I was amazed. That it was the dacoit who had shown me this murderous attention I could not doubt. But where in heaven's name *was* he? He could not humanly have remained below water for so long; yet he certainly was not above, was not upon the surface, concealed amongst the reeds, nor hidden upon the bank.

There, in the bright sunshine, a consciousness of the eerie possessed me. It was with an uncomfortable feeling that my phantom foe might be aiming a second knife at my back that I turned away and hastened towards Smith. My fearful expectations were not realized, and I picked up the little weapon which had so narrowly missed me, and with it in my hand rejoined my friend.

He was standing with one arm closely clasped about the apparently exhausted woman, and her dark eyes were fixed upon him with an extraordinary expression.

"What does it mean, Smith?" I began.

But he interrupted me.

"Where is the dacoit?" he demanded rapidly.

"Since he seemingly possesses the attributes of a fish," I replied, "I cannot pretend to say."

The gipsy woman lifted her eyes to mine and laughed. Her laughter was musical, not that of such an old hag as Smith held captive; it was familiar too.

I started, and looked closely into the wizened face.

"He's tricked you," said Smith, an angry note in his voice. "What is that you have in your hand?"

I showed him the knife, and told him how it had come into my possession.

"I know," he rapped. "I saw it. He was in the water not three yards from where you stood. You must have seen him. Was there nothing visible?"

"Nothing."

The woman laughed again, and again I wondered.

"A wildfowl," I added; "nothing else."

"A wildfowl," snapped Smith. "If you will consult your recollections of the habits of wildfowl you will see that this particular specimen was a *rara avis*. It's an old trick, Petrie, but a good one, for it is used in decoying. A dacoit's head was concealed in that fowl. It's useless. He has certainly made good his escape by now."

"Smith," I said, something crestfallen, "why are you detaining this gipsy woman?"

"Gipsy woman!" he laughed, hugging her tightly as she made an impatient movement. "Use your eyes, old man."

He jerked the frowsy wig from her head, and beneath was a cloud of disordered hair that shimmered in the sunlight.

"A wet sponge will do the rest," he said.

Into my eyes, widely opened in wonder, looked the dark eyes of the captive; and beneath the disguise I picked out the charming features of the slave girl. There were tears on the whitened lashes, and she was submissive now.

"This time," said my friend hardly, "we have fairly captured her—and we will hold her."

From somewhere upstream came a faint call.

"The dacoit!"

Nayland Smith's lean body straightened; he stood alert, strung up.

Another call answered, and a third responded. Then followed the flatly shrill note of a police whistle, and I noted a column of black vapour rising beyond the wall, mounting straight to heaven as the smoke of a welcome offering.

The surrounded mansion was in flames!

"Curse it!" rapped Smith. "So this time we were right. But, of course, he has had ample opportunity to remove his effects. I knew that. The man's daring is incredible. He has given himself till the very last moment—and we blundered upon two of the outposts."

"I lost one."

"No matter. We have the other. I expect no further arrests, and the house will have been so well fired by the Doctor's servants that nothing can save it. I fear its ashes will afford us no clue, Petrie; but we have secured a lever which should serve to disturb Fu-Manchu's world."

He glanced at the queer figure which hung submissively in his arms. She looked up proudly.

"You need not hold me so tight," she said, in her soft voice. "I will come with you."

That I moved amid singular happenings, you, who have borne with me thus far, have learned, and that I witnessed many curious scenes; but of the many such scenes in that race-drama wherein Nayland Smith and Dr. Fu-Manchu played the leading parts, I remember none more bizarre than the one at my rooms that afternoon.

Without delay, and without taking the Scotland Yard men into our confidence, we hurried our prisoner back to London, for my friend's authority was supreme. A strange trio we were, and one which excited no little comment; but the journey came to an end at last. Now we were in my unpretentious sitting-room—the room wherein Smith first had unfolded to me the story of Dr. Fu-Manchu and of the great secret society which sought to upset the balance of the world— to place Europe and America beneath the sceptre of Cathay.

I sat with my elbows upon the writing-table, my chin in my hands. Smith restlessly paced the floor, relighting his blackened briar a dozen times in as many minutes. In the big armchair the psuedo-gipsy was curled up. A brief toilet had converted the wizened old woman's face into that of a fascinatingly pretty girl. Wildly picturesque she looked in her ragged Romany garb. She held a cigarette in her fingers and watched us through lowered lashes.

Seemingly, with true Oriental fatalism, she was quite reconciled to her fate, and ever and anon she would bestow upon me a glance from her beautiful eyes which few men, I say with confidence, could have sustained unmoved. Though I could not be blind to the emotions of that passionate Eastern soul, yet I strove not to think of them. Accomplice of an arch-murderer she might be; but she was dangerously lovely.

"That man who was with you," said Smith, suddenly turning upon her, "was in Burma up till quite recently. He murdered a fisherman thirty miles above Prome only a month before I left. The D.S.P. had placed a thousand rupees on his head. Am I right?"

The girl shrugged her shoulders.

"Suppose— What then?" she asked.

"Suppose I handed you over to the police?" suggested Smith. But he spoke without conviction, since in the recent past we both had owed our lives to her.

"As you please," she replied. "The police would learn nothing."

"You do not belong to the Far East," my friend said abruptly. "You may have Eastern blood in your veins, but you are no kin of Fu-Manchu."

"That is true," she admitted, and knocked the ash from her cigarette.

"Will you tell me where to find Fu-Manchu?"

She shrugged her shoulders again, glancing eloquently in my direction.

Smith walked to the door.

"I must make out my report, Petrie," he said. "Look after the prisoner."

And as the door closed softly behind him I knew what was expected of me; but, honestly, I shirked my responsibility. What attitude should I adopt? How should I go about my delicate task? In a quandary, I stood watching the girl whom singular circumstances saw captive in my rooms.

"You do not think we would harm you?" I began awkwardly. "No harm shall come to you. Why will you not trust us?"

She raised her brilliant eyes.

"Of what avail has your protection been to some of those others," she said, "those others whom *he* has sought for?"

Alas! it had been of none, and I knew it well. I thought I grasped the drift of her words.

"You mean that if you speak, Fu-Manchu will find a way of killing you?"

"Of killing *me*!" she flashed scornfully. "Do I seem one to fear for myself?"

"Then what do you fear?" I asked in surprise.

She looked at me oddly.

"When I was seized and sold for a slave," she answered, "my sister was taken too, and my brother—a child." She spoke the word with a tender intonation, and her slight accent rendered it the more soft. "My sister died in the desert. My brother lived. Better, far better, that he had died too."

Her words impressed me intensely.

"Of what are you speaking?" I questioned. "You speak of slave-raids, of the desert. Where did these things take place? Of what country are you?"

"Does it matter?" she questioned in turn. "Of what country am I? A slave has no country, no name."

"No name!" I cried.

"You may call me Kâramanèh," she said. "As Kâramanèh I was sold to Dr. Fu-Manchu, and my brother also he purchased. We were cheap at the price he paid." She laughed shortly, wildly.

"But he has spent a lot of money to educate me. My brother is all that is left to me in the world to love, and he is in the power of Dr. Fu-Manchu. You understand? It is upon him the blow will fall. You ask me to fight against Fu-Manchu. You talk of protection. Did your protection save Sir Crichton Davey?"

I shook my head sadly.

"You understand now why I cannot disobey my master's orders—why, if I would, I dare not betray him."

I walked to the window and looked out. How could I answer her arguments? What could I say? I heard the rustle of her ragged skirts, and she who called herself Kâramanèh stood beside me. She laid her hand upon my arm.

"Let me go," she pleaded. "He will kill him! He will kill him!"

Her voice shook with emotion.

"He cannot revenge himself upon your brother when you are in no way to blame," I said angrily. "We arrested you; you are not here of your own free will."

She drew her breath sharply, clutching at my arm, and in her eyes I could read that she was forcing her mind to some arduous decision.

"Listen." She was speaking rapidly, nervously. "If I help you to take Dr. Fu-Manchu—tell you where he is to be found *alone*—will you promise me, solemnly promise me, that you will immediately go to the place where I shall guide you and release my brother; that you will let us both go free?"

"I will," I said, without hesitation. "You may rest assured of it."

"But there is a condition," she added.

"What is it?"

"When I have told you where to capture him you must release me."

I hesitated. Smith often had accused me of weakness where this girl was concerned. What now was my plain duty? That she would utterly decline to speak under any circumstances unless it suited her to do so, I felt assured. If she spoke the truth, in her proposed bargain there was no personal element; her conduct I now viewed in a new light. Humanity, I thought, dictated that I accept her proposal; policy also.

"I agree," I said, and looked into her eyes, which were aflame now with emotion, an excitement perhaps of anticipation, perhaps of fear.

She laid her hands upon my shoulders.

"You will be careful?" she said pleadingly.

"For your sake," I replied, "I shall."

"Not for my sake."

"Then for your brother's."

"No." Her voice had sunk to a whisper. "For your own."

CHAPTER SEVENTEEN

THE HULK OFF THE FLATS

A cool breeze met us, blowing from the lower reaches of the Thames. Far behind us twinkled the dim lights of Low's Cottages, the last regular habitations abutting upon the marshes. Between us and the cottages stretched half a mile of lush land through which at this season there were, however, numerous dry paths; before us the flats again, a dull, monotonous expanse beneath the moon, with the promise of the cool breeze that the river flowed around the bend ahead. It was very quiet. Only the sound of our footsteps, as Nayland Smith and I tramped steadily toward our goal, broke the stillness of that lonely place.

Not once but many times, within the last twenty minutes, I had thought that we were ill-advised to adventure alone upon the capture of the formidable Chinese doctor; but we were following out our compact with Kâramanèh; and one of her stipulations had been that the police must not be acquainted with her share in the matter.

A light came into view far ahead of us.

"That's the light, Petrie," said Smith. "If we keep that straight before us, according to our information we shall strike the hulk."

I grasped the revolver in my pocket, and the presence of the little weapon was curiously reassuring. I have endeavoured, perhaps in extenuation of my own fears, to explain how about Dr. Fu-Manchu there rested an atmosphere of horror, peculiar, unique. He was not as other men. The dread that he inspired in all with whom he came in contact, the terrors which he controlled and hurled at whomsoever cumbered his path, rendered him an object supremely sinister. I despair of conveying to those who may read this account any but the coldest conception of the man's evil power.

Smith stopped suddenly and grasped my arm. We stood listening.

"What?" I asked.

"You heard nothing?"

I shook my head.

Smith was peering back over the marshes in his oddly alert way. He turned to me, and his face wore a peculiar expression.

"You don't think it's a trap?" he jerked. "We are trusting her blindly."

Strange it may seem, but something within me rose in arms against the innuendo.

"I don't," I said shortly.

He nodded. We pressed on.

Ten minutes' steady tramping brought us within sight of the Thames. Smith and I both had noticed how Fu-Manchu's activities centred always about the London river. Undoubtedly it was his highway, his line of communication along which he moved his mysterious forces. The opium den off Shadwell Highway; the mansion upstream, at that hour a smouldering shell; now the hulk lying off the marshes. Always he made his headquarters upon the river. It was significant; and even if tonight's expedition should fail, this was a clue for our future guidance.

"Bear to the right," directed Smith. "We must reconnoitre before making our attack."

We took a path that led directly to the river bank. Before us lay the grey expanse of water, and out upon it moved the busy shipping of the great mercantile city. But this life of the river seemed widely removed from us. The lonely spot where we stood had no kinship with human activity. Its dreariness illuminated by the brilliant moon, it looked indeed a fit setting for an act in such a drama as that wherein we played our parts. When I had lain in the East End opium den, when upon such another night as this I had looked out upon a peaceful Norfolk countryside; the world of living men, had come to me.

Silently Smith stared out at the distant moving lights.

"Kâramanèh merely means a slave," he said irrelevantly.

I made no comment.

"There's the hulk," he added.

The bank upon which we stood dipped in mud sloped to the level of the running tide. Seaward it rose higher, and by a narrow inlet— for we perceived that we were upon a kind of promontory—a rough pier showed. Beneath it was a shadowy shape in the patch of gloom which the moon threw far out upon the softly eddying water. Only one dim light was visible amid this darkness.

"That will be the cabin," said Smith.

Acting upon our prearranged plan we turned and walked up on to the staging above the hulk. A wooden ladder led out and down to the deck below, and was loosely lashed to a ring on the pier. With every motion of the tidal waters the ladder rose and fell, its rungs creaking harshly against the crazy railing.

"How are we going to get down without being detected?" whispered Smith.

"We've got to risk it," I said grimly.

Without further words my friend climbed around on to the ladder and commenced to descend. I waited until his head disappeared below the level, and, clumsily enough, prepared to follow him.

The hulk at that moment giving an unusually heavy heave, I stumbled, and for one breathless moment looked down upon the glittering surface streaking the darkness beneath me. My foot had slipped, and but that I had a firm grip upon the top rung, that instant, most probably, had marked the end of my share in the fight with Fu-Manchu. As it was I had a narrow escape. I felt something slip from my hip pocket, but the weird creaking of the ladder, the groans of the labouring hulk, and the lapping of the waves about the staging drowned the sound of the splash as my revolver dropped into the river.

Rather white-faced, I think, I joined Smith on the deck. He had witnessed my accident, but—

"We must risk it," he whispered in my ear. "We dare not turn back now."

He plunged into the semi-darkness, making for the cabin, I perforce following.

At the bottom of the ladder we came fully into the light streaming out from the singular apartment at the entrance to which we found ourselves. It was fitted up as a laboratory. A glimpse I had of shelves loaded with jars and bottles, of a table strewn with scientific paraphernalia, with retorts, with tubes of extraordinary shapes, holding living organisms, and with instruments—some of them of a form unknown to my experience. I saw too that books, papers and rolls of parchment littered the bare wooden floor. Then Smith's voice rose above the confused sounds about me, incisive, commanding:

"I have you covered, Dr. Fu-Manchu!"

For Fu-Manchu sat at the table.

The picture that he presented at that moment is one which persistently clings in my memory. In his long, yellow robe, his mask-like, intellectual face bent forward amongst the riot of singular appliances before him, his great, high brow gleaming in the light of the shaded lamp above, and with the abnormal eyes, filmed and green, raised to us, he seemed a figure from the realms of delirium.

But, most amazing circumstance of all, he and his immediate surroundings tallied, almost identically, with the dream-pictures which had come to me as I lay chained in the cell!

Some of the large jars about the place held anatomy specimens A faint smell of opium hung in the air, and playing with the tassel of one of the cushions upon which, as upon a divan, Fu-Manchu was seated, leapt and chattered the little marmoset.

That was an electric moment. I was prepared for anything—for anything except for what really happened.

The Doctor's wonderful, evil face betrayed no hint of emotion. The lids flickered over the filmed eyes, and their greenness grew momentarily brighter, and filmed over again.

"Put up your hands!" rapped Smith, "and attempt no tricks." His voice quivered with excitement. "The game's up, Fu-Manchu. Find something to tie him with, Petrie."

I moved forward to Smith's side, and was about to pass him in the narrow doorway. The hulk moved beneath our feet like a living thing—groaning, creaking—and the water lapped about the rotten woodwork with a sound infinitely dreary.

"Put up your hands!" ordered Smith imperatively.

Fu-Manchu slowly raised his hands, and a smile dawned upon the impassive features—a smile that had no mirth in it, only menace, revealing as it did his even, discoloured teeth, but leaving the filmed eyes inanimate, dull, inhuman.

He spoke softly, sibilantly.

"I would advise Dr. Petrie to glance behind him before he moves."

Smith's keen grey eyes never for a moment quitted the speaker. The gleaming barrel moved not a hair's breadth. But I glanced quickly over my shoulder—and stifled a cry of pure horror.

A wicked, pock-marked face, with wolfish fangs bared, and jaundiced eyes squinting obliquely into mine, was within two inches of me. A lean, brown hand and arm, the great thews standing up like cords, held a crescent-shaped knife a fraction of an inch above my jugular vein. A slight movement must have despatched me; a sweep of the fearful weapon, I doubt not, would have severed my head from my body.

"Smith!" I whispered hoarsely, "don't look around. For God's sake keep him covered. But a dacoit has his knife at my throat!"

Then, for the first time, Smith's hand trembled. But his glance never wavered from the malignant, emotionless countenance of Dr. Fu-Manchu. He clenched his teeth hard, so that the muscles stood out prominently upon his jaw.

I suppose that silence which followed my awful discovery prevailed but a few seconds. To me those seconds were each a lingering death. There, below, in that groaning hulk, I knew more of icy terror than any of our meetings with the murder-group had brought to me before; and through my brain throbbed a thought: the girl had betrayed us!

"You supposed that I was alone?" suggested Fu-Manchu. "So I was."

Yet no trace of fear had broken through the impassive yellow mask when we had entered.

"But my faithful servant followed you," he added. "I thank him. The honours, Mr. Smith, are mine, I think?"

Smith made no reply. I divined that he was thinking furiously. Fu-Manchu moved his hand to caress the marmoset, which had leapt playfully upon his shoulder, and crouched there gibing at us in a whistling voice.

"Don't stir!" said Smith savagely. "I warn you!"

Fu-Manchu kept his hand raised.

"May I ask how you discovered my retreat?" he asked.

"This hulk has been watched since dawn," lied Smith brazenly.

"So?" The Doctor's filmed eyes cleared for a moment. "And today you compelled me to burn a house, and you have captured one of my people, too. I congratulate you. She would not betray me though lashed with scorpions."

The great gleaming knife was so near to my neck that a sheet of note-paper could scarcely have been slipped between blade and vein, I think; but my heart throbbed even more wildly when I heard those words.

"An impasse," said Fu-Manchu. "I have a proposal to make. I assume that you would not accept my word for anything?"

"I would not," replied Smith promptly.

"Therefore," pursued the Chinaman, and the occasional guttural alone marred his perfect English, "I must accept yours. Of your resources outside this cabin I know nothing. You, I take it, know as little of mine. My Burmese friend and Dr. Petrie will lead the way, then; you and I will follow. We will strike out across the marsh for, say, three hundred yards. You will then place your pistol on the ground, pledging me your word to leave it there. I shall further require your assurance that you will make no attempt upon me until I have retraced my steps. I and my good servant will withdraw, leaving you, at the expiration of the specified period, to act as you see fit. Is it agreed?"

Smith hesitated. Then:

"The dacoit must leave his knife also," he stipulated.

Fu-Manchu smiled his evil smile again.

"Agreed. Shall I lead the way?"

"No!" rapped Smith. "Petrie and the dacoit first; then you; I last."

A guttural word of command from Fu-Manchu, and we left the cabin, with its evil odours, its mortuary specimens, and its strange instruments, and in the order arranged mounted to the deck.

"It will be awkward on the ladder," said Fu-Manchu. "Dr. Petrie, I will accept your word to adhere to the terms."

"I promise," I said, the words almost choking me.

We mounted the rising and dipping ladder; all reached the pier, and strode out across the flats, the Chinaman always under close cover of Smith's revolver. Around about our feet, now leaping ahead, now gambolling back, came and went the marmoset. The dacoit, dressed solely in a dark loin-cloth, walked beside me, carrying his huge knife, and sometimes glancing at me with his blood-lustful eyes. Never before, I venture to say, had an autumn moon lighted such a scene in that place.

"Here we part," said Fu-Manchu, and spoke another word to his follower.

The man threw his knife upon the ground.

"Search him, Petrie," directed Smith. "He may have a second concealed."

The Doctor consented; and I passed my hands over the man's scanty garments.

"Now search Fu-Manchu."

This also I did. And never have I experienced a similar sense of revulsion from any human being. I shuddered, as though I had touched a venomous reptile.

Smith threw down his revolver.

"I curse myself for an honourable fool," he said. "No one could dispute my right to shoot you dead where you stand."

Knowing him as I did, I could tell from the suppressed passion in Smith's voice that only by his unhesitating acceptance of my friend's word, and implicit faith in his keeping it, had Dr. Fu-Manchu escaped just retribution at that moment. Fiend though he was, I admired his courage; for all this he too must have known.

The Doctor turned, and with the dacoit walked back. Nayland Smith's next move filled me with surprise. For just as, silently, I was thanking God for my escape, my friend began shedding his coat, collar and waistcoat.

"Pocket your valuables, and do the same," he muttered hoarsely. "We have a poor chance, but we are both fairly fit. Tonight, Petrie, we literally have to run for our lives."

We live in a peaceful age, wherein it falls to the lot of few men to owe their survival to their fleetness of foot. At Smith's words I realized in a flash that such was to be our fate tonight.

I have said that the hulk lay off a sort of promontory. East and west, then, we had nothing to hope for. To the south was Fu-Manchu; and even as, stripped of our heavier garments, we started to run northward, the weird signal of a dacoit rose on the night and was answered—was answered again.

"Three, at least," hissed Smith, "three armed dacoits. Hopeless."

"Take the revolver," I cried. "Smith, it's—"

"No," he rapped, through clenched teeth. "A servant of the Crown in the East makes his motto: 'Keep your word, though it break your neck!' I don't think we need fear it being used against us.

Fu-Manchu avoids noisy methods."

So back we ran, over the course by which, earlier, we had come. It was, roughly, a mile to the first building—a deserted cottage— and another quarter of a mile to any that was occupied. Our chance of meeting a living soul, other than Fu-Manchu's dacoits, was practically *nil*.

At first we ran easily, for it was the second half-mile that would decide our fate. The professional murderers who pursued us ran like panthers, I knew; and I dared not allow my mind to dwell upon those yellow figures with the curved, gleaming knives. For a long time neither of us looked back.

On we ran, and on—silently, doggedly.

Then a hissing breath from Smith warned me what to expect.

Should I, too, look back? Yes. It was impossible to resist the horrid fascination.

I threw a quick glance over my shoulder.

And never while I live shall I forget what I saw. Two of the pursuing dacoits had outdistanced their fellow (or fellows), and were actually within three hundred yards of us.

More like dreadful animals they looked than human beings, running bent forward, with their faces curiously uptilted. The brilliant moonlight' gleamed upon bared teeth, as I could see, even at that distance, even in that quick, agonized glance, and it gleamed upon the crescent-shaped knives.

"As hard as you can go now," panted Smith. "We must make an attempt to break into the empty cottage. Only chance."

I had never in my younger days been a notable runner; for Smith I cannot speak. But I am confident that the next half-mile was done in time that would not have disgraced a crack man. Not once again did either of us look back. Yard upon yard we raced forward together! My heart seemed to be bursting. My leg muscles throbbed with pain. At last, with the empty cottage in sight, it came to that pass with me when another three yards looks as unattainable as three miles. Once I stumbled.

"My God!" came from Smith, weakly.

But I recovered myself. Bare feet pattered close upon our heels, and panting breaths told how even Fu-Manchu's bloodhounds were hard put to it by the killing pace we had made.

"Smith," I whispered, "look in front. Someone!"

As through a red mist I had seen a dark shape detach itself from the shadows of the cottage, and merge into them again. It could only be another dacoit; but Smith, not heeding, or not hearing, my faintly whispered words, crashed open the gate and hurled himself blindly at the door.

It burst open before him with a resounding boom, and he pitched forward into the interior darkness. Flat upon the floor he lay, for as, with a last effort, I gained the threshold and dragged myself within, I almost fell over his recumbent body.

Madly I snatched at the door. His foot held it open. I kicked the foot away, and banged the door to. As I turned, the leading dacoit, his eyes starting from their sockets, his face the face of a demon, leapt through the gateway.

That Smith had burst the latch I felt assured, but by some divine accident my weak hands found the bolt. With the last ounce of strength spared to me I thrust it home in the rusty socket—as a full six inches of shining steel split the middle panel and protruded above my head.

I dropped, sprawling, beside my friend.

A terrific blow shattered every pane of glass in the solitary window, and one of the grinning animal faces looked in.

"Sorry, old man," whispered Smith, and his voice was barely audible. Weakly he grasped my hand. "My fault. I shouldn't have let you come."

From the corner of the room where the black shadows lay flicked a long tongue of flame. Muffled, staccato, came the report. And the yellow face at the window was blotted out.

One wild cry, ending in a rattling gasp, told of a dacoit gone to his account.

A grey figure glided past me and was silhouetted against the broken window.

Again the pistol sent its message into the night, and again came the reply to tell how well and truly that message had been delivered.

In the stillness, intense by sharp contrast, the sound of bare soles pattering upon the path outside stole to me. Two runners, I thought there were, so that four dacoits must have been upon our trail. The room was full of pungent smoke. I staggered to my feet as the grey figure with the revolver turned toward me. Something familiar there was in that long grey garment, and now I perceived why I had thought so.

It was my grey rain-coat.

"Kâramanèh," I whispered.

And Smith, supporting himself uprightly with difficulty, and holding fast to the ledge beside the door, muttered something hoarsely, which sounded like "God bless her!"

The girl trembling now, placed her hands upon my shoulders with that quaint, pathetic gesture peculiarly her own.

"I followed you," she said. "Did you not know I should follow you? But I had to hide because of another who was following also. I had but just reached this place when I saw you running towards me."

She broke off and turned to Smith.

"This is your pistol." she said naïvely. "I found it in your bag. Will you please take it!"

He took it without a word. Perhaps he could not trust himself to speak.

"Now go. Hurry!" she said. "You are not safe yet."

"But you?" I asked.

"You have failed," she replied. "I must go back to him. There is no other way."

Strangely sick at heart for a man who had just had a miraculous escape from death, I opened the door. Coatless, dishevilled figures, my friend and I stepped out into the moonlight.

Hideous under the pale rays lay the two dead men, their glazed eyes upcast to the peace of the blue heavens. Kâramanèh had shot to kill, for both had bullets in their brains. If God ever planned a more complex nature than hers, a nature more tumultuous with conflicting passions, I cannot conceive of it. Yet her beauty was of the sweetest; and in some respects she had the heart of a child—this girl who could shoot so straightly.

"We must send the police tonight," said Smith. "Or the papers—"

"Hurry," came the girl's voice commandingly from the darkness of the cottage.

It was a singular situation. My very soul rebelled against it. But what could we do?

"Tell us where we can communicate," began Smith.

"Hurry. I shall be suspected. Do you want him to kill me?"

We moved away. All was very still now, and the lights glimmered faintly ahead. Not a wisp of cloud brushed the moon's disc.

"Good-night, Kâramanèh," I whispered softly.

CHAPTER EIGHTEEN

"ANDAMAN—SECOND"

To pursue further the adventure on the marshes would be a task at once useless and thankless. In its actual and in its dramatic significance it concluded with our parting from Kâramanèh. And in that parting I learnt what Shakespeare meant by "sweet sorrow".

There was a world, I learnt, upon the confines of which I stood, a world whose very existence hitherto had been unsuspected. Not the least of the mysteries which peeped from the darkness was the mystery of the heart of Kâramanèh. I sought to forget her. I sought to remember her. Indeed, in the latter task I found one more congenial, yet in the direction and extent of the ideas which it engendered, one that led me to a precipice.

East and West may not intermingle. As a student of world-policies, as a physician, I admitted, could not deny, that truth. Again, if Kâramanèh were to be credited, she had come to Fu-Manchu a slave; had fallen into the hands of the raiders; had crossed the desert with the slave-drivers; had known the house of the slave dealer. Could it be? With the fading of the crescent of Islam I had thought such things to have passed.

But if it were so?

At the mere thought of a girl so deliciously beautiful in the brutal power of slavers, I found myself grinding my teeth—closing my eyes in a futile attempt to blot out the pictures called up.

Then, at such times, I would find myself discrediting her story. Again, I would find myself wondering, vaguely, why such problems persistently haunted my mind. But always, my heart had an answer. And I was a medical man, who sought to build up a family practice!—who, in brief, a very short time ago, had thought himself past the hot follies of youth and entered upon that staid phase of life wherein the daily problems of the medical profession hold absolute sway and such seductive follies as dark eyes and red lips find no place—are excluded!

But it is foreign from the purpose of this plain record to enlist sympathy for the recorder. The topic upon which, here, I have ventured to touch was one fascinating enough to me; I cannot hope that it holds equal charm for any other. Let us return to that which it is my duty to narrate and let us forget my brief digression.

It is a fact, singular but true, that few Londoners know London. Under the guidance of my friend, Nayland Smith, I had learned, since his return from Burma, how there are haunts in the very heart of the metropolis whose existence is unsuspected by all but the few; places unknown even to the ubiquitous copy-hunting pressman.

Into a quiet thoroughfare not two minutes' walk from the pulsing life of Leicester Square, Smith led the way. Before a door sandwiched in between two dingy shop-fronts he paused and turned to me.

"Whatever you see or hear," he cautioned, "express no surprise."

A cab had dropped us at the corner. We both wore dark suits and fez caps with black silk tassels. My complexion had been artificially reduced to a shade resembling the deep tan of my friend's. He rang the bell beside the door.

Almost immediately it was opened by a negro woman—gross, hideously ugly.

Smith uttered something in voluble Arabic. As a linguist his attainments were a constant source of surprise. The jargons of the East, Far and Near, he spoke like his mother tongue. The woman immediately displayed the utmost servility, ushering us into an ill-lighted passage, with every evidence of profound respect. Following this passage, and passing an inner door, from beyond whence proceeded bursts of discordant music, we entered a little room, bare of furniture, with coarse matting for mural decoration, and a patternless red carpet on the floor. In a niche burnt a common metal lamp.

The negress left us, and close upon her departure entered a very aged man with a long patriarchal beard, who greeted my friend with dignified courtesy. Following a brief conversation, the aged Arab—for such he appeared to be—drew aside a strip of matting, revealing a dark recess. Placing his finger upon his lips, he silently invited us to enter.

We did so, and the mat was dropped behind us. The sounds of crude music were now much plainer, and as Smith slipped a little shutter side I gave a start of surprise.

Beyond lay a fairly large apartment, having divans or low seats around three of its walls. These divans were occupied by a motley company of Turks, Egyptians, Greeks, and others; and I noted two Chinese. Most of them smoked cigarettes, and some were drinking. A girl was performing a sinuous dance upon the square carpet occupying the centre of the floor, accompanied by a young negro woman upon a guitar and by several members of the assembly who clapped their hands to the music or hummed a low, monotonous melody.

Shortly after our entrance into the passage the dance terminated, and the dancer fled through a curtained door at the further end of the room. A buzz of conversation arose.

"It is a sort of combined *Wekâleh* and place of entertainment for a certain class of Oriental resident in, or visiting, London," Smith whispered. "The old gentleman who has just left us is the proprietor or host. I have been here before on several occasions, but have always drawn blank."

He was peering out eagerly into the strange club-room.

"Whom do you expect to find here?" I asked.

"It is a recognized meeting-place," said Smith in my ear. "It is almost a certainty that some of the Fu-Manchu group use it at times."

Curiously I surveyed all those faces which were visible from the spy-hole. My eyes rested particularly upon the two Chinamen.

"Do you recognize anyone?" I whispered.

"S-sh!"

Smith was craning his neck so as to command a sight of the doorway. He obstructed my view, and only by his tense attitude and some subtle wave of excitement which he communicated to me did I know that a new arrival was entering.

The hum of conversation died away, and in the ensuing silence I heard the rustle of draperies. The newcomer was a woman, then. Fearful of making any noise, I yet managed to get my eyes to the level of the shutter.

A woman in an elegant flame-coloured opera-cloak was crossing the floor and coming in the direction of the spot where we were concealed. She wore a soft silk scarf about her head, a fold partly draped across her face. A momentary view I had of her—and wildly incongruous she looked in that place—and she had disappeared from sight, having approached some one invisible who sat upon the divan immediately beneath our point of vantage.

From the way in which the company gazed toward her, I divined that she was no habituée of the place, but that her presence there was as greatly surprising to those in the room as it was to me.

Whom could she be, this elegant lady who visited such a haunt— who, it would seem, was so anxious to disguise her identity, but who was dressed for a society function rather than for a midnight expedition of so unusual a character?

I began a whispered question, but Smith tugged at my arm to silence me. His excitement was intense. Had his keener powers enabled him to recognize the unknown?

A faint but most peculiar perfume stole to my nostrils, a perfume which seemed to contain the very soul of Eastern mystery. Only one woman known to me used that perfume—Kâramanèh.

Then it was she!

At last my friend's vigilance had been rewarded. Eagerly I bent forward. Smith literally quivered in anticipation of a discovery.

Again the strange perfume was wafted to our hiding-place; and, glancing neither to right nor left, I saw Kâramanèh—for that it was she I no longer doubted —recross the room and disappear.

"The man she spoke to," hissed Smith. "We must see him! We must have him!"

He pulled the mat aside and stepped out into the anteroom. It was empty. Down the passage he led, and we were almost come to the door of the big room when it was thrown open and a man came rapidly out, opened the street door before Smith could reach him, and was gone, slamming it fast.

I can swear that we were not four seconds behind him, but when we gained the street it was empty. Our quarry had disappeared as if by magic. A big car was just turning the corner toward Leicester Square.

"That is the girl," rapped Smith, "but where in heaven's name is the man to whom she brought the message? I would give a hundred pounds to know what business is afoot. To think that we have had such an opportunity and have thrown it away!"

Angry and nonplussed he stood at the corner, looking in the direction of the crowded thoroughfare into which the car had been driven, tugging at the lobe of his ear, as was his habit in such moments of perplexity, and sharply clicking his teeth together. I, too, was very thoughtful. Clues were few enough in those days of our war with that giant antagonist. The mere thought that our trifling error of judgment tonight in tarrying a moment too long might mean the victory of Fu-Manchu, might mean the turning of the balance which a wise providence had adjusted between the white and yellow races, was appalling.

To Smith and I, who knew something of the secret influences at work to overthrow the Indian Empire, to place, it might be, the whole of Europe and America beneath an Eastern rule, it seemed that a great yellow hand was stretched out over London. Dr. Fu-Manchu was a menace to the civilized world. Yet his very existence remained unsuspected by the millions whose fate he sought to command.

"Into what dark scheme have we had a glimpse?" said Smith. "What State secret is to be filched? What faithful servant of the British Raj to be spirited away? Upon whom now has Fu-Manchu set his death seal?"

"Kâramanèh on this occasion may not have been acting as an emissary of the Doctor."

"I feel assured that she was, Petrie. Of the many whom this yellow cloud may at any moment envelop, to which one did her message refer? The man's instructions were urgent. Witness his hasty departure. Curse it!" He dashed his right clenched fist into the palm of his left hand. "I never had a glimpse of his face, first to last. To think of the hours I have spent in that place, in anticipation of just such a meeting—only to bungle the opportunity when it arose!"

Scarce heeding what course we followed, we had come now to Piccadilly Circus, and had walked out into the heart of the night's traffic. I just dragged Smith aside in time to save him from the off-front wheel of a big Mercédès. Then the traffic was blocked, and we found ourselves dangerously penned in amidst the press of vehicles.

Somehow we extricated ourselves, jeered at by taxi-drivers, who naturally took us for two simple Oriental visitors; and just before that impassable barrier, the arm of a London policeman, was lowered and the stream moved on, a faint breath of perfume became perceptible to me.

The cabs and cars about us were actually beginning to move again, and there was nothing for it but a hasty retreat to the kerb. I could not pause to glance behind, but instinctively I knew that someone—someone who used that rare, fragrant essence—was leaning from the window of the car.

"*Andaman—second!*" floated a soft whisper.

We gained the pavement as the pent-up traffic roared upon its way.

Smith had not noticed the perfume worn by the unseen occupant of the car, had not detected the whispered words. But I had no reason to doubt my senses, and I knew beyond question that Kârarnanèh had been within a yard of us, had recognized us, and had uttered those words for our guidance.

On regaining my rooms, we devoted a whole hour to considering what *"Andaman—second"* could possibly mean.

"Hang it all!" cried Smith, "it might mean anything—the result of a race, for instance."

He burst into one of his rare laughs, and began to stuff broad-cut mixture into his briar. I could see that he had no intention of turning in.

"I can think of no one—no one of note—in London at present upon whom it is likely that Fu-Manchu would make an attempt," he said, "I except ourselves."

We began methodically to go through the long list of names which we had compiled and to review our elaborate notes. When, at last, I turned in, the night had given place to a new day. But sleep evaded me, and *"Andaman—second"* danced like a mocking phantom through my brain.

Then I heard the telephone bell. I heard Smith speaking.

A minute afterwards he was in my room, his face very grim.

"I knew as well as if I'd seen it with my own eyes that some black business was afoot last night," he said. "And it was; within pistol-shot of us! Some one has got at Frank Norris West. Inspector Weymouth has just been on the phone."

"Norris West!" I cried, "the American aviator—and inventor—"

"Of the West aero-torpedo—yes. He's been offering it to the English War Office, and they have delayed too long."

I got out of bed.

"What do you mean?"

"I mean that its potentialities have attracted the attention of Dr. Fu-Manchu!"

Those words operated electrically. I do not know how long I was in dressing, how long a time elapsed ere the cab for which Smith had phoned arrived, how many precious minutes were lost upon the journey; but, in a nervous whirl, these things slipped into the past, like the telegraph poles seen from the window of an express, and still in that tensed state, we came upon the scene of this newest outrage.

Mr. Norris West, whose lean, stoic face had latterly figured so often in the daily Press, lay upon the floor in the little entrance hall of his chambers, flat upon his back, with the telephone receiver in his hand.

The outer door had been forced by the police. They had had to remove a piece of the panelling to get at the bolt. A medical man was leaning over the recumbent figure in the striped pyjama suit, and Inspector Weymouth stood watching him as Smith and I entered.

"He has been heavily drugged," said the doctor, sniffing at West's lips, "but I cannot say what drug has been used. It isn't chloroform or anything of that nature. He can safely be left to sleep it off, I think."

I agreed, after a brief examination.

"It's most extraordinary," said Weymouth. "He rang up the Yard about an hour ago and said his chambers had been invaded by Chinamen. Then the man at the phone plainly heard him fall. When we got here his front door was bolted, as you've seen, and the windows are three floors up. Nothing is disturbed."

"The plans of the aero-torpedo?" rapped Smith.

"I take it they are in the safe in his bedroom," replied the detective, "and that is locked all right. I think he must have taken an overdose of something and had illusions. But in case there was anything in what he mumbled (you could hardly understand him) I thought it as well to send for you."

"Quite right," said Smith rapidly. His eyes shone like steel. "Lay him on the bed, Inspector."

It was done, and my friend walked into the bedroom.

Save that the bed was disordered, showing that West had been sleeping in it, there were no evidences of the extraordinary invasion mentioned by the drugged man. It was a small room—the chambers were of that kind which are let furnished—and very neat. A safe with a combination lock stood in a corner. The window was open about a foot at the top.

Smith tried the safe and found it fast. He stood for a moment clicking his teeth together, by which I knew him to be perplexed. He walked over to the window and threw it up. We both looked out.

"You see," came Weymouth's voice, "it is altogether too far from the court below for our cunning Chinese friends to have fixed a ladder with one of their bamboo-rod arrangements. And, even if they could get up there, it's too far down from the roof—two more stories—for them to have fixed it from there."

Smith nodded thoughtfully, at the same time trying the strength of an iron bar which ran from side to side of the window-sill. Suddenly he stooped, with a sharp exclamation. Bending over his shoulder I saw what it was that had attracted his attention.

Clearly imprinted upon the dust-coated grey stone of the sill was a confused series of marks—tracks—call them what you will.

Smith straightened himself and turned a wondering look upon me

"What is it, Petrie?" he said amazedly. "Some kind of bird has been here, and recently."

Inspector Weymouth in turn examined the marks.

"I never saw bird tracks like these, Mr. Smith," he muttered.

Smith was tugging at the lobe of his ear.

"No," he returned reflectively, "come to think of it, neither did I."

He twisted around, looking at the man on the bed.

"Do you think it was all an illusion?" asked the detective.

"What about those marks on the window-sill?" jerked Smith.

He began restlessly pacing about the room, sometimes stopping before the locked safe and frequently glancing at Norris West.

Suddenly he walked out and briefly examined the other apartments, only to return again to the bedroom.

"Petrie," he said, "we are losing valuable time. West must be aroused!"

Inspector Weymouth stared.

Smith turned to me impatiently. The doctor summoned by the police was gone. "Is there no means of arousing him, Petrie?" he said.

"Doubtless," I replied, "he could be revived if one but knew what drug he had taken."

My friend began his restless pacing again, and suddenly pounced upon a little phial of tablets which had been hidden behind some books on a shelf near the bed. He uttered a triumphant exclamation.

"See what we have here, Petrie!" he directed, handing the phial to me. "It bears no label."

I crushed one of the tablets in my palm and applied my tongue to the powder.

"Some preparation of chloral hydrate," I pronounced.

"A sleeping draught?" suggested Smith eagerly.

"We might try," I said, and scribbled a formula upon a leaf of my note-book. I asked Weymouth to send the man who accompanied him to call up the nearest chemist and procure the antidote.

During the man's absence Smith stood contemplating the unconscious inventor, a peculiar expression upon his bronzed face.

"*Andaman—second*," he muttered. "Shall we find the key to the riddle here, I wonder?"

Inspector Weymouth, who had concluded, I think, that the mysterious telephone call was due to mental aberration on the part of Norris West, was gnawing at his moustache impatiently when his assistant returned. I administered the powerful restorative, and although, as later transpired, chloral was not responsible for West's condition, the antidote operated successfully.

Norris West struggled into a sitting position, and looked about him with haggard eyes.

"The Chinamen! The Chinamen!" he muttered.

He sprang to his feet, glaring wildly at Smith and I, reeled, and almost fell.

"It is all right," I said, supporting him. "I'm a doctor. You have been unwell."

"Have the police come?" he burst out. "The safe—try the safe!"

"It's all right," said Inspector Weymouth. "The safe is locked—unless some one else knows the combination, there's nothing to worry about."

"No one else knows it," said West, and staggered unsteadily to the safe. Clearly his mind was in a dazed condition, but, setting his jaw with a curious expression of grim determination, he collected his thoughts and opened his safe.

He bent down, looking in.

In some way the knowledge came to me that the curtain was about to rise on a new and surprising act in the Fu-Manchu drama.

"God!" he whispered—we could scarcely hear him—"the plans are gone!"

CHAPTER NINETEEN

NORRIS WEST'S STORY

I have never seen a man quite so surprised as Inspector Weymouth. "This is absolutely incredible!" he said. "There's only one door to your chambers. We found it bolted from the inside."

"Yes," groaned West, pressing his hand to his forehead. "I bolted it myself at eleven o'clock, when I came in."

"No human being could climb up or down to your windows. The plans of the aero-torpedo were inside the safe."

"I put them there myself," said West, "on returning from the War Office, and I had occasion to consult them after I had come in and bolted the door. I returned them to the safe and locked it. That it was still locked you saw for yourselves, and no one else in the world knows the combination."

"But the plans have gone," said Weymouth. "It's magic! How was it done? What happened last night, sir? What did you mean when you rang us up?"

Smith during this colloquy was pacing rapidly up and down the room. He turned abruptly to the aviator.

"Every fact you can remember, Mr. West, please," he said tersely, "and be as brief as you possibly can."

"I came in, as I said," explained West, "about eleven o'clock, and, having made some notes relating to an interview arranged for this morning, I locked the plans in the safe and turned in."

"There was no one hidden anywhere in your chambers?" snapped Smith.

"There was not," replied West. "I looked. I invariably do. Almost immediately, I went to sleep."

"How many chloral tabloids did you take?" I interrupted.

Norris West turned to me with a slow smile.

"You're acute, doctor," he said. "I took two. It's a bad habit, but I can't sleep without. They are specially made up for me by a firm in Philadelphia.

"How long sleep lasted, when it became filled with uncanny dreams, and when those dreams merged into reality, I do not know—shall never know, I suppose. But out of the dreamless void a face came to me—closer—closer—and peered into mine.

"I was in that curious condition wherein one knows that one is dreaming and seeks to awaken to escape. But a nightmare-like oppression held me. So I must lie and gaze into the seared yellow face that hung over me, for it would drop so close that I could trace the cicatrized scar running from the left ear to the corner of the mouth, and drawing up the lip like the lip of a snarling cur. I could look into the malignant, jaundiced eyes; I could hear the dim whispering of the distorted mouth—whispering that seemed to counsel something—something evil. That whispering intimacy was indescribably repulsive. Then the wicked yellow face would be withdrawn, and would recede until it became as a pin's head in the darkness far above me—almost like a glutinous, liquid thing.

"Somehow I got upon my feet, or dreamed I did—God knows where dreaming ended and reality began. Gentlemen, maybe you'll conclude I went mad last night, but as I stood holding on to the bed-rail I heard the blood throbbing through my arteries with a noise like a screw-propeller. I started laughing. The laughter issued from my lips with a shrill whistling sound that pierced me with physical pain and seemed to wake the echoes of the whole block. I thought, myself, I was going mad, and I tried to command my will—to break the power of the choral—for I concluded that I had accidentally taken an overdose.

"Then the walls of my bedroom started to recede, till at last I stood holding on to a bed which had shrunk to the size of a doll's cot, in the middle of a room like Trafalgar Square! That window yonder was such a long way off I could scarcely see it, but I could just detect a Chinaman—the owner of the evil yellow face—creeping through it. He was followed by another, who was enormously tall—so tall that, as they came towards me (and it seemed to take them something like half an hour to cross this incredible apartment in my dream), the second Chinaman seemed to tower over me like a cypress-tree.

"I looked up to his face—his wicked, hairless face. Mr. Smith, whatever age I live to, I'll never forget that face I saw last night—or did I see it? God knows! The pointed chin, the great dome of a forehead, and the eyes—heavens above, the huge green eyes—!"

He shook like a sick man, and I glanced at Smith significantly. Inspector Weymouth was stroking his moustache, and his mingled expression of incredulity and curiosity was singular to behold.

"The pumping of my blood," continued West, "seemed to be bursting my body; the room kept expanding and contracting. One time the ceiling would be pressing down on my head, and the

Chinamen—sometimes I thought there were two of them, sometimes twenty—became dwarfs; the next instant it shot up like a roof of a cathedral.

" 'Can I be awake,' I whispered, 'or am I dreaming?'

"My whisper went sweeping in windy echoes about the walls, and was lost in the shadowy distances up under the invisible roof.

" 'You are dreaming—yes.' It was the Chinaman with the green eyes who was addressing me, and the words that he uttered appeared to occupy an immeasurable time in the utterance. 'But at will I can render the subjective objective.' I don't think I can have dreamed those singular words, gentlemen?

"And then he fixed the green eyes upon me the blazing green eyes. I made no attempt to move. They seemed to be draining me of something vital—bleeding me of every drop of mental power. The whole nightmare room grew green, and I felt that I was being absorbed into its greenness.

"I can see what you think. And even in my delirium—if it was delirium—I thought the same. Now comes the climax of my experience—my vision—I don't know what to call it. I *saw* some *words issuing* from my own mouth!"

Inspector Weymouth coughed discreetly. Smith whisked around upon him.

"This will be outside your experience, Inspector, I know," he said, "but Mr. Norris West's statement does not surprise me in the least. I know to what the experience was due."

Weymouth stared incredulously, but a drawing perception of the truth was come to me, too.

"How I *saw a sound* I just won't attempt to explain; I simply tell you I saw it. Somehow I knew I had betrayed myself—given something away."

"You gave away the secret of the lock combination!" rapped Smith.

"Eh!" grunted Weymouth.

But West went on hoarsely:

"Just before the blank came a name flashed before my eyes. It was 'Bayard Taylor'."

At that I interrupted West.

"I understand!" I cried. "I understand! Another name has just occurred to me, Mr. West—that of the Frenchman, Moreau."

"You have solved the mystery," said Smith. "It was natural Mr. West should have thought of the American traveller, Bayard Taylor, though. Moreau's book is purely scientific. He has probably never read it."

"I fought with the stupor that was overcoming me," continued West, "striving to associate that vaguely familiar name with the fantastic things through which I moved. It seemed to me that the room was empty again. I made for the hall, for the telephone. I could scarcely drag my feet along. It seemed to take me half an hour to get there. I remember calling up Scotland Yard, and I remember no more."

There was a short, tense interval.

In some respects I was nonplussed; but, frankly, I think Inspector Weymouth considered West insane. Smith, his hands locked behind his back, stared out of the window.

"*Andaman—second,*" he said suddenly. "Weymouth, when is the first train to Tilbury?"

"Five twenty-two from Fenchurch Street," replied the Scotland Yard man promptly.

"Too late!" rapped my friend. "Jump in a taxi and pick up two good men to leave for China at once! Then go and charter a special to Tilbury to leave in twenty-five minutes. Order another cab to wait outside for me."

Weymouth was palpably amazed, but Smith's tone was imperative. The inspector departed hastily.

I stared at Smith, not comprehending what prompted this singular course.

"Now that you can think clearly, Mr. West," he said, "of what does your experience remind you? The errors of perception regarding time; the idea of *seeing a sound*; the illusion that the room alternately increased and diminished in size; your fit of laughter, and the recollection of the name, Bayard Taylor. Since evidently you are familiar with that author's work—*The Land of the Saracen*, is it not?—these symptoms of the attack should be familiar, I think."

Norris West pressed his hands to his evidently aching head,

"Bayard Taylor's book," he said dully. "Yes! ... I know of what my brain sought to remind me—Taylor's account of his experience under hashish. Mr. Smith, someone doped me with hashish!"

Smith nodded grimly.

"*Cannabis indica*," I said—"Indian hemp. That is what you were drugged with. I have no doubt that now you experience a feeling of nausea and intense thirst, with aching in the muscles, particularly the deltoid? I think you must have taken at least fifteen grains."

Smith stopped his perambulations immediately in front of West, looking into his dulled eyes.

"Someone visited your chambers last night," he said slowly, "and for your chloral tablets substituted some containing hashish, or perhaps not pure hashish. Fu-Manchu is a profound chemist."

Norris West started.

"Someone substituted—" he began.

"Exactly," said Smith looking at him keenly, "someone who was here yesterday. Have you any idea whom it could have been?"

West hesitated. "I had a visitor in the afternoon," he said, seemingly speaking the words unwillingly, "but—"

"A lady?" jerked Smith. "I suggest that it was a lady."

West nodded.

"You're quite right," he admitted. "I don't know how you arrived at the conclusion, but a lady whose acquaintance I made recently—a foreign lady—"

"Kâramenèh!" snapped Smith.

"I don't know what you mean in the least; but she came here—knowing this to be my present address—to ask me to protect her from a mysterious man who had followed her right from Charing Cross. She said he was down in the lobby, and naturally I asked her to wait here whilst I went and sent him about his business."

He laughed shortly.

"I am over-old," he said, "to be guyed by a woman. You spoke just now of some one called Fu-Manchu. Is that the crook I'm indebted to for the loss of my plans? I've had attempts made by agents of two European governments, but a Chinaman is a novelty."

"This Chinaman," Smith assured him, "is the greatest novelty of his age. You recognize your symptoms now from Bayard Taylor's account?"

"Mr. West's statement," I said "ran closely parallel with portions of Moreau's book on *Hashish Hallucinations*. Only Fu-Manchu, I think, would have thought of employing Indian hemp. I doubt, though, if it was the pure *Cannabis indica*. At any rate, it acted as an opiate—"

"And drugged Mr. West," interrupted Smith, "sufficiently to enable Fu-Manchu to enter unobserved."

"Whilst it produced symptoms which rendered him an easy subject for the Doctor's influence. It is difficult in this case to separate hallucination from reality, but I think, Mr. West, that Fu-Manchu must have exercised a hypnotic influence upon your drugged brain. We have evidence that he dragged from you the secret of the combination."

"God knows we have!" said West. "But who is this Fu-Manchu, and how—how in the name of wonder did he get into my chambers?"

Smith pulled out his watch. "That," he said rapidly, "I cannot delay to explain if I'm to intercept the man who has the plans. Come along, Petrie; we must be at Tilbury within the hour. There is just a bare chance."

CHAPTER TWENTY

SOME THEORIES AND A FACT

It was with my mind in a condition of unique perplexity that I hurried with Nayland Smith into the cab which waited and dashed off through the streets in which the busy life of London just stirred into being. I suppose I need not say that I could penetrate no further into this, Fu-Manchu's latest plot, than the drugging of Norris West with hashish? Of his having been so drugged with Indian hemp—that is, converted temporarily into a maniac—would have been evident to any medical man who had heard his statement and noted the distressing after-effects which conclusively pointed to Indian hemp poisoning. Knowing something of the Chinese doctor's powers, I could understand that he might have extracted from West the secret of the combination by sheer force of will whilst the American was under the influence of the drug. But I could not understand how Fu-Manchu had gained access to locked chambers on the third story of a building.

"Smith," I said, "those bird tracks on the window-sill—they furnish the key to a mystery which is puzzling me."

"They do," said Smith, glancing impatiently at his watch. "Consult your memories of Dr. Fu-Manchu's habits—especially your memories of his pets."

I reviewed in my mind the creatures gruesome and terrible which surrounded the Chinaman—the scorpions, the bacteria, the noxious things which were the weapons wherewith he visited death upon whomsoever opposed the establishment of a potential Yellow Empire. But no one of them could account for the imprints upon the dust of West's window-sill.

"You puzzle me, Smith," I confessed. "There is much in this extraordinary case that puzzles me. I can think of nothing to account for the marks."

"Have you thought of Fu-Manchu's marmoset?" asked Smith.

"The monkey!" I cried.

"They were the footprints of a small ape," my friend continued. "For a moment I was deceived as you were, and believed them to be the tracks of a large bird; but I have seen the footprints of apes before now, and a marmoset, though an American variety, I believe, is not unlike some of the apes of Burma."

"I am still in the dark," I said.

"It is pure hypothesis," continued Smith, "but here is the theory—in lieu of a better one it covers the facts. The marmoset—and it is contrary from the character of Fu-Manchu to keep any creature for mere amusement—is trained to perform certain duties.

"You observed the waterspout running up beside the window; you observed the iron bar intended to prevent a window-cleaner from falling out? For an ape the climb from the court below to the sill above was a simple one. He carried a cord, probably attached to his body. He climbed on to the sill, over the bar, and climbed down again. By means of this cord a rope was pulled up over the bar; by means of the rope one of those ladders of silk and bamboo. One of the Doctor's servants ascended—probably to ascertain if the hashish had acted successfully. That was the yellow dream-face which West saw bending over him. Then followed the Doctor, and to his giant will the drugged brain of West was a pliant instrument which he bent to his own ends. The court would be deserted at that hour of the night, and, in any event, directly after the ascent the ladder probably was pulled up, only to be lowered again when West had revealed the secret of his own safe and Fu-Manchu had secured the plans. The reclosing of the safe and the removing of the hashish tablets, leaving no clue beyond the delirious ravings of a drug slave—for so anyone unacquainted with the East must have construed West's story—is particularly characteristic. His own tablets were returned, of course. The sparing of his life alone is a refinement of art which points to a past master."

"Kâramanèh was the decoy again?" I said shortly.

"Certainly. Hers was the task to ascertain West's habits and to substitute the tablets. She it was who waited in the luxurious car— infinitely less likely to attract attention at that hour in that place than a modest taxi—and received the stolen plans. She did her work well."

"Poor Kâramanèh; she had no alternative! I said I would have given a hundred pounds for a sight of the messenger's face—the man to whom she handed them. I would give a thousand, now!"

"*Andaman—second,*" I said. "What did she mean?"

"Then it has not dawned upon you?" cried Smith excitedly, as the cab turned into the station. "The *Andaman,* of the Oriental Navigation Company's line, leaves Tilbury with the next tide for China ports. Our man is a second-class passenger. I am wiring to delay her departure, and the special should get us to the docks inside forty minutes."

Very vividly I can reconstruct in my mind that dash to the docks through the early autumn morning. My friend being invested with extraordinary powers from the highest authorities, by Inspector Weymouth's instructions the line had been cleared all the way.

Something of the tremendous importance of Nayland Smith's mission came home to me as we hurried on to the platform, escorted by the station-master, and the five of us—for Weymouth had two other C.I.D. men with him—took our seats in the special.

Off we went on top speed, roaring through stations, where a glimpse might be had of wondering officials upon the platforms, for a special train was a novelty on the line. All ordinary traffic arrangements were held up until we had passed through, and we reached Tilbury in time which I doubt not constituted a record.

Then, at the docks was the great liner, delayed in her passage to the Far East by the will of my royally empowered companion. It was novel, and infinitely exciting.

"Mr. Commissioner Nayland Smith?" said the captain interrogatively, when we were shown into his room, and looked from one to another, and back to the telegraph form which he held in his hand.

"The same, Captain," said my friend briskly. "I shall not detain you a moment. I am instructing the authorities at all ports east of Suez to apprehend one of your second-class passengers, should he leave the ship. He is in possession of plans which practically belong to the British Government."

"Why not arrest him now?" asked the seaman bluntly.

"Because I don't know him. All second-class passengers' baggage will be searched as they land. I am hoping something from that, if all else fails. But I want you privately to instruct your stewards to watch any passenger of Oriental nationality, and to co-operate with the two

Scotland Yard men who are joining you for the voyage. I look to you to recover these plans, Captain."

"I will do my best," the captain assured him.

Then, from amid the heterogeneous group on the dockside, we were watching the liner depart, and Nayland Smith's expression was a very singular one—Inspector Weymouth stood with us, a badly puzzled man—when occurred the extraordinary incident which to this day remains inexplicable, for, clearly heard by all three of us, a guttural voice said:

"Another victory for China, Mr. Nayland Smith!"

I turned as though I had been stung. Smith turned also. My eyes passed from face to face of the group about us. None was familiar. No one apparently had moved away.

But the voice was the voice of *Doctor Fu-Manchu.*

As I write of it, now, I can appreciate the difference between that happening, as it appealed to us, and as it must appeal to you who merely read of it. It is beyond my powers to convey the sense of the uncanny which the episode created. Yet, even as I think of it, I feel again, though in lesser degree, the chill which seemed to creep through my veins that day.

From my brief history of the wonderful and evil man who once walked, by the many unsuspected, in the midst of the people of England—near whom you, personally, may at some time unwittingly have been—I am aware that much must be omitted. I have no space for lengthy examinations of the many points but ill illuminated with which it is dotted. This incident at the docks is but one such point.

Another is the singular vision which appeared to me whilst I lay in the cellar of the house near Windsor. It has since struck me that it possessed peculiarities akin to those of a hashish hallucination. Can it be that we were drugged on that occasion with Indian hemp?

Cannabis indica is a treacherous narcotic, as every medical man knows full well; but Fu-Manchu's knowledge of the drug was far in advance of our slow science. West's experience proved so much.

I may have neglected opportunities—later, you shall judge if I did so—opportunities to glean for the West some of the strange knowledge of the secret East. Perhaps at a future time I may rectify my errors. Perhaps that wisdom—the wisdom stored up by Fu-Manchu—is lost for ever. There is, however, at least a bare possibility of its survival, in part; and I do not wholly despair of one day publishing a scientific sequel to this record of our dealing with the Chinese doctor.

CHAPTER TWENTY-ONE

THE HOME OF FU-MANCHU

Time wore on and seemingly brought us no nearer, or very little nearer, to our goal. So carefully had my friend Nayland Smith excluded the matter from the Press that, whilst public interest was much engaged with some of the events in the skein of mystery which he was come from Burma to unravel, outside the Secret Service and the special department of Scotland Yard few people recognized that the several murders, accomplished and attempted, robberies and disappearances formed each a link in a chain; fewer still were aware that a baneful presence was in our midst, that a past master of the evil arts lay concealed somewhere in the metropolis; searched for by the keenest wits which the authorities could direct to the task, but eluding all—triumphant, contemptuous.

One link in that chain Smith himself for long failed to recognize. Yet it was a big and important link.

"Petrie," he said to me one morning, "listen to this:

" '... In sight of Shanghai—a dark night. On board the deck of a junk passing close to seaward of the *Andaman* a blue flare started up.

A minute later there was a cry of "Man overboard!"

" 'Inquiry showed the missing man to be a James Edwards, second class, booked to Shanghai. I think the name was assumed. The man was some sort of Oriental, and we had had him under close observation....'

"That's the end of their report," said Smith.

He referred to the two C.I.D. men who had joined the *Andaman* at the moment of her departure from Tilbury.

He carefully lighted his pipe.

"*Is* it a victory for China, Petrie?" he said softly.

"Until the great war reveals her secret resources—and I pray that the day be not in my time—we shall never know," I replied.

Smith began striding up and down the room.

"Whose name," he jerked abruptly, "stands now at the head of our danger list?"

He referred to a list which we had compiled of the notable men intervening between the evil genius who secretly had invaded London and the triumph of his cause—the triumph of the yellow races.

I glanced at our notes.

"Lord Southery," I replied.

Smith tossed the morning paper across to me.

"Look," he said shortly. "He's dead."

I read the account of the peer's death, and glanced at the long obituary notice; but no more than glanced at it. He had but recently returned from the East, and now, after a short illness, had died from some affection of the heart. There had been no intimation that his illness was of a serious nature, and even Smith, who watched over his flock—the flock threatened by the wolf, Fu-Manchu—with jealous zeal, had not suspected that the end was so near.

"Do you think he died a natural death, Smith?" I asked.

My friend reached across the table and rested the tip of a long finger upon one of the sub-headings to the account:

SIR FRANK NARCOMBE SUMMONED TOO LATE!

"You see," said Smith, "Southery died during the night, but Sir Frank Narcombe, arriving a few minutes later, unhesitatingly pronounced death to be due to syncope, and seems to have noticed nothing suspicious."

I looked at him thoughtfully.

"Sir Frank is a great physician," I said slowly, "but we must remember he would be looking for nothing suspicious."

"We must remember," rapped Smith, "that if Dr. Fu-Manchu is responsible for Southery's death, except to the eye of an expert there would be nothing suspicious to see. Fu-Manchu leaves no clues."

"Are you going around?" I asked.

Smith shrugged his shoulders.

"I think not," he replied. "Either a greater one than Fu-Manchu has taken Lord Southery, or the yellow Doctor has done his work so well that no trace remains of his presence in the matter."

Leaving his breakfast untasted, he wandered aimlessly about the room, littering the hearth with matches as he constantly relighted his pipe, which went out every few minutes.

"It's no good, Petrie," he burst out suddenly, "it cannot be a coincidence. We must go around and see him."

An hour later we stood in the silent room, with its drawn blinds and its deathful atmosphere, looking down at the pale intellectual face of Henry Stradwick, Lord Southery, the greatest engineer of his day. The mind that lay behind that splendid brow had planned the construction of the railway for which Russia had paid so great a price, had conceived the scheme for the canal which, in the near future, was to bring two great continents a full week's journey nearer one to the other. But now it would plan no more.

"He had latterly developed symptoms of *angina pectoris*," explained the family physician, "but I had not anticipated a fatal termination so soon. I was called about two o'clock this morning, and found Lord Southery in a dangerously exhausted condition. I did all that was possible, and Sir Frank Narcombe was sent for. But shortly before his arrival the patient expired."

"I understand, Doctor, that you had been treating Lord Southery for *angina pectoris*?" I said.

"Yes," was the reply, "for some months."

"You regard the circumstances of his end as entirely consistent with a death from that cause?"

"Certainly, do you observe anything unusual yourself? Sir Frank Narcombe quite agrees with me. There is surely no room for doubt?"

"No," said Smith, tugging reflectively at the lobe of his left ear. "We do not question the accuracy of your diagnosis in any way, sir."

"But am I not right in supposing that you are connected with the police?" asked the physician.

"Neither Dr. Petrie nor myself are in any way connected with the police," answered Smith. "But, nevertheless, I look to you to regard our recent questions as confidential."

As we were leaving the house, hushed awesomely in deference to the unseen visitor who had touched Lord Southery with grey, cold fingers, Smith paused, detaining a black-coated man who passed us on the stairs.

"You were Lord Southery's valet?

The man bowed.

"Were you in the room at the moment of his fatal seizure?"

"I was, sir."

"Did you see or hear anything unusual—anything unaccountable?"

"Nothing, sir."

"No strange sounds outside the house, for instance?"

The man shook his head, and Smith, taking my arm, passed out into the street

"Perhaps this business is making me imaginative," he said, "but there seems to be something tainting the air in yonder—something peculiar to houses whose doors bear the invisible death-mark of Fu-Manchu."

"You are right, Smith!" I cried. "I hesitated to mention the matter, but I, too, have developed some other sense which warns me of the Doctor's presence. Although there is not a scrap of confirmatory evidence, I am sure that he has brought about Lord Southery's death as if I had seen him strike the blow,"

It was in that torturing frame of mind—chained, helpless, in our ignorance, or by reason of the Chinaman's supernormal genius—that we lived throughout the ensuing days. My friend began to look like a man consumed by a burning fever. Yet, we could not act.

In the growing dark of an evening shortly following I stood idly turning over some of the works exposed for sale outside a second-hand bookseller's in New Oxford Street. One dealing with the secret societies of China struck me as being likely to prove instructive, and I was about to call the shopman when I was startled to feel a hand clutch my arm.

I turned around rapidly—and was looking into the darkly beautiful eyes of Kâramanèh! She—whom I had seen in so many guises—was dressed in a perfectly fitting walking habit, and had much of her wonderful hair concealed beneath a fashionable hat.

She glanced about her apprehensively.

"Quick! Come around the corner. I must speak to you," she said, her musical voice thrilling with excitement.

I never was quite master of myself in her presence. He must have been a man of ice who could have been, I think, for her beauty had all the bouquet of rarity; she was a mystery—and mystery adds charm to a woman. Probably she should have been under arrest, but I know I would have risked much to save her from it.

As we turned into a quiet thoroughfare she stopped and said:

"I am in distress. You have often asked me to enable you to capture Dr. Fu-Manchu. I am prepared to do so."

I could scarcely believe that I heard aright.

"Your brother—" I began.

She seized my arm entreatingly, looking into my eyes.

"You are a doctor," she said. "I want you to come and see him now."

"What! Is he in London?"

"He is at the house of Dr. Fu-Manchu."

"And you would have me—"

"Accompany me there, yes."

Nayland Smith, I doubted not, would have counselled me against trusting my life in the hands of this girl with the pleading eyes. Yet I did so, and with little hesitation; for shortly we were travelling eastward in a closed cab. Kâramanèh was very silent, but always when I turned to her I found her big eyes fixed upon me with an expression in which there was pleading, in which there was sorrow, in which there was something else—something indefinable, yet strangely disturbing. The cabman she had directed to drive to the lower end of the Commercial Road, the neighbourhood of the new docks, and the scene of one of our early adventures with Dr. Fu-Manchu. The mantle of dusk had closed about the squalid activity of the East End streets as we neared our destination. Aliens of every shade of colour were into the glare of the lamps upon the main road about us now, emerging from burrow-like alleys. In the short space of the drive we had passed from the bright world of the West into the dubious underworld of the East.

I do not know that Kâramanèh moved; but in sympathy, as we neared the abode of the sinister Chinaman, she crept nearer to me, and when the cab was discharged, and together we walked down a narrow turning leading riverward, she clung to me fearfully, hesitated, and even seemed upon the point of turning back. But, on overcoming her fear or repugnance, she led on, through a maze of alleyways and courts, wherein I hopelessly lost my bearings, so that it came home to me how wholly I was in the hands of this girl whose history was so full of shadows, whose real character was so inscrutable, whose beauty, whose charm, truly might mask the cunning of a serpent.

I spoke to her.

"*S-sh!*" She laid her hand upon my arm, enjoining me to silence.

The high, drab brick wall of what looked like some part of a dock building loomed above us in the darkness, and the indescribable stenches of the Lower Thames were borne to my nostrils through a gloomy, tunnel-like opening, beyond which whispered the river. The muffled clangour of waterside activity was about us. I heard a key grate in a lock, and Kâramanèh drew me into the shadow of an open door, entered, and closed it behind her.

For the first time I perceived, in contrast to the odours of the court without, the fragrance of the peculiar perfume which now I had come to associate with her. Asbolute darkness was about us, and by this perfume alone I knew that she was near to me, until her hand touched mine, and I was led along an uncarpeted passage and up an uncarpeted stair. A second door was unlocked, and I found myself in an exquisitely furnished room, illuminated by the soft light of a shaded lamp which stood upon a low, inlaid table amidst a perfect ocean of silken cushions, strewn upon a Persian carpet, whose yellow richness was lost in the shadows beyond the circle of light.

Kâramanèh raised a curtain draped before a doorway, and stood listening intently for a moment.

The silence was unbroken.

Then something stirred amid the wilderness of cushions, and two tiny bright eyes looked up at me. Peering closely, I succeeded in distinguishing, crouched in that soft luxuriance, a little ape. It was Dr. Fu-Manchu's marmoset.

"This way," whispered Kâramanèh.

Never, I thought, was a staid medical man committed to a more unwise enterprise, but so far I had gone, and no consideration of prudence could now be of avail.

The corridor beyond was thickly carpeted. Following the direction of a faint light which gleamed ahead, it proved to extend as a balcony across one end of a spacious apartment. Together we stood high up there in the shadows, and looked down upon such a scene as I never could have imagined to exist within many a mile of that district.

The place below was even more richly appointed than the room into which first we had come. Here, as there, piles of cushions formed splashes of gaudy colour about the floor. Three lamps hung by chains from the ceiling, their light softened by rich silk shades. One wall was almost entirely occupied by glass cases containing chemical apparatus, tubes, retorts, and other less orthodox indications of Dr. Fu-Manchu's pursuits, whilst close against another lay the most extraordinary object of a sufficiently extraordinary room—a low couch, upon which was extended the motionless form of a boy. In the light of a lamp which hung directly above him his olive face

showed an almost startling resemblance to that of Kâramanèh—
save that the girl's colouring was more delicate. He had black, curly
hair, which stood out prominently against the white covering upon
which he lay, his hands crossed upon his breast.

Transfixed with astonishment, I stood looking down upon him.
The wonders of *The Arabian Nights* were wonders no longer, for here,
in East End London, was a true magician's palace, lacking not its
beautiful slave, lacking not its enchanted prince!

"It is Azîz, my brother," said Kâramanèh.

We passed down a stairway on to the floor of the apartment.
Kâramanèh knelt and bent over the boy, stroking his hair and
whispering to him lovingly. I, too, bent over him; and I shall never
forget the anxiety in the girl's eyes as she watched me eagerly whilst
I made a brief examination.

Brief, indeed, for even ere I had touched him I knew that the
comely shell held no spark of life. But Kâramanèh fondled the cold
hands, and spoke softly in that Arabic tongue which long before I
had divined must be her native language.

Then, as I remained silent, she turned and looked at me, read the
truth in my eyes, and rose from her knees, stood rigidly upright, and
clutched me tremblingly.

"He is not dead—he is *not* dead!" she whispered; and shook me
as a child might, seeking to arouse me to a proper understanding.
"Oh, tell me he is not—"

"I cannot," I replied gently; "for indeed he is."

"No!" she said, wild-eyed, and raising her hands to her face as
though half distraught. "You do not understand—yet you are a
doctor. You do not understand—"

She stopped, moaning to herself and looking from the handsome
face of the boy to me. It was pitiful; it was uncanny. But sorrow for

the girl predominated in my mind. Then from somewhere I heard a sound which I had heard before in houses occupied by Dr. Fu-Manchu—that of a muffled gong.

"Quick!" Kâramanèh had me by the arm. "Up! He has returned!"

She fled up the stairs to the balcony, I close at her heels. The shadows veiled us, the thick carpet deadened the sound of our tread, or certainly we must have been detected by the man who entered the room we had just quitted.

It was Dr. Fu-Manchu!

Yellow-robed, immobile, the inhuman green eyes glittering catlike, even, it seemed, before the light struck them, he threaded his way through the archipelago of cushions and bent over the couch of Azîz.

Kâramanèh dragged me down on to my knees.

"Watch!" she whispered. "Watch!"

Dr. Fu-Manchu felt for the pulse of the boy whom a moment since I had pronounced dead, and, stepping to the tall glass case, took out a long-necked flask of chased gold, and from it, into a graduated glass, he poured some drops of an amber liquid wholly unfamiliar to me. I watched him with all my eyes, and noted how high the liquid rose in the measure. He charged a needle-syringe, and, bending again over Azîz, made an injection.

Then all the wonders I had heard of this man became possible, and with an awe which any other physician who had examined Azîz must have felt, I admitted him a miracle-worker. For as I watched, all but breathless, the dead came to life! The glow of health crept upon the olive cheek—the boy moved—he raised his hands above his head—he sat up, supported by the Chinese doctor!

Fu-Manchu touched some hidden bell. A hideous yellow man with a scarred face entered, carrying a tray upon which were a bowl containing some steaming fluid, apparently soup, what looked like oaten cakes, and a flask of red wine.

As the boy, exhibiting no more unusual symptoms than if he had just awakened from a normal sleep, commenced his repast, Kâramanèh drew me gently along the passage into the room which we had first entered. My heart leapt wildly as the marmoset bounded past us to drop hand over hand to the lower apartment in search of its master.

"You see," said Kâramanèh, her voice quivering, "he is not dead! But without Fu-Manchu he is dead to me. How can I leave him when he holds the life of Azîz in his hand?"

"You must get me that flask, or some of its contents," I directed. "But tell me, how does he produce the appearance of death?"

"I cannot tell you," she replied. "I do not know. It is something in the wine. In another hour Azîz will be again as you saw him. But see." And, opening a little ebony box, she produced a phial half filled with the amber liquid.

"Good!" I said, and slipped it into my pocket. "When will be the best time to seize Fu-Manchu and to restore your brother?"

"I will let you know," she whispered, and, opening the door, pushed me hurriedly from the room. "He is going away tonight to the north; but you must not come tonight. Quick! Quick! Along the passage. He may call me at any moment."

So, with the phial in my pocket containing a potent preparation unknown to Western science, and with a last long look into the eyes of Kâramanèh, I passed out into the narrow alley, out from the fragrant perfumes of that mystery house into the place of Thames-side stenches.

CHAPTER TWENTY-TWO

WE GO NORTH

"We must arrange for the house to be raided without delay," said Smith. "This time we are sure of our ally—"

"But we must keep our promise to her," I interrupted.

"You can look after that, Petrie," my friend said. "I will devote the whole of my attention to Dr. Fu-Manchu!" he added grimly.

Up and down the room he paced, gripping the blackened briar between his teeth, so that the muscles stood squarely upon his jaws. The bronze which spoke of the Burmese sun enhanced the brightness of his grey eyes.

"What have I all along maintained?" he jerked, looking back at me across his shoulder— "that, although Kâramanèh was one of the strongest weapons in the Doctor's armoury, she was one which some day would be turned against him. That day has dawned."

"We must await word from her."

"Quite so."

He knocked out his pipe on the grate. Then:

"Have you any idea of the nature of the fluid in the phial?"

"Not the slightest. And I have none to spare for analytical purposes."

Nayland Smith began stuffing mixture into the hot pipe-bowl, and dropping an almost equal quantity on the floor.

"I cannot rest, Petrie," he said, "I am itching to get to work. Yet, a false move, and—"

He lighted his pipe, and stood staring from the window.

"I shall, of course, take a needle-syringe with me," I explained.

Smith made no reply.

"If I but knew the composition of the drug which produced the semblance of death," I continued, "my fame would long survive my ashes."

My friend did not turn. But:

"She said it was something he put in the wine?" he jerked.

"In the wine, yes."

Silence fell. My thoughts reverted to Kâramanèh, whom Dr. Fu-Manchu held in bonds stronger than any slave-chains. For, with Azîz, her brother, suspended between life and death, what could she do save obey the mandates of the cunning Chinaman? What perverted genius was his! If that treasury of obscure wisdom which he, perhaps alone of living men, had rifled, could but be thrown open to the sick and suffering, the name of Dr. Fu-Manchu would rank with the golden ones in the history of healing.

Nayland Smith suddenly turned, and the expression upon his face amazed me.

"Look out the next train to L—!" he rapped.

"To L—? What—?"

"There's the Bradshaw. We haven't a minute to waste."

In his voice was the imperative note I knew so well; in his eyes was the light which told of an urgent need for action—a portentous truth suddenly grasped.

"One in half an hour—the last."

"We must catch it."

No further word or explanation he vouchsafed, but darted off to dress; for he had spent the afternoon pacing the room, in his dressing-gown, and smoking without intermission.

Out and to the corner we hurried and leapt into the first taxi upon the rank. Smith enjoined the man to hasten, and we were off—all in that whirl of feverish activity which characterized my friend's movements in times of important action. He sat glancing impatiently from the window and twitching at the lobe of his ear.

"I know you will forgive me, old man," he said, "but there is a little problem which I am trying to work out in my mind. Did you bring the things I mentioned?"

"Yes."

Conversation lapsed, until, just as the cab turned into the station, Smith said:

"Should you consider Lord Southery to have been the first constructive engineer of his time, Petrie?"

"Undoubtedly," I replied.

"Greater than Von Homber, of Berlin?"

"Possibly not. But Van Homber has been dead for three years."

"Three years, is it?"

"Roughly."

"Ah!"

We reached the station in time to secure a non-corridor compartment to ourselves, and to allow Smith leisure carefully to inspect the occupants of all the others, from the engine to the guard's van. He was muffled up to the eyes, and he warned me to keep out of sight in the corner of the compartment. In fact, his behaviour had me bursting with curiosity. The train having started:

"Don't imagine, Petrie," said Smith, "that I am trying to lead you blindfolded in order later to dazzle you with my perspicacity. I am simply afraid that this may be a wild-goose chase. The idea upon which I am acting does not seem to have struck you. I wish it had. The fact would argue in favour of its being sound."

"At present I am hopelessly mystified."

"Well, then, I will not bias you toward my view. But just study the situation, and see if you can arrive at the reason for this sudden journey. I shall be distinctly encouraged if you succeed."

But I did not succeed, and since Smith obviously was unwilling to enlighten me, I pressed him no more. The train stopped at Rugby, where he was engaged with the stationmaster in making some mysterious arrangements. At L—, however, their object became plain, for a high-power car was awaiting us, and into this we hurried, and ere the greater number of passengers had reached the platform were being driven off at headlong speed along the moon-bathed roads.

Twenty minutes' rapid travelling, and a white mansion leapt into the line of sight, standing out vividly against its woody backing.

"Stradwick Hall," said Smith, "The home of Lord Southery. We are first—but Dr. Fu-Manchu was on the train."

Then the truth dawned upon the gloom of my perplexity.

CHAPTER TWENTY-THREE

THE VAULT

"Your extraordinary proposal fills me with horror, Mr. Smith!"

The sleek little man in the dress suit, who looked like a head waiter (but was the trusted legal adviser of the house of Southery) puffed at his cigar indignantly. Nayland Smith, whose restless pacing had led him to the far end of the library, turned, a remote but virile figure, and looked back to where I stood by the open hearth with the solicitor.

"I am in your hands, Mr. Henderson," he said, and advanced upon the latter, his grey eyes ablaze. "Save for the heir, who is abroad on foreign service, you say there is no kin of Lord Southery to consider. The word rests with you. If I am wrong, and you agree to my proposal, there is none whose susceptibilities will suffer—"

"My own, sir!"

"If I am right, and you prevent me from acting, you become a murderer, Mr. Henderson."

The lawyer started, staring nervously up at Smith, who now towered over him menacingly.

"Lord Southery was a lonely man," continued my friend. "If I could have placed my proposition before one of his blood, I do not doubt what my answer had been. Why do you hesitate? Why do you experience this feeling of horror?"

Mr. Henderson stared down into the fire. His constitutionally ruddy face was pale.

"It is entirely irregular, Mr. Smith. We have not the necessary powers—"

Smith snapped his teeth together impatiently, snatching his watch from his pocket and glancing at it.

"I am vested with the necessary powers. I will give you a written order, sir."

"The proceeding savours of paganism. Such a course might be admissible in China, in Burma—"

"Do you weigh a life against such quibbles? Do you suppose that, granting *my* irresponsibility, Dr. Petrie would countenance such a thing if he doubted the necessity?"

Mr. Henderson looked at me with pathetic hesitance.

"There are guests in the house—mourners who attended the ceremony today. They—"

"Will never know, if we are in error," interrupted Smith. "Good God! why do you delay?"

"You wish it to be kept secret?"

"You and I, Mr. Henderson, and Dr. Petrie will go now. We require no other witnesses. We are answerable only to our consciences."

The lawyer passed his hand across his damp brow.

"I have never in my life been called upon to come to so momentous a decision in so short a time," he confessed.

But, aided by Smith's indomitable will, he made his decision, and it led to we three, looking and feeling like conspirators, hurrying across the park beneath a moon whose placidity was a rebuke to the turbulent passions which reared their strangle-growth in the garden of England. Not a breath of wind stirred amid the leaves. The calm of perfect night soothed everything to slumber. Yet, if Smith were right (and I did not doubt him) the green eyes of Dr. Fu-Manchu had looked upon the scene; and I found myself marvelling that its beauty had not wilted. Even now the dread Chinaman must be near to us.

As Mr. Henderson unlocked the ancient iron gates he turned to Nayland Smith. His face twitched oddly.

"Witness that I do this unwillingly," he said—"most unwillingly."

"Mine be the responsibility," was the reply.

Smith's voice quivered, responsive to the nervous vitality pent up within that lean frame. He stood motionless, listening—and I knew for whom he listened. He peered about him to right and left—and I knew whom he expected but dreaded to see.

Above us now the trees looked down with a solemnity different from the aspect of the monarchs of the park, and the nearer we came to our journey's end the more sombre and lowering bent the verdant arch—or so it seemed.

By that path, patched now with pools of moonlight, Lord Southery had passed upon his bier, with the sun to light his going; by that path several generations of Stradwicks had gone to their last resting-place.

To the doors of the vault the moonrays found free access. No branch, no leaf, intervened. Mr. Henderson's face looked ghastly. The keys which he carried rattled in his hand.

"Light the lantern," he said unsteadily.

Nayland Smith, who again had been peering suspiciously about into the shadows, struck a match and lighted the lantern which he carried. He turned to the solicitor.

"Be calm, Mr. Henderson," he said sternly. "It is your plain duty to your client."

"God be my witness that I doubt it," replied Henderson, and opened the door.

We descended the steps. The air beneath was damp and chill. It touched us as with clammy fingers; and the sensation was not wholly physical.

Before the narrow mansion which now sufficed Lord Southery, the great engineer whom kings had honoured, Henderson reeled and clutched at me for support. Smith and I had looked to him for no aid in our uncanny task, and rightly.

With averted eyes he stood over by the steps of the tomb, whilst my friend and myself set to work. In the pursuit of my profession I had undertaken labours as unpleasant, but never amid an environment such as this. It seemed that generations of Stradwicks listened to each turn of every screw.

At last it was done, and the pallid face of Lord Southery questioned the intruding light. Nayland Smith's hand was as steady as a rigid bar when he raised the lantern. Later, I knew, there would be a sudden releasing of the tension of will—a reaction physical and mental—but not until his work was finished.

That my own hand was steady I ascribed to one thing solely— professional zeal. For, under conditions which, in the event of failure and exposure, must have led to an unpleasant inquiry by the British Medical Association, I was about to attempt an experiment never before essayed by a physician of the white races.

Though I failed, though I succeeded, that it ever came before the B.M.A., or any other council, was improbable; in the former event, all but impossible. But the knowledge that I was about to practise charlatanry, or what any one of my fellow-practitioners must have designated as such, was with me. Yet so profound had my belief become in the extraordinary being whose existence was a danger to the world, that I revelled in my immunity from official censure. I was glad that it had fallen to my lot to take one step—though blindly—into the *future* of medical science.

So far as my skill bore me, Lord Southery was dead. Unhesitatingly, I would have given a death certificate, save for two considerations. The first, although his latest scheme ran contrary from the interests of Dr. Fu-Manchu, his genius, diverted into other channels, would serve the yellow group better than his death. The second, I had seen the boy Azîz raised from a state as like death as this.

From the phial of amber-hued liquid which I had with me, I charged a needle-syringe. I made the injection, and waited.

"If he is really dead!" whispered Smith. "It seems incredible that he can have survived for three days without food. Yet I have known a fakir to go for a week."

Mr. Henderson groaned.

Watch in hand, I stood observing the grey face.

A second passed; another; a third. In the fourth the miracle began. Over the seemingly cold clay crept the hue of pulsing life. It came in waves in waves which corresponded with the throbbing of the awakened heart; which swept fuller and stronger; which filled and quickened the chilled body.

As rapidly we freed the living man from the trappings of the dead one, Southery, uttering a stiffled scream, sat up, looked about him with half-glazed eyes, and fell back.

"My God!" cried Smith.

"It is all right," I said, and had time to note how my voice had assumed a professional tone. "A little brandy from my flask is all that is necessary now."

"You have two patients, Doctor," rapped my friend.

Mr. Henderson had fallen in a swoon to the floor of the vault.

"Quiet," whispered Smith; "*he* is here."

He extinguished the light.

I supported Lord Southery. "What has happened?" he kept moaning. "Where am I? Oh God! what has happened?"

I strove to reassure him in a whisper, and placed my travelling coat about him. The door at the top of the mausoleum steps we had reclosed but not relocked. Now, as I upheld the man whom literally we had rescued from the grave, I heard the door reopen. To aid Henderson I could make no move. Smith was breathing hard beside me. I dared not think what was about to happen, nor what its effects might be upon Lord Southery in his exhausted condition.

Through the Memphian dark of the tomb cut a spear of light, touching the last stone of the stairway.

A guttural voice spoke some words rapidly, and I knew that Dr. Fu-Manchu stood at the head of the stairs. Although I could not see my friend, I became aware that Nayland Smith had his revolver in his hand, and I reached into my pocket for mine.

At last the cunning Chinaman was about to fall into a trap. It would require all his genius, I thought, to save him tonight. Unless his suspicions were aroused by the unlocked door, his capture was imminent. Someone was descending the steps.

In my right hand I held my revolver, and with my left arm about Lord Southery, I waited through ten such seconds of suspense as I have rarely known.

The spear of light plunged into the well of darkness again.

Lord Southery, Smith and myself were hidden by the angle of the wall; but full upon the purplish face of Mr. Henderson the beam shone. In some way it penetrated to the murk of his mind; and he awakened from his swoon with a hoarse cry, struggled to his feet, and stood looking up the stair in a sort of frozen horror.

Smith was past him at a bound. Something flashed toward him as the light was extinguished. I saw him duck, and heard the knife ring upon the floor.

I managed to move sufficiently to see at the top, as I fired up the stairs, the yellow face of Dr. Fu-Manchu, to see the gleaming, chatoyant eyes, greenly terrible, as they sought to pierce the gloom. A flying figure was racing up, three steps at a time (that of a brown man scantily clad). He stumbled and fell, by which I knew that he was hit; but went on again, Smith hard on his heels.

"Mr. Henderson!" I cried, "relight the lantern and take charge of Lord Southery. Here is my flask on the floor. I rely upon you."

Smith's revolver spoke again as I went bounding up the stair. Black against the square of moonlight, I saw him stagger, I saw him fall. As he fell, for the third time I heard the crack of his revolver.

Instantly I was at his side. Somewhere along the black aisle beneath the trees receding footsteps pattered.

"Are you hurt, Smith?" I cried anxiously.

He got upon his feet.

"He has a dacoit with him," he replied, and showed me the long curved knife which he held in his hand, a full inch of the blade bloodstained. "A near thing for me, Petrie."

I heard the whir of a restarted motor.

"We have lost him," said Smith.

"But we have saved Lord Southery," I said. "Fu-Manchu will credit us with a skill as great as his own."

"We must get to the car," Smith muttered, "and try to overtake them. Ugh! my left arm is useless."

"It would be mere waste of time to attempt to overtake them," I argued, "for we have no idea in which direction they will proceed."

"I have a very good idea," snapped Smith. "Stradwick Hall is less than ten miles from the coast. There is only one practicable means of conveying an unconscious man secretly from here to London."

"You think he meant to take him from here to London?"

"Prior to shipping him to China; I think so. His clearing-house is probably on the Thames."

"A boat?"

"A yacht, presumably, is lying off the coast in readiness. Fu-Manchu may even have designed to ship him direct to China."

Lord Southery, a bizarre figure, my travelling coat wrapped about him, and supported by his solicitor, who was almost as pale as himself, emerged from the vault into the moonlight.

"This is a triumph for you, Smith," I said.

The throb of Fu-Manchu's car died into faintness and was lost in the night's silence.

"Only half a triumph," he replied. "But we still have another chance—the raid on his house. When will the word come from Kâramanèh?"

Southery spoke in a weak voice.

"Gentlemen," he said, "it seems I am raised from the dead."

It was the weirdest moment of the night wherein we heard that newly buried man speak from the gate of his tomb.

"Yes," replied Smith slowly, "and spared from the fate of heaven alone knows how many men of genius. The yellow society lacks a Southery, but that Dr. Fu-Manchu was in Germany three years ago I have reason to believe; so that, even without visiting the grave of your great Teutonic rival, who suddenly died at about that time, I venture to predict that they have a Von Homber. And the futurist group in China knows how to *make* men work!"

CHAPTER TWENTY-FOUR

AZÍZ

From the rescue of Lord Southery my story bears me mercilessly on to other things. I may not tarry, as more leisurely penmen, to round my incidents; they were not of my choosing. I may not pause to make you better acquainted with the figures of my drama; its scheme is none of mine. Often enough, in those days, I found a fitness in the lines of Omar:

> We are no other than a moving row
> Of Magic Shadow-shapes that come and go
>   Round with the Sun-illuminated Lantern held
> In Midnight by the Master of the Show.

But "the Master of the Show," in this case, was Dr. Fu-Manchu!

I have been asked many times since the days with which these records deal: Who *was* Dr. Fu-Manchu? Let me confess here that my final answer must be postponed. I can only indicate, at this place, the trend of my reasoning, and leave my reader to form whatever conclusion he pleases.

What group can we isolate and label as responsible for the overthrow of the Manchus? The casual student of modern Chinese history will reply: "Young China". This is unsatisfactory. What do you mean by Young China? In my own hearing Fu-Manchu had disclaimed, with scorn, association with the whole of that movement; and assuming that the name were not an assumed one, he clearly can have been no anti-Manchu, no Republican.

The Chinese Republican is of the Mandarin class, but of a new generation which veneers its Confucianism with Western polish. These youthful and unbalanced reformers, in conjunction with older but no less ill-balanced provincial politicians, may be said to represent Young China. Amid such turmoils as this we invariably look for, and invariably find, a Third Party. In my opinion, Dr. Fu-Manchu was one of the leaders of such a party.

Another question often put to me was: where did the Doctor hide during the time that he pursued his operations in London? This is more susceptible of explanation. For a time Nayland Smith supposed, as I did myself, that the opium den adjacent to the old Ratcliff Highway was the Chinaman's base of operations; later we came to believe that the mansion near Windsor was his hiding-place, and later still, the hulk lying off the downstream flats. But I think I can state with confidence that the spot which he had chosen for his home was neither of these, but the East End riverside building which I was the first to enter. Of this I am all but sure; for the reason that it not only was the home of Fu-Manchu, of Kâramanèh, and of her brother Azîz, but the home of something else—of something which I shall speak of later.

The dreadful tragedy (or series of tragedies) which attended the raid upon the place will always mark in my memory the supreme horror of a horrible case. Let me endeavour to explain what occurred.

By the aid of Kâramanèh, you have seen how we had located the whilom warehouse, which, from the exterior, was so drab and dreary, but which within was a place of wondrous luxury. At the moment selected by our beautiful accomplice, Inspector Weymouth and a body of detectives entirely surrounded it; a river police launch lay off the wharf which opened from it on the riverside; and this upon a singularly black night, than which a better could not have been chosen.

"You will fulfil your promise to me?" said Kâramaneh, and looked up into my face.

She was enveloped in a big, loose cloak, and from the shadow of the hood her wonderful eyes gleamed out like stars.

"What do you wish us to do?" asked Nayland Smith.

"You—and Dr. Petrie," she replied swiftly, "must enter first, and bring out Azîz. Until he is safe—until he is out of that place—you are to make no attempt upon—"

"Upon Dr. Fu-Manchu?" interrupted Weymouth; for Kâramanèh hesitated to pronounce the dreaded name, as she always did. "But how can we be sure that there is no trap laid for us?"

The Scotland Yard man did not entirely share my confidence in the integrity of this Eastern girl whom he knew to have been a creature of the Chinaman's.

"Azîz lies in the private room," she explained eagerly, her old accent more noticeable than usual. "There is only one of the Burmese men in the house, and he—he dare not enter without orders!"

"But Fu-Manchu?"

"We have nothing to fear from him. He will be your prisoner within ten minutes from now! I have no time for words—you must believe!" She stamped her foot impatiently.

"And the dacoit?" snapped Smith.

"He also."

"I think perhaps I'd better come in, 100," said Weymouth slowly.

Kâramanèh shrugged her shoulders with quick impatience, and unlocked the door in the high brick wall which divided the gloomy, evil-smelling court from the luxurious apartments of Dr. Fu-Manchu.

"Make no noise," she warned. And Smith and myself followed her along the uncarpeted passage beyond.

Inspector Weymouth, with a final word of instruction to his second in command, brought up the rear. The door was reclosed; a few paces beyond a second was unlocked. Passing through a small room, unfurnished, a further passage led us to a balcony. The transition was startling.

Darkness was about us now, and silence: a perfumed, slumberous darkness—a silence full of mystery. For, beyond the walls of the apartment whereon we looked down, waged the unceasing battle of sounds that is the hymn of the great industrial river. About the scented confines which bounded us now, floated the smoke-laden vapours of the Lower Thames.

From the metallic but infinitely human clangour of dock-side life, from the unpleasant but homely odours which prevail where ships swallow in and belch out the concrete evidences of commercial prosperity, we had come into this incensed stillness, where one shaded lamp painted dim enlargements of its Chinese silk upon the nearer walls, and left the greater part of the room the darker for its contrast.

Nothing of the Thames-side activity—of the riveting and scraping—the bumping of bales—the bawling of orders—the hiss of steam—penetrated to this perfumed place. In the pool of tinted light lay the deathlike figure of the dark-haired boy, Kâramanèh's muffled form bending over him.

"At last I stand in the house of Dr. Fu-Manchu!" whispered Smith.

Despite the girl's assurance, we knew that proximity to the

sinister Chinaman must be fraught with danger. We stood, not in the lion's den, but in the serpent's lair.

From the time when Nayland Smith had come from Burma in pursuit of this advance-guard, of a cogent Yellow Peril, the face of Dr. Fu-Manchu rarely had been absent from my dreams day or night. The millions might sleep in peace—the millions in whose cause we laboured!—but we who knew the reality of the danger knew that a veritable octopus whose head was that of Dr. Fu-Manchu, whose tentacles were dacoity, thuggee, modes of death secret and swift, which in the darkness plucked men from life and left no clue behind.

"Kâramanèh!" I called softly.

The muffled form beneath the lamp turned so that the soft light fell upon the darkly lovely face of the slave girl. She who had been a pliant instrument in the hands of Fu-Manchu now was to be the means whereby society should be rid of him.

She raised her finger warningly; then beckoned me to approach.

My feet sinking in the rich pile of the carpet, I came through the gloom of the great apartment into the patch of light, and, Kâramanèh beside me, stood looking down upon the boy; dead so far as Western lore had power to judge, but kept alive in that deathlike trance by the uncanny skill of the Chinese doctor.

"Be quick!" she said, "be quick! Awaken him! I am afraid."

From the case which I carried I took out a needle-syringe and phial containing a small quantity of amber-hued liquid. It was a drug not to be found in the British Pharmacopoeia. Of its constitution I knew nothing. Although I had had the phial in my possession for some days I had not dared to devote any of its precious contents to analytical purposes. The amber drops spelt life for the boy Azîz, spelt success for the mission of Nayland Smith, spelt ruin for the fiendish Chinaman.

I raised the white coverlet. The boy, fully dressed, lay with his arms crossed upon his breast. I discerned the mark of previous injections as, charging the syringe from the phial, I made what I hoped would be the last of such experiments upon him. I would have given half of my small worldly possessions to have known the real nature of the drug which was now coursing through the veins of Azîz—which was tinting the greyed face with the olive tone of life; which, so far as my medical training bore me, was restoring the dead to life.

But such was not the purpose of my visit. I was come to remove from the house of Dr. Fu-Manchu the living chain which bound Kâramanèh to him. Azîz alive and free, the Doctor's hold upon the slave girl would be broken.

My lovely companion, her hands convulsively clasped, knelt and devoured with her eyes the face of the boy who was passing through the most amazing physiological change in the history of therapeutics. The peculiar perfume which she wore—which seemed to be a part of her—which always I associated with her—was faintly perceptible. Kâramanèh was breathing rapidly.

"You have nothing to fear," I whispered, "see, he is reviving. In a few moments all will be well with him."

The hanging lamp with its garishly coloured shade swung gently above us, wafted, it seemed, by some draught which passed through the apartment. The boy's heavy lids began to quiver, and Kâramanèh nervously clutched my arm, and held me so whilst we watched for the long-lashed eyes to open. The stillness of the place was positively unnatural; it seemed inconceivable that all about us was the discordant activity of the commercial East End. Indeed, this eerie silence was becoming oppressive; it began to appal me.

Inspector Weymouth's wondering face peeped over my shoulder.

"Where *is* Dr. Fu-Manchu?" I whispered, as Nayland Smith in turn appeared beside me. "I cannot understand the silence of the house—"

"Look about," replied Kâramanèh, never taking her eyes from the face of Azîz.

I peered around the shadowy walls. Tall glass cases there were, shelves and niches; where once, from the gallery above, I had seen the tubes and retorts, the jars of unfamiliar organisms, the books of unfamiliar lore, the impedimenta of the occult student and man of science —the visible evidences of Fu-Manchu's presence. Shelves—cases—niches—were bare. Of the complicated appliances unknown to civilized laboratories wherewith he pursued his strange experiments, of the tubes wherein he isolated the bacilli of unclassified diseases, of the yellow-bound volumes for a glimpse at which (had they known of their contents) the great men of Harley Street would have given a fortune—no trace remained. The silken cushions; the inlaid tables; all were gone.

The room was stripped, dismantled. Had Fu-Manchu fled? The silence assumed a new significance. His dacoits and kindred ministers of death—all must have fled too.

"You have let him escape us!" I said rapidly. "You promised to aid us to capture him to send us a message—and you have delayed until—"

"No," she said, "no!" and clutched at my arm again. "Oh! is he not reviving slowly? Are you sure you have made no mistake?"

Her thoughts were all for the boy; and her solicitude touched me. Again I examined Azîz, the most remarkable patient of my professional career.

As I counted the strengthening pulse, he opened his dark eyes— which were so like the eyes of Kâramanèh—and, with the girl's eager arms tightly about him, sat up, looking wonderingly around.

Kâramanèh pressed her cheek to his, whispering loving words in that softly spoken Arabic which had first betrayed her nationality to Nayland Smith. I handed her my flask, which I had filled with wine.

"My promise is fulfilled!" I said. "You are free! Now for Fu-Manchu! But first let us admit the police to this house; there is something uncanny in its stillness."

"No," she replied. "First let my brother be taken out and placed in safety. Will you carry him?"

She raised her face to that of Inspector Weymouth, upon which was written awe and wonder.

The burly detective lifted the boy as tenderly as a woman, passed through the shadows to the stairway, ascended, and was swallowed up in the gloom. Nayland Smith's eyes gleamed feverishly. He turned to Kâramanèh.

"You are not playing with us?" he said harshly. "We have done our part; it remains for you to do yours."

"Do not speak so loudly," the girl begged. "*He* is near us—and, oh God, I fear him so!"

"Where is he?" persisted my friend.

Kâramanèh's eyes were glassy with fear now.

"You must not touch him until the police are here," she said—but from the direction of her quick, agitated glances I knew that, her brother safe, now she feared for me, and for me alone. Those glances set my blood dancing; for Kâramanèh was an Eastern jewel which any man of flesh and blood must have coveted had he known it to lie within his reach. Her eyes were twin lakes of mystery which, more than once, I had known the desire to explore.

"Look—beyond that curtain"—her voice was barely audible—"but do not enter. Even as he is, I fear him."

Her voice, her palpable agitation, prepared us for something extraordinary. Tragedy and Fu-Manchu were never far apart. Though we were two, and help was so near, we were in the abode of the most cunning murderer who ever came out of the East.

It was with strangely mingled emotions that I crossed the thick carpet, Nayland Smith beside me, and drew aside the draperies concealing a door, to which Kâramanèh had pointed. Then, upon looking into the dim place beyond, all else save what it held was forgotten.

We looked upon a small, square room, the walls draped with fantastic Chinese tapestry, the floor strewn with cushions; and reclining in a corner, where the faint, blue light from a lamp, placed upon a low table, painted grotesque shadows about the cavernous face—was Dr. Fu-Manchu!

At sight of him my heart leapt—and seemed to suspend its functions, so intense was the horror which this man's presence inspired in me. My hand clutching the curtain, I stood watching him. The lids veiled the malignant green eyes, but the thin lips seemed to smile. Then Smith silently pointed to the hand, which held a little pipe. A sickly perfume assailed my nostrils, and the explanation of the hushed silence, and the ease with which we had thus far executed our plan, came to me, The cunning mind was torpid—lost in a brutish world of dreams.

Fu-Manchu was in an opium sleep!

The dim light traced out a network of tiny lines, which covered the yellow face from the pointed chin to the top of the great domed brow, and formed deep shadow pools in the hollows beneath his eyes. At last we had triumphed. The man's ruling vice had wrought his downfall.

I could not determine the depth of his obscene trance; and mastering some of my repugnance, and forgetful of Kâramanèh's warning, I was about to step forward into the room, loaded with its nauseating opium fumes, when a soft breath fanned my cheek.

"Do not go in!" came Kâramanèh's warning voice—hushed—trembling.

Her little hand grasped my arm. She drew Smith and myself back from the door.

"There is danger there!" she whispered, "Do not enter that room! The police must reach him in some way—and drag him out! Do not enter that room!"

The girl's voice quivered hysterically; her eyes blazed into savage flame. The fierce resentment born of dreadful wrongs was consuming her now; but fear of Fu-Manchu held her yet. Inspector Weymouth came down the stairs and joined us.

"I have sent the boy to Ryman's room at the station," he said. "The divisional surgeon will look after him until you arrive Dr. Petrie. All is ready now. The launch is just off the wharf and every side of the place under observation, Where's our man?"

He drew a pair of handcuffs from his pocket and raised his eyebrows interrogatively. The absence of sound—of any demonstration from the elusive Chinaman whom he was there to arrest—puzzled him.

Nayland Smith jerked his thumb towards the curtain.

At that, and before we could utter a word, Weymouth stepped to the draped door. He was a man who drove straight at his goal and saved reflections for subsequent leisure. I think, moreover, that the atmosphere of the place (stripped as it was it retained its heavy, voluptuous perfume) had begun to get a hold upon him. He was anxious to shake it off; to be up and doing.

He pulled the curtain aside and stepped into the room. Smith and I perforce followed him. Just within the door the three of us stood looking across at the limp thing which had spread terror throughout the Eastern and Western world. Helpless as Fu-Manchu was, he inspired terror now, though the giant intellect was inert—stupefied.

In the dimly lit apartment we had quitted I heard Kâramanèh utter a stifled scream. But it came too late.

As though cast up by a volcano, the silken cushions, the inlaid table with its blue-shaded lamp, the garish walls, the sprawling figure with the ghastly light playing upon its features—quivered, and shot upward!

So it seemed to me; though, in the ensuing instant, I remembered, too late, a previous experience of the floors of Fu-Manchu's private apartments; I knew what has indeed befallen us. A trap had been released beneath our feet.

I recall falling—but have no recollection of the end of my fall—of the shock marking the drop. I only remember fighting for my life against a stifling something which had me by the throat. I knew that I was being suffocated, but my hands met only the deathly emptiness.

Into a poisonous well of darkness I sank. I could not cry out. I was helpless. Of the fate of my companions I knew nothing—could surmise nothing.

Then ... all consciousness ended.

CHAPTER TWENTY-FIVE

THE FUNGI CELLARS

I was being carried along a dimly lighted, tunnel-like place, slung, sackwise, across the shoulder of a Burman. He was not a big man, but he supported my considerable weight with apparent ease. A deadly nausea held me, but the rough handling had served to restore me to consciousness. My hands and feet were closely lashed. I hung limply as a wet towel; I felt that this spark of tortured life which had flickered up in me must ere long finally become extinguished.

A fancy possessed me, in these the first moments of my restoration to the world of realities, that I had been smuggled into China; and as I swung head downward I told myself that the huge, puffy things which strewed the path were a species of giant toadstool, unfamiliar to me and possibly peculiar to whatever district of China I now was in.

The air was hot, steamy, and loaded with a smell as of rotting vegetation. I wondered why my bearer so scrupulously avoided touching any of the unwholesome-looking growths in passing through what seemed a succession of cellars, but steered a tortuous course among the bloated, unnatural shapes, lifting his bare brown feet with catlike delicacy.

He passed under a low arch, dropped me roughly to the ground and ran back. Half stunned, I lay watching the agile brown body melt into the distances of the cellars. Their walls and roof seemed to emit a faint, phosphorescent light.

"Petrie!" came a weak voice from somewhere ahead … "Is that you, Petrie?"

It was Nayland Smith!

"Smith!" I said, and strove to sit up. But the intense nausea overcame me, so that I all but swooned.

I heard his voice again, but could attach no meaning to the words which he uttered. A sound of terrific blows reached my ears, too.

The Burman reappeared, bending under the heavy load which he bore. For, as he picked his way through the bloated things which grew upon the floors of the cellars, I realized that he was carrying the inert body of Inspector Weymouth. And I found myself comparing the strength of the little brown man with that of a Nile beetle, which can raise many times its own weight.

Then, behind him, appeared a second figure, which immediately claimed the whole of my errant attention.

"Fu-Manchu!" hissed my friend, from the darkness which concealed him.

It was indeed none other than Fu-Manchu—the Fu-Manchu whom we had thought to be helpless. The deeps of the Chinaman's cunning—the fine quality of his courage—were forced upon me as amazing facts.

He had assumed the appearance of a drugged opium-smoker so well as to dupe me—a medical man; so well as to dupe Kâramanèh— whose experience of the noxious habit probably was greater than my own. And, with the gallows dangling before him, he had waited—played the part of a lure—whilst a body of police actually surrounded the place!

I have since thought that the room probably was one which he actually used for opium debauches, and the device of the trap was intended to protect him during the comatose period.

Now, holding a lantern above his head, the deviser of the trap whereinto we, mouselike, had blindly entered, came through the cellars, following the brown man who carried Weymouth. The faint rays of the lantern (it apparently contained a candle) revealed a veritable forest of the gigantic fungi—poisonously coloured—hideously swollen—climbing from the floor up the slimy walls—clinging like horrid parasites to such part of the arched roof as was visible to me.

Fu-Manchu picked his way through the fungi ranks as daintily as though the distorted, tumid things had been viper-headed.

The resounding blows which I had noted before, and which had never ceased, culminated in a splintering crash. Dr. Fu-Manchu and his servant, who carried the apparently insensible detective, passed in under the arch, Fu-Manchu glancing back once along the passages. The lantern he extinguished, or concealed; and whilst I waited, my mind dully surveying memories of all the threats which this uncanny being had uttered, a distant clamour came to my ears.

Then, abruptly, it ceased. Dr. Fu-Manchu had closed a heavy door; and to my surprise I perceived that the greater part of it was of glass. The will-o'-the-wisp glow which played around the fungi, rendered the vista of the cellars faintly luminous, and visible to me from where I lay. Fu-Manchu spoke softly. His voice, its guttural note alternating with a sibilance on certain words, betrayed no traces of agitation. The man's unbroken calm had in it something inhuman. For he had just perpetrated an act of daring unparalleled in my experience, and in the clamour now shut out by the glass door I tardily recognized the entrance of the police into some barricaded part of the house—the coming of those who would save us—who would hold the Chinese doctor for the hangman!

"I have decided," he said deliberately, "that you are more worthy of my attention than I had formerly supposed. A man who can solve the secret of the Golden Elixir" (I had not solved it; I had merely stolen some) "should be a valuable acquisition to my Council. The extent of the plans of Mr. Commissioner Nayland Smith and of the English Scotland Yard it is incumbent upon me to learn. Therefore, gentlemen, you live—for the present!"

"And you'll swing," came Weymouth's hoarse voice, "in the near future! You and all your yellow gang!"

"I trust not," was the placid reply. "Most of my people are safe: some are shipped as lascars upon the liners; others have departed by different means. Ah!"

That last word was the only one indicative of excitement which had yet escaped him. A disc of light danced among the brilliant poison hues of the passages but no sound reached us; by which I knew that the glass door must fit almost hermetically. It was much cooler here than in the place through which we had passed, and the nausea began to leave me, my brain to grow more clear. Had I known what was to follow I should have cursed the lucidity of mind which now came to me; I should have prayed for oblivion—to be spared the sight of that which ensued.

"It's Logan!" cried Inspector Weymouth; and I could tell that he was struggling to free himself of his bonds. From his voice it was evident that he too was recovering from the effects of the narcotic which had been administered to us all.

"Logan!" he cried. "Logan! This way—*help!*"

But the cry beat back upon us in that enclosed space, and seemed to carry no further than the invisible walls of our prison.

"The door fits well," came Fu-Manchu's mocking voice. "It is fortunate for us all that it is so. This is my observation window, Dr. Petrie, and you are about to enjoy a unique opportunity of studying fungology. I have already drawn your attention to the anaesthetic properties of the *lyco-perdon,* or Common Puff-ball. You may have recognized the fumes? The chamber into which you rashly precipitated yourselves was charged with them. By a process of my own I have greatly enhanced the value of the Puff-ball in this respect. Your friend, Mr. Weymouth, proved the most obstinate subject; but he succumbed in fifteen seconds."

"Logan! Help! *Help!* This way, man!"

Something very like fear sounded in Weymouth's voice now. Indeed, the situation was so uncanny that it almost seemed unreal. A group of men had entered the farthermost cellar, led by one who bore an electric pocket-lamp. The hard, white ray danced from bloated grey fungi to others of nightmare shape, of dazzling, venomous brilliance. The mocking, lecture-room voice continued:

"Note the snowy growth upon the roof, Doctor. Do not be deceived by its size. It is a giant variety of my own culture and is of the order *empusa.* You, in England, are familiar with the death of the common house-fly—which is found attached to the window-pane by a coating of white mould. I have developed the spores of this mould and have produced a giant species. Observe the interesting effect of the strong light upon my orange and blue *amanita* fungus!"

Hard beside me I heard Nayland Smith groan. Weymouth had become suddenly silent. For my own part, I could have shrieked in pure horror. *For I knew what was coming.* I realized in one agonized instant the significance of the dim lantern, of the careful progress through the subterranean fungi grove, of the care with which Fu-Manchu and his servant had avoided touching any of the growths. I knew, now, that Dr. Fu-Manchu was the greatest fungologist the world had ever known; was a poisoner to whom the Borgias were as children—and I knew that the detectives blindly were walking into a valley of death.

Then it began—the unnatural scene—the saturnalia of murder.

Like to many bombs the brilliantly coloured caps of the huge toatstool-like things alluded to by the Chinaman exploded, as the white ray sought them out in the darkness which alone preserved their existence. A brownish cloud—I could not determine whether liquid or powdery—arose in the cellar.

I tried to close my eyes—or to turn them away from the reeling forms of the men who were trapped in that poison-hole. It was useless: I must look.

The bearer of the lamp had dropped it, but the dim, eerily illuminated gloom endured scarce a second. A bright light sprang up—doubtless at the touch of the fiendish being who now resumed speech:

"Observe the immediate symptoms of delirium, Doctor!"

Out there, beyond the glass door, the unhappy victims were laughing—tearing their garments from their bodies—leaping—waving their arms—were become *maniacs*!

"We will now release the ripe spores of giant *empusa*," continued the wicked voice. "The air of the second cellar being supercharged with oxygen, they immediately germinate. Ah! it is a triumph! That process is the scientific triumph of my life!"

Like powdered snow the white spores fell from the roof, frosting the writhing shapes of the already poisoned men. Before my horrified gaze, *the fungus grew;* it spread from the head to the feet of those it touched; it enveloped them as in glittering shrouds …

"They die like flies!" screamed Fu-Manchu, with a sudden febrile excitement; and I felt assured of something I had long suspected: that that magnificent, perverted brain was the brain of a homicidal maniac—though Smith would never accept the theory.

"It is my fly-trap!" shrieked the Chinaman. "And I am the god of destruction!"

CHAPTER TWENTY-SIX

WE LOSE WEYMOUTH

The clammy touch of the mist revived me. The culmination of the scene in the poison cellars, together with the effects of the fumes which I had inhaled again, had deprived me of consciousness. Now I knew that I was afloat on the river. I still was bound: furthermore, a cloth was wrapped tightly about my mouth, and I was secured to a ring in the deck.

By moving my aching head to the left I could look down into the oily water; by moving it to the right I could catch a glimpse of the empurpled face of Inspector Weymouth, who, similarly bound and gagged, lay beside me, but only of the feet and legs of Nayland Smith. For I could not turn my head sufficiently far to see more.

We were aboard an electric launch. I heard the hated guttural voice of Fu-Manchu, subdued now to its habitual calm, and my heart leapt to hear the voice that answered him. It was that of Kâramanèh. His triumph was absolute. Clearly his plans for departure were complete; his slaughter of the police in the underground passages had been a final reckless demonstration of which the Chinaman's

241

subtle cunning would have been incapable had he not known his escape from the country to be assured.

What fate was in store for us? How would he avenge himself upon the girl who had betrayed him to his enemies? What portion awaited those enemies? He seemed to have formed the singular determination to smuggle me into China—but what did he purpose in the case of Weymouth, and in the case of Nayland Smith?

All but silently we were feeling our way through the mist. Astern died the clangour of dock and wharf into a remote discord. Ahead hung the foggy curtain veiling the traffic of the great waterway; but through it broke the calling of sirens, the tinkling of bells.

The gentle movement of the screw ceased altogether. The launch lay heaving slightly upon the swells.

A distant throbbing grew louder—and something advanced upon us through the haze.

A bell rang, and muffled by the fog a voice proclaimed itself—a voice which I knew. I felt Weymouth writhing impotently beside me; heard him mumbling incoherently; and I knew that he, too, had recognized the voice.

It was that of Inspector Ryman of the river police; and their launch was within biscuit-throw of that upon which we lay!

"'Hoy! 'Hoy!"

I trembled. A feverish excitement claimed me. They were hailing us. We carried no lights; but now—and ignoring the pain which shot from my spine to my skull I craned my neck to the left—the port light of the police launch glowed angrily through the mist.

I was unable to utter any save mumbling sounds, and my companions were equally helpless. It was a desperate position. Had the police seen us, or had they hailed at random?

The light drew nearer.

"Launch, 'hoy!"

They had seen us! Fu-Manchu's guttural voice spoke shortly—and our screw began to revolve again; we leapt ahead to the bank of darkness. Faint grew the light of the police launch—and was gone. But I heard Ryman's voice shouting.

"Full speed!" came faintly through the darkness. "Port! Port!"

Then the murk closed down, and with our friends far astern of us we were racing deeper into the fog banks—speeding seaward; though of this I was unable to judge at the time.

On we raced, and on, sweeping over growing swells. Once, a black, towering shape dropped down upon us. Far above, lights blazed, bells rang, vague cries pierced the fog. The launch pitched and rolled perilously, but weathered the wash of the liner which so nearly had concluded this episode. It was such a journey as I had taken once before, early in our pursuit of the genius of the Yellow Peril; but this was infinitely more terrible, for now we were utterly in Fu-Manchu's power.

A voice mumbled in my ear. I turned my bound up face; and Inspector Weymouth raised his hands in the dimness and partly slipped the bandage from his mouth.

"I've been working at the cords since we left those filthy cellars," he whispered, "My wrists are all cut, but when I've got out a knife and freed my ankles—"

Smith had kicked him with his bound feet. The detective slipped the bandage back to position and placed his hands behind him again. Dr. Fu-Manchu, wearing a heavy overcoat but no hat, came aft. He was dragging Kâramanèh by the wrists. He seated himself on the cushions near to us, pulling the girl down beside him. Now I could see her face—and the expression in her beautiful eyes made me writhe.

Fu-Manchu was watching us, his discoloured teeth faintly visible in the dim light, to which my eyes were becoming accustomed.

"Dr. Petrie," he said, "you shall be my honoured guest at my home in China. You shall assist me to revolutionize chemistry. Mr. Smith, I fear you know more of my plans than I had deemed it possible for you to have learnt, and I am anxious to know if you have a confidant. Where your memory fails you, and my files and wire jackets prove ineffectual, Inspector Weymouth's recollections may prove more accurate."

He turned to the cowering girl—who shrank away from him in pitiful, abject terror.

"In my hands, Doctor," he continued, "I hold a needle charged with a rare culture. It is the link between the bacilli and the fungi. You have seemed to display an undue interest in the peach and pearl which render my Kâramanèh so delightful, in the supple grace of her movements and the sparkle of her eyes. You can never devote your whole mind to those studies which I have planned for you whilst such distractions exist. A touch of this keen point, and the laughing Kâramanèh becomes the shrieking hag—the maniacal, mowing—"

Then, with an ox-like rush, Weymouth was upon him!

Kâramanèh, wrought upon past endurance, with a sobbing cry sank to the deck—and lay still. I managed to twist into a half-sitting posture, and Smith rolled aside as the detective and the Chinaman crashed down together.

Weymouth had one big hand at the Doctor's yellow throat; with his left he grasped the Chinaman's right. It held the needle.

Now, I could look along the length of the little craft, and, so far as it was possible to make out in the fog, only one other was aboard— the half-clad brown man who navigated her—and who had carried us through the cellars. The murk had grown denser and now shut us in like a box. The throb of the motor—the hissing breath of the two who fought—with so much at issue—these sounds and the wash of the water alone broke the eerie stillness.

By slow degrees, and with a reptilian agility horrible to watch, Fu-Manchu was neutralizing the advantage gained by Weymouth. His clawish fingers were fast in the big man's throat; the right hand with its deadly needle was forcing down the left of his opponent. He had been underneath, but now he was gaining the upper place. His powers of physical endurance must have been truly marvellous. His breath was whistling through his nostils significantly, but Weymouth was palpably tiring.

The latter suddenly changed his tactics. By a supreme effort, to which he was spurred, I think, by the growing proximity of the needle, he raised Fu-Manchu—by throat and arm—and pitched him sideways.

The Chinaman's grip did not relax, and the two wrestlers dropped, a writhing mass, upon the port cushions. The launch heeled over, and my cry of horror was crushed back into my throat by the bandage. For, as Fu-Manchu sought to extricate himself, he over-balanced—fell back—and, bearing Weymouth with him, slid into the river! The mist swallowed them up.

There are moments of which no man can recall his mental impressions, moments so acutely horrible that, mercifully, our memory retains nothing of the emotions they occasioned. This was one of them. A chaos ruled in my mind. I had a vague belief that the Burman, forward, glanced back, Then the course of the launch was changed.

How long intervened between the tragic end of that gargantuan struggle and the time when a black wall leapt suddenly up before us I cannot pretend to state.

With a sickening jerk we ran aground. A loud explosion ensued, and I clearly remember seeing the brown man leap out into the fog—which was the last I saw of him.

Water began to wash aboard.

Fully alive to our imminent peril, I fought with the cords that bound me; but I lacked poor Weymouth's strength of wrist, and I began to accept as a horrible and imminent possibility a death from drowning within six feet of the bank.

Beside me, Nayland Smith was straining and twisting. I think his object was to touch Kâramanèh, in the hope of arousing her. Where he failed in his project, the inflowing water succeeded. A silent prayer of thankfulness came from my very soul when I saw her stir—when I saw her raise her hands to her head—and saw the big, horror-bright eyes gleam through the mist veil.

CHAPTER TWENTY-SEVEN

WEYMOUTH'S HOME

We quitted the wrecked launch but a few seconds before her stern settled down into the river. Where the mud-bank upon which we found ourselves was situated we had no idea. But at least it was terra firma—and we were free from Dr. Fu-Manchu.

Smith stood looking out toward the river,

"My God!" he groaned. "My God!"

He was thinking, as I was, of Weymouth.

And when, an hour later, the police boat located us (on the mud-flats below Greenwich) and we heard that the toll of the poison cellars was eight men, we also heard news of our brave companion.

"Back there in the fog, sir," reported Inspector Ryman, who was in charge, and his voice was under poor command, "there was an uncanny howling, and peals of laughter that I'm going to dream about for weeks—"

Kâramanèh, who nestled beside me like a frightened child, shivered; and I knew that the needle had done its work, despite Weymouth's giant strength.

Smith swallowed noisily.

"Pray God the river has that yellow Satan," he said. "I would sacrifice a year of my life to see his rat's body on the end of a grappling-iron!"

We were a sad party that steamed through the fog homeward that night. It seemed almost like deserting a staunch comrade to leave the spot—so nearly as we could locate it—where Weymouth had put up that last gallant fight. Our helplessness was pathetic, and although, had the night been clear as crystal, I doubt if we could have acted otherwise, it came to me that this stinking murk was a new enemy which drove us back in coward retreat.

But so many were the calls upon our activity, and so numerous the stimulants to our initiative in those times, that soon we had matter to relieve our minds from this stress of sorrow.

There was Kâramanèh to be considered—Kâramanèh and her brother. A brief counsel was held, whereat it was decided that for the present they should be lodged at a hotel.

"I shall arrange," Smith whispered to me, for the girl was watching us, "to have the place patrolled night and day."

"You cannot suppose—"

"Petrie! I cannot and dare not suppose Fu-Manchu dead until with my own eyes I have seen him so!"

Accordingly we conveyed the beautiful Oriental girl and her brother away from that luxurious abode in its sordid setting. I will not dwell upon the final scene in the poison cellars lest I be accused of accumulating horror for horror's sake. Members of the fire brigade, helmed against contagion, brought out the bodies of the victims wrapped in their living shrouds ...

From Kâramanèh we learnt much of Fu-Manchu, little of herself.

"What am I? Does my poor history matter—to any one?" was her answer to questions respecting herself.

And she would droop her lashes over her dark eyes.

The dacoits whom the Chinaman had brought to England originally numbered seven, we learned. As you, having followed me thus far, will be aware, we had thinned the ranks of the Burmans. Probably only one now remained in England. They had lived in a camp in the grounds of the house near Windsor (which, as we had learned at the time of its destruction, the Doctor had bought outright). The Thames had been his highway.

Other members of the group had occupied quarters in various parts of the East End, where sailormen of all nationalities congregate. Shen-Yan's had been the East End headquarters. He had employed the hulk from the time of his arrival, as a laboratory for a certain class of experiment undesirable in proximity to a place of residence.

Nayland Smith asked the girl on one occasion if the Chinaman had had a private sea-going vessel, and she replied in the affirmative. She had never been on board, however, had never even set eyes upon it, and could give us no information respecting its character. It had sailed for China.

"You are sure," asked Smith keenly, "that it has actually left?"

"I understood so, and that we were to follow by another route."

"It would have been difficult for Fu-Manchu to travel by a passenger boat?"

"I cannot say what were his plans."

In a state of singular uncertainty, then, readily to be understood, we passed the days following the tragedy which had deprived us of our fellow-worker.

Vividly I recall the scene at poor Weymouth's home on the day that we visited it. I then made the acquaintance of the inspector's brother. Nayland Smith gave him a detailed account of the last scene.

"Out there in the mist," he concluded wearily, "it all seemed very unreal."

"I wish to God it had been!"

"Amen to that, Mr. Weymouth. But your brother made a gallant finish. If ridding the world of Fu-Manchu were the only good deed to his credit, his life had been well spent."

James Weymouth smoked awhile in thoughtful silence. Though but four and a half miles S.S.E. of St. Paul's, the quaint little cottage, with its rustic garden, shadowed by the tall trees which had so lined the village street before motor buses were, a spot as peaceful and secluded as any in broad England. But another shadow lay upon it today—chilling, fearful. An incarnate evil had come out of the dim East and in its dying malevolence had touched this home.

"There are two things I don't understand about it, sir," continued Weymouth. "What was the meaning of the horrible laughter which the river police heard in the fog? And where are the bodies?"

Kâramanèh, seated beside me, shuddered at the words. Smith, whose restless spirit granted him little repose, paused in his aimless wanderings about the room and looked at her.

In these latter days of his Augean labours to purge England of the unclean thing which had fastened upon her, my friend was more lean and nervous-looking than I had ever known him. His long residence in Burma had rendered him spare and had burnt his naturally dark skin to a coppery hue; but now his grey eyes had grown feverishly bright and his face so lean as at times to appear positively emaciated.

"This lady may be able to answer your first question," he said. "She and her brother were for some time in the household of Dr. Fu-Manchu. In fact, Mr. Weymouth, Kâramanèh, as her name implies, was a slave."

Weymouth glanced at the beautiful, troubled face with scarcely veiled distrust.

"You don't look as though you had come from China, miss," he said, with a sort of unwilling admiration.

"I do not come from China," replied Kâramanèh. "My father was a pure Bedawee. But my history does not matter." (At times there was something imperious in her manner, and to this her musical accent added force.) "When your brave brother, Inspector Weymouth, and Dr. Fu-Manchu were swallowed up by the river, Fu-Manchu held a poisoned needle in his hand. The laughter meant that the needle had done its work. Your brother had become mad!"

Weymouth turned aside to hide his emotion.

"What was on the needle?" he asked huskily.

"It was something which he prepared from the venom of some creature found in certain Chinese swamps," she answered. "It produces madness, but not always death."

"He would have had a poor chance," said Smith, "even had he been in complete possession of his senses. At the time of the encounter we must have been some considerable distance from shore, and the fog was impenetrable."

"But how do you account for the fact that neither of the bodies has been recovered?"

"Ryman of the river police tells me that persons lost at that point are not always recovered—or not until a considerable time later."

There was a faint sound from the room above. The news of that tragic happening out in the mist upon the Thames had prostrated poor Mrs. Weymouth.

"She hasn't been told half the truth," said her brother-in-law. "She doesn't know about—the poisoned needle. What kind of fiend was this Dr. Fu-Manchu?" He burst into a sudden blaze of furious resentment. "John never told me much, and you have let mighty little leak into the papers. What was he? Who was he?"

Half he addressed the words to Smith, half to Kâramanèh.

"Dr. Fu-Manchu," replied the former, "was the ultimate expression of Chinese cunning: a phenomenon such as occurs but once in many generations. He was a superman of incredible genius, who, had he willed, could have revolutionized science. There is a superstition in some parts of China according to which, under certain peculiar conditions (one of which is proximity to a deserted burial-ground) an evil spirit of incredible age may enter into the body of a new-born infant. All my efforts thus far have not availed me to trace the genealogy of the man called Dr. Fu-Manchu. Even Kâramanèh cannot help me in this. But I have sometimes thought that he was a member of a certain very old Kiangsu family—and that the peculiar conditions I have mentioned prevailed at his birth!"

Smith, observing our looks of amazement, laughed shortly, and quite mirthlessly.

"Poor old Weymouth!" he jerked. "I suppose my labours are finished; but I am far from triumphant. Is there any improvement in Mrs. Weymouth's condition?"

"Very little," was the reply. "She has lain in a semiconscious state since the news came. No one had any idea she would take it so. At one time we were afraid her brain was going. She seemed to have delusions."

Smith spun around upon Weymouth.

"Of what nature?" he asked rapidly.

The other pulled nervously at his moustache.

"My wife has been staying with her," he explained, "since—it happened; and for the last three nights poor John's widow has cried out at the same time—half-past two—that someone was knocking on the door."

"What door?"

"That door yonder—the street door."

All our eyes turned in the direction indicated.

"John often came home at half-past two from the Yard," continued Weymouth; "so we naturally thought poor Mary was wandering in her mind. But last night—and it's not to be wondered at—my wife couldn't sleep, and she was wide awake at half-past two."

"Well?"

Nayland Smith was standing before him, alert, bright-eyed.

"She heard it too!"

The sun was streaming into the cosy little sitting-room; but I will confess that Weymouth's words chilled me uncannily. Kâramanèh laid her hand upon mine in a quaint, childish fashion peculiarly her own. Her hand was cold, but its touch thrilled me. For Kâramanèh was not a child, but a rarely beautiful girl—a pearl of the East such as many a monarch has fought for.

"What then?" asked Smith.

"She was afraid to move—afraid to look from the window!"

My friend turned and stared hard at me.

"A subjective hallucination, Petrie?"

"In all probability," I replied. "You should arrange that your wife be relieved in her trying duties, Mr. Weymouth. It is too great a strain for an inexperienced nurse."

CHAPTER TWENTY-EIGHT

THE KNOCKING ON THE DOOR

Of all that we had hoped for in our pursuit of Fu-Manchu how little had we accomplished. Excepting Kâramanèh and her brother (who were victims and not creatures of the Chinese doctor's) not one of the formidable group had fallen alive into our hands. Dreadful crimes had marked Fu-Manchu's passage through the land. Not one half of the truth (and nothing of the later developments) had been made public. Nayland Smith's authority was sufficient to control the Press.

In the absence of such a veto a veritable panic must have seized upon the entire country; since a monster—a thing more than humanly evil—existed in our midst.

Always Fu-Manchu's secret activities had centred about the great waterway. There was much of poetic justice in his end; for the Thames had claimed him who so long had used the stream as a highway for the passage to and fro for his secret forces. Gone now were the yellow men who had been the instruments of his evil will; gone was the giant intellect which had controlled the complex murder machine. Kâramanèh, whose beauty he had used as a lure, at last was free, and no more with her smile would tempt men to death—that her brother might live.

Many there are, I doubt not, who will regard the Eastern girl with horror. I ask their forgiveness in that I regarded her quite differently. No man having seen her could have condemned her unheard. Many, having looked into her lovely eyes, had they found there what I found, must have forgiven her almost any crime.

That she valued human life but little was no matter for wonder. Her nationality—her history—furnished adequate excuse for an attitude not condonable in a European equally cultured.

But indeed let me confess that hers was a nature incomprehensible to me in some respects. The soul of Kâramanèh was a closed book to my shortsighted Western eyes. But the body of Kâramanèh was exquisite; her beauty of a kind that was a key to the most extravagant rhapsodies of Eastern poets. Her eyes held a challenge wholly Oriental in its appeal; her lips, even in repose, were a taunt. And, herein, East is West and West is East.

Finally, despite her lurid history, despite the scornful self-possession of which I knew her capable, she was an unprotected girl—in years, I believe, a mere child—whom Fate had cast in my way. At her request, we had booked passages for her brother and herself to Egypt. The boat sailed in three days. But Kâramanèh's beautiful eyes were sad; often I detected tears on the black lashes. Shall I endeavour to describe my own tumultuous, warring emotions? It would be useless, since I know it to be impossible. For in those dark eyes burned a fire I might not see; those silken lashes veiled a message I dared not read.

Nayland Smith was not blind to the facts of the complicated situation. I can truthfully assert that he was the only man of my acquaintance who, having come in contact with Kâramanèh, had kept his head.

We endeavoured to divert her mind from the recent tragedies by a round of amusements, though with poor Weymouth's body still at the mercy of unknown waters Smith and I made but a poor show of gaiety; and I took a gloomy pride in the admiration which our lovely companion everywhere excited. I learnt, in those days, how rare a thing in nature is a really beautiful woman.

One afternoon we found ourselves at an exhibition of watercolours in Bond Street. Kâramanèh was intensely interested in the subjects of the drawings—which were entirely Egyptian. As usual, she furnished matter for comment amongst the other visitors, as did the boy, Azîz, her brother, anew upon the world from his living grave in the house of Dr. Fu-Manchu.

Suddenly Azîz clutched at his sister's arm, whispering rapidly in Arabic. I saw her peachlike colour fade; saw her become pale and wild-eyed—the haunted Kâramanèh of the old days. She turned to me.

"Dr. Petrie—he says that Fu-Manchu is here!"

"Where?"

Nayland Smith rapped out the, question violently, turning in a flash from the picture which he was examining.

"In this room!" she whispered, glancing furtively, affrightedly, about her. "Something tells Azîz when *he* is near—and I too feel strangely afraid. Oh, can it be that he is not dead!"

She held my arm tightly. Her brother was searching the room with big, velvet black eyes. I studied the faces of the several visitors; and Smith was staring about him with the old alert look, and tugging nervously at the lobe of his ear. The name of the giant foe of the white race instantaneously had strung him up to a pitch of supreme intensity.

Our united scrutinies discovered no figure which could have been that of the Chinese doctor. Who could mistake that long, gaunt shape, with the high, mummy-like shoulders, and the indescribable gait, which I can only liken to that of an awkward cat?

Then, over the heads of a group of people who stood by the doorway, I saw Smith peering at someone—at someone who passed across the outer room. Stepping aside, I too obtained a glimpse of this person.

As I saw him, he was a tall, old man, wearing a black Inverness coat and a rather shabby silk hat. He had long white hair and a patriarchal beard, wore smoked glasses and walked slowly, leaning upon a stick.

Smith's gaunt face paled. With a rapid glance at Kâramanèh, he made off across the room. Could it be Dr. Fu-Manchu?

Many days had passed since, already half-choked by Inspector Weymouth's iron grip, Fu-Manchu, before our own eyes, had been swallowed up by the Thames. Even now men were seeking his body, and that of his last victim. Nor had we left any stone unturned. Acting upon information furnished by Kâramanèh, the police had searched every known haunt of the murder group. But everything pointed to the fact that the group was disbanded and dispersed; that the lord of strange deaths who had ruled it was noYet Smith was not satisfied. Neither, let me confess, was I. Every port was watched; and in suspected districts a kind of house-to-house patrol had been instituted. Unknown to the great public, in those days a secret war waged—a war in which all the available forces of the authorities took the field against one man! But that one man was the evil of the East incarnate.

When we rejoined him, Nayland Smith was talking to the commissionaire at the door. He turned to me.

"That is Professor Jenner Monde," he said. "The sergeant here knows him well'

The name of the celebrated Orientalist of course was familiar to me, although I had never before set eyes upon him.

"The Professor was out East the last time I was there, sir," stated the commissionaire. "I often used to see him. But he's an eccentric old gentleman. Seems to live in a world of his own. He's recently back from China, I think."

Nayland Smith stood clicking his teeth together in irritable hesitation. I heard Kâramanèh sigh, and, looking at her, I saw that her cheeks were regaining their natural colour.

She smiled in pathetic apology.

"If he was here he is gone," she said. "I am not afraid now."

Smith thanked the commissionaire for his information and we quitted the gallery.

"Professor Jenner Monde," muttered my friend, "has lived so long in China as almost to be a Chinaman. I have never met him— never seen him, before; but I wonder—"

"You wonder what, Smith?"

"I wonder if he could possibly be an ally of the Doctor's!"

I stared at him in amazement.

"If we are to attach any importance to the incident at all," I said, "we must remember that the boy's impression—and Kâramanèh's— was that Fu-Manchu was present in person."

"I *do* attach importance to the incident, Petrie; they are naturally sensitive to such impressions. But I doubt if even the abnormal organization of Azîz could distinguish between the hidden presence of a creature of the Doctor's and that of the Doctor himself. I shall make a point of calling upon Professor Jenner Monde."

But Fate had ordained that much should happen ere Smith made his proposed call upon the Professor.

Kâramanèh and her brother safely lodged in their hotel (which was watched night and day by four men under Smith's orders), we returned to my quiet suburban rooms.

"First," said Smith, "let us see what we can find out respecting Professor Monde."

He went to the telephone and called up New Scotland Yard. There followed some little delay before the requisite information was obtained. Finally, however, we learnt that the Professor was something of a recluse, having few acquaintances and fewer friends.

He lived alone in chambers in New Inn Court, Carey Street. A charwoman did such cleaning as was considered necessary by the Professor, who employed no regular domestic. When he was in London he might be seen fairly frequently at the British Museum, where his shabby figure was familiar to the officials. When he was not in London—that is, during the greater part of each year—no one knew where he went. He never left any address to which letters might be forwarded.

"How long has he been in London now?" asked Smith.

So far as could be ascertained from New Inn Court, (replied Scotland Yard) roughly, a week.

My friend left the telephone and began restlessly to pace the room. The charred briar was produced and stuffed with that broad-cut Latakia mixture of which Nayland Smith consumed close upon a pound a week. He was one of those untidy smokers who leave tangled tufts hanging from the pipe-bowl and when they light up strew the floor with smouldering fragments.

A ringing came, and shortly afterwards a girl entered.

"Mr. James Weymouth to see you, sir."

"Hullo!" rapped Smith. "What's this?"

Weymouth entered, big and florid, and in some respects singularly like his brother, in others as singularly unlike. Now, in his black suit, he was a sombre figure; and in the blue eyes I read a fear suppressed.

"Mr. Smith," he began, "there's something uncanny going on at Maple Cottage."

Smith wheeled the big armchair forward.

"Sit down, Mr. Weymouth," he said. "I am not entirely surprised. But you have my attention. What has occurred?"

Weymouth took a cigarette from the box which I proffered and poured out a peg of whisky. His hand was not quite steady.

"That knocking," he explained. "It came again the night after you were there, and Mrs. Weymouth—my wife, I mean—felt that she couldn't spend another night there alone—"

"Did she look out of the window?" I asked.

"No, Doctor; she was afraid. But I spent last night downstairs in the sitting-room—and I looked out!"

He took a gulp from his glass. Nayland Smith, seated on the edge of the table, his extinguished pipe in his hand, was watching keenly.

"I'll admit I didn't look out at once," Weymouth resumed. "There was something so uncanny, gentlemen, in that knocking—knocking—in the dead of the night. I thought"—his voice shook—"of poor Jack, lying somewhere amongst the slime of the river—and, oh, my God! it came to me that it was Jack who was knocking—and I dare not think what he—what it—would look like!"

He leant forward, his chin in his hand. For a few moments we were all silent.

"I know I funked," he continued huskily. "But when the wife came to the head of the stairs and whispered to me: 'There it is again. What in heaven's name can it be?'—I started to unbolt the door. The knocking had stopped. Everything was very still. I heard Mary—*his* widow—

sobbing upstairs; that was all. I opened the door a little bit at a time."

Pausing again, he cleared his throat, and went on:

"It was a bright night, and there was no one there—not a soul. But somewhere down the lane, as I looked out into the porch, I heard most awful groans! They got fainter and fainter. Then—I could have sworn I heard *someone laughing!* My nerves cracked up at that, and I shut the door again."

The narration of his weird experience revived something of the natural fear which it had occasioned. He raised his glass, with unsteady hand, and drained it.

Smith struck a match and relighted his pipe. He began to pace the room again. His eyes were literally on fire.

"Would it be possible to get Mrs. Weymouth out of the house before tonight? Remove her to your place, for instance?" he asked abruptly.

Weymouth looked up in surprise.

"She seems to be in a very low state," he replied. He glanced at me. "Perhaps Dr. Petrie would give us an opinion?"

"I will come and see her," I said. "But what is your idea, Smith?"

"I want to hear that knocking!" he rapped. "But in what I may see fit to do I must not be handicapped by the presence of a sick woman."

"Her condition at any rate will admit of our administering an opiate," I suggested. "That would meet the situation?"

"Good!" cried Smith. He was intensely excited now. "I rely upon you to arrange something, Petrie. Mr. Weymouth"—he turned to our visitor—"I shall be with you this evening not later than twelve o'clock."

Weymouth appeared to be greatly relieved. I asked him to wait whilst I prepared a draught for the patient. When he was gone:

"What do you think this knocking means, Smith?" I asked.

He tapped out his pipe on the side of the grate and began with nervous energy to refill it again from the dilapidated pouch.

"I dare not tell you what I hope, Petrie," he replied—"nor what I fear."

CHAPTER TWENTY-NINE

THE ONE WHO KNOCKED

Dusk was falling when we made our way in the direction of Maple Cottage. Nayland Smith appeared to be keenly interested in the character of the district. A high and ancient wall bordered the road along which we walked for a considerable distance. Later it gave place to a rickety fence.

My friend peered through a gap in the latter.

"There is quite an extensive estate here," he said, "not yet cut up by the builder. It is well wooded on one side, and there appears to be a pool lower down."

The road was a quiet one, and we plainly heard the tread—quite unmistakable—of an approaching policeman. Smith continued to peer through the hole in the fence, until the officer drew up level with us. Then:

"Does this piece of ground extend down to the village, constable?" he inquired.

Quite willing for a chat, the man stopped, and stood with his thumbs thrust in his belt.

"Yes, sir. They tell me three new roads will be made through it between here and the hill."

"It must be a happy hunting ground for tramps?"

"I've seen some suspicious-looking coves about at times. But after dusk an army might be inside there and nobody the wiser."

"Burglaries frequent in the houses backing on to it?"

"Oh no. A favourite game in these parts is snatching loaves and bottles of milk from the doors, first thing, as they're delivered. There's been an extra lot of it lately. My mate who relieves me has got special instructions to keep his eye open in the mornings!" The man grinned. "It wouldn't be a very big case even if he caught anybody!"

"No," said Smith absently, "perhaps not. Your business must be a dry one this warm weather. Good night."

"Good night, sir," replied the constable, richer by half a crown—"and thank you."

Smith stared after him for a moment, tugging reflectively at the lobe of his ear.

"I don't know that it wouldn't be a big case, after all," he murmured. "Come on, Petrie."

Not another word did he speak, until we stood at the gate of Maple Cottage. There a plain-clothes man was standing, evidently awaiting Smith. He touched his hat.

"Have you found a suitable hiding-place?" asked my companion rapidly.

"Yes, sir," was the reply. "Kent—my mate—is there now. You'll notice that he can't be seen from here."

"No," agreed Smith, peering all about him. "He can't. Where is he?"

"Behind the broken wall," explained the man, pointing. "Through that ivy there's a clear view of the cottage door."

"Good. Keep your eyes open. If a messenger comes for me, he is to be intercepted, you understand. No one must be allowed to disturb us. You will recognize the messenger. He will be one of your fellows. Should he come—hoot three times, as much like an owl as you can."

We walked up to the porch of the cottage. In response to Smith's ringing came James Weymouth, who seemed greatly relieved by our arrival.

"First," said my friend briskly, "you had better run up and see the patient."

Accordingly, I followed Weymouth upstairs and was admitted by his wife to a neat little bedroom where the grief-stricken woman lay, a wanly pathetic sight.

"Did you administer the draught, as directed?" I asked.

Mrs. James Weymouth nodded. She was a kindly looking woman, with the same dread haunting her hazel eyes as that which lurked in her husband's blue ones.

The patient was sleeping soundly. Some whispered instructions I gave to the faithful nurse and descended to the sitting-room. It was a warm night, and Weymouth sat by the open window, smoking. The dim light from the lamp on the table lent him an almost startling likeness to his brother; and for a moment I stood at the foot of the stairs scarce able to trust my reason. Then he turned his face fully toward me, and the illusion was lost.

"Do you think she is likely to wake, Doctor?" he asked.

"I think not," I replied.

Nayland Smith stood upon the rug before the hearth, swinging from one foot to the other, in his nervously restless way. The room was foggy with the fumes of tobacco, for he too was smoking. At intervals of some five to ten minutes, his blackened briar (which

I never knew him to clean or scrape) would go out. I think Smith used more matches than any other smoker I have ever met, and he invariably carried three boxes in various pockets of his garments.

The tobacco habit is infectious, and, seating myself in an armchair, I lighted a cigarette. For this dreary vigil I had come prepared with a bunch of rough notes, a writing-block, and a fountain pen. I settled down to work upon my record of the Fu-Manchu case.

Silence fell upon Maple Cottage. Save for the shuddering sigh which whispered through the over-hanging cedars, and Smith's eternal match-striking, nothing was there to disturb me in my task. Yet I could make little progress. Between my mind and the chapter upon which I was at work a certain sentence persistently intruded itself. It was as though an unseen hand held the written page closely before my eyes. This was the sentence:

"Imagine a person, tall, lean, and feline, high-shouldered, with a brow like Shakespeare and a face like Satan, a close-shaven skull, and long, magnetic eyes of the true cat-green: invest him with all the cruel cunning of an entire Eastern race, accumulated in one giant intellect ..."

Dr. Fu-Manchu! Fu-Manchu as Smith had described him to me on that night which now seemed so remotely distant—the night upon which I had learned of the existence of the wonderful and evil being born of that secret quickening which stirred in the womb of the yellow races.

As Smith, for the ninth or tenth time, knocked out his pipe on a bar of the grate, the cuckoo clock in the kitchen proclaimed the hour.

"Two," said James Weymouth.

I abandoned my task, replacing notes and writing-block in the bag I had with me. Weymouth adjusted the lamp, which had begun to smoke.

I tiptoed to the stairs and, stepping softly, ascended to the sick-room. All was quiet, and Mrs. Weymouth whispered to me that the patient still slept soundly. I returned to find Nayland Smith pacing about the room in that state of suppressed excitement habitual with him in the approach of any crisis.

At a quarter-past two the breeze dropped entirely, and such a stillness reigned all about us as I could not have supposed possible so near to the ever-throbbing heart of the metropolis. Plainly I could hear Weymouth's heavy breathing. He sat at the window and looked out into the black shadows under the cedars. Smith ceased his pacing and stood again on the rug very still. He was listening! I doubt not we were all listening.

Some faint sound broke the impressive stillness, coming from the direction of the village street. It was a vague, indefinite disturbance, brief, and upon it ensued a silence more marked than ever. Some minutes before Smith had extinguished the lamp. In the darkness I heard his teeth snap sharply together.

The call of an owl sounded very clearly three times.

I knew that to mean that a messenger was come; but from whence or bearing what tidings I knew not. My friend's plans were incomprehensible to me; nor had I pressed him for any explanation of their nature, knowing him to be in that high-strung and somewhat irritable mood which claimed him at times of uncertainty—when he doubted the wisdom of his actions, the accuracy of his surmises. He gave no sign.

Very faintly I heard a clock strike the half-hour. A soft breeze stole again through the branches above. The wind I thought must be in a new quarter since I had not heard the clock before. In so lonely a spot it was difficult to believe that the bell was that of St. Paul's. Yet such was the fact.

And hard upon the ringing followed another sound—a sound we all had expected, had waited for; but at whose coming no one of us, I think, retained complete mastery of himself.

Breaking up the silence in a manner that set my heart wildly leaping it came—an imperative knocking on the door!

"My God!" groaned Weymouth—but he did not move from his position at the window.

"Stand by, Petrie!" said Smith.

He strode to the door—and threw it widely open.

I know I was very pale. I think I cried out as I fell back—retreated with clenched hands from before *that* which stood on the threshold.

It was a wild, unkempt figure, with straggling beard, hideously staring eyes. With its hands it clutched at its hair—at its chin; plucked at its mouth. No moonlight touched the features of this unearthly visitant, but scanty as was the illumination we could see the gleaming teeth—and the wildly glaring eyes.

It began to laugh—peal after peal—hideous and shrill.

Nothing so terrifying had ever smote upon my ears. I was palsied by the horror of the sound.

Then Nayland Smith pressed the button of an electric torch which he carried. He directed the disc of white light fully upon the face in the doorway.

"Oh, God!" cried Weymouth. "It's John!"—and again and again; "Oh, God! Oh, God!"

Perhaps for the first time in my life I really believed (nay, I could not doubt) that a thing of another world stood before me. I am ashamed to confess the extent of the horror that came upon me. James Weymouth raised his hands, as if to thrust away from him that awful thing in the door. He was babbling—prayers, I think, but wholly incoherent.

"Hold him, Petrie!"

Smith's voice was low. (When we were past thought or intelligent action, he, dominant and cool, with that forced calm for which, a crisis over, he always paid so dearly, was thinking of the woman who slept above.)

He leapt forward; and in the instant that he grappled with the one who had knocked I knew the visitant for a man of flesh and blood—a man who shrieked and fought like a savage animal, foamed at the mouth and gnashed his teeth in horrid frenzy; knew him for a madman—knew him for the victim of Fu-Manchu—not dead, but living—for Inspector Weymouth—a maniac!

In a flash I realized all this and sprang to Smith's assistance. There was a sound of racing footsteps, and the men who had been watching outside came running into the porch. A third was with them; and the five of us (for Weymouth's brother had not yet grasped the fact that a man and not a spirit shrieked and howled in our midst) clung to the infuriated madman, yet barely held our own with him.

"The syringe, Petrie!" gasped Smith. "Quick! You must manage to make an injection!"

I extricated myself and raced into the cottage for my bag. A hypodermic syringe ready charged I had brought with me at Smith's request. Even in that thrilling moment I could find time to admire the wonderful foresight of my friend, who had divined what would befall—isolated the strange, pitiful truth from the chaotic circumstances which saw us at Maple Cottage that night.

Let me not enlarge upon the end of the awful struggle. At one time I despaired (we all despaired) of quieting the poor, demented creature. But at last it was done; and the gaunt, bloodstained savage whom we had known as Detective-Inspector Weymouth lay passive upon the couch in his own sitting-room. A great wonder possessed my mind for the genius of the uncanny being who with the scratch of a needle had made a brave and kindly man into this unclean, brutish thing.

Nayland Smith, gaunt and wild-eyed, and trembling yet with his tremendous exertions, turned to the man whom I knew to be the messenger from Scotland Yard.

"Well?" he rapped.

"He is arrested, sir," the detective reported. "They have kept him at his chambers as you ordered."

"Has she slept through it?" said Smith to me. (I had just returned from a visit to the room above.)

I nodded.

"Is *he* safe for an hour or two?"—indicating the figure on the couch.

"For eight or ten," I replied grimly.

"Come, then. Our night's labours are not nearly complete."

CHAPTER THIRTY

FLAMES

Later was forthcoming evidence to show that poor Weymouth had lived a wild life, in hiding among the thick bushes of the tract of land which lay between the village and the suburb on the neighbouring hill. Literally, he had returned to primitive savagery and some of his food had been that of the lower animals, though he had not scrupled to steal, as we learned when his lair was discovered.

He had hidden himself cunningly; but witnesses appeared who had seen him, in the dusk, and fled from him. They never learnt that the object of their fear was Inspector John Weymouth. How, having escaped death in the Thames, he had crossed London unobserved, we never knew; but his trick of knocking upon his own door at half-past two each morning (a sort of dawning of sanity mysteriously linked with old custom) will be a familiar class of symptom to all students of alienation.

I revert to the night when Smith solved the mystery of the knocking.

In a car which he had in waiting at the end of the village we sped through the deserted streets to New Inn Court. I, who had followed Nayland Smith through the failures and successes of his mission, knew that tonight he had surpassed himself; had justified the confidence placed in him by the highest authorities.

We were admitted to an untidy room—that of a student, a traveller and a crank—by a plain-clothes officer. Amid picturesque and disordered fragments of a hundred ages, in a great carven chair placed before a towering statue of the Buddha, sat a handcuffed man. His white hair and beard were patriarchal; his pose had great dignity. But his expression was entirely masked by the smoked glasses which he wore.

Two other detectives were guarding the prisoner.

"We arrested Professor Jenner Monde as he came in, sir," reported the man who had opened the door. "He has made no statement. I hope there isn't a mistake."

"I hope not," rapped Smith.

He strode across the room. He was consumed by a fever of excitement. Almost savagely he tore away the beard, tore off the snowy wig—dashed the smoked glasses upon the floor.

A great, high brow was revealed, and green, malignant eyes, which fixed themselves upon him with an expression I can never forget.

It was Dr. Fu-Manchu!

One intense moment of silence ensued—of silence which seemed to throb. Then:

"What have you done with Professor Monde?" demanded Smith.

Dr. Fu-Manchu showed his even, yellow teeth in the singularly evil smile which I knew so well. A manacled prisoner, he sat as unruffled as a judge upon the bench. In truth and in justice I am compelled to say that Fu-Manchu was absolutely fearless.

"He has been detained in China," he replied, in smooth, sibilant tones—"by affairs of great urgency. His well-known personality and ungregarious habits have served me well here!"

Smith, I could see, was undetermined how to act; he stood tugging at his ear and glancing from the impassive Chinaman to the wondering detectives.

"What are we to do, sir?" one of them asked.

"Leave Dr. Petrie and myself alone with the prisoner until I call you."

The three withdrew. I divined now what was coming.

"Can you restore Weymouth's sanity?" rapped Smith abruptly "I cannot save you from the hangman, nor"—his fists clenched convulsively "would I if I could; but—"

Fu-Manchu fixed his brilliant eyes upon him.

"Say no more, Mr. Smith," he interrupted; "you misunderstand me. I do not quarrel with that, but what I have done from conviction and what I have done of necessity are separated—are seas apart. The brave Inspector Weymouth I wounded with a poisoned needle, in self-defence; but I regret his condition as greatly as you do. I respect such a man There is an antidote to the poison of the needle."

"Name it," said Smith.

Fu-Manchu smiled again.

"Useless," he replied. "I alone can prepare it. My secrets shall die with me. I will make a sane man of Inspector Weymouth, but no one else shall be in the house but he and I."

"It will be surrounded by police," interrupted Smith grimly.

"As you please," said Fu-Manchu. "Make your arrangements. In that ebony case upon the table are the instruments for the cure. Arrange for me to visit him where and when you will—"

"I distrust you utterly. It is some trick," jerked Smith.

Dr. Fu-Manchu rose slowly and drew himself up to his great height. His manacled hands could not rob him of the uncanny dignity which was his. He raised them above his head with a tragic gesture, and fixed his piercing gaze upon Nayland Smith.

"The God of Cathay hear me," he said, with a deep, guttural note in his voice—"I swear—"

The most awful visitor who ever threatened the peace of England, the end of the visit of Fu-Manchu was characteristic—terrible—inexplicable.

Strange to relate, I did not doubt that this weird being had conceived some kind of admiration or respect for the man to whom he had wrought so terrible an injury. He was capable of such sentiments, for he entertained some similar one in regard to myself.

A cottage further down the village street than Weymouth's was vacant, and in the early dawn of that morning became the scene of *outré* happenings. Poor Weymouth, still in a comatose condition, we removed there (Smith having secured the key from the astonished agent). I suppose so strange a specialist never visited a patient before—certainly not under such conditions.

For into the cottage, which had been entirely surrounded by a ring of police, Dr. Fu-Manchu was admitted from the closed car in which, his work of healing complete, he was to be borne to prison—to death!

Law and justice were suspended by my royally empowered friend that the enemy of the white race might heal one of those who had hunted him down!

No curious audience was present, for sunrise was not yet come; no concourse of excited students followed the hand of the Master; but within that surrounded cottage was performed one of those miracles of science which in other circumstances had made the fame of Dr. Fu-Manchu to live for ever.

Inspector Weymouth, dazed, dishevelled, clutching his head as a man who had passed through the Valley of the Shadow—but sane—sane!—walked out into the porch!

He looked towards us—his eyes wild, but not with the fearsome wildness of insanity.

"Mr. Smith!" he cried—and staggered down the path—"Dr. Petrie! What—"

There came a deafening explosion. From *every* visible window of the deserted cottage flames burst forth!

"*Quick!*" Smith's voice rose almost to a scream—"into the house!"

He raced up the path, past Inspector Weymouth, who stood swaying there like a drunken man. I was close upon his heels. Behind me came the police.

The door was impassable! Already it vomited a deathly heat, borne upon stifling fumes like those of the mouth of the Pit. We burst a window. The room within was a furnace!

"My God!" cried someone. "This is supernatural!"

"Listen!" cried another. "Listen!"

The crowd which a fire can conjure up, at any hour of day or night, out of the void of nowhere, was gathering already. But upon all descended a pall of silence.

From the heart of the holocaust a voice proclaimed itself—a voice raised, not in anguish but in *triumph!* It chanted barbarically—and was still.

The abnormal flames rose higher—leaping forth from every window.

"The alarm!" said Smith hoarsely. "Call up the brigade!"

I come to the close of my chronicle, and feel that I betray a trust—the trust of my reader. For having limned, in the colours at my command, the fiendish Chinese doctor, I am unable to conclude my task as I should desire, unable, with any consciousness of finality, to write Finis to the end of my narrative.

It seems to me sometimes that my pen is but temporarily idle— that I have but dealt with a single phase of a movement having a hundred phases. One sequel I hope for, and against all the promptings of logic and Western bias. If my hope shall be realized I cannot, at this time, pretend to state.

The future, 'mid its many secrets, holds this precious one from me.

I ask you, then, to absolve me from the charge of ill completing my work; for any curiosity with which this narrative may leave the reader burdened is shared by the writer.

With intent, I have rushed you from the chambers of Professor Jenner Monde to that closing episode at the deserted cottage; I have made the pace hot in order to impart to these last pages of my account something of the breathless scurry which characterized those happenings.

My canvas may seem sketchy: it is my impression of the reality. No hard details remain in my mind of the dealings of that night:— Fu-Manchu arrested—Fu-Manchu, manacled, entering the cottage on his mission of healing; Weymouth, miraculously rendered sane, coming forth; the place in flames.

And then?

To a shell the cottage burned, with an incredible rapidity which pointed to some hidden agency; to a shell about ashes which held *no trace of human bones!*

It has been asked of me: Was there no possibility of Fu-Manchu's having eluded us in the ensuing confusion? Was there no loophole of escape?

I reply, that so far as I was able to judge, a rat could scarce have quitted the building undetected. Yet that Fu-Manchu had, in some incomprehensible manner and by some mysterious agency, produced those abnormal flames, I cannot doubt. Did he voluntarily ignite his own funeral pyre?

As I write there lies before me a soiled and creased sheet of vellum. It bears some lines traced in a cramped, peculiar, and all but illegible hand. This fragment was found by Inspector Weymouth (to this day a man mentally sound) in a pocket of his ragged garments.

When it was written I leave you to judge. How it came to be where Weymouth found it calls for no explanation.

To Mr. Commissioner NAYLAND SMITH and DR PETRIE—
Greeting! I am recalled home by One who may not be denied. In much that I came to do I have failed. Much that I have done I would undo; some little I have undone. Out of fire I came—the smouldering fire of a thing one day to be a consuming flame; in fire I go. Seek not my ashes. I am the lord of the fires! Farewell.

FU-MANCHU

Whom has been with me in my several meetings with the man who penned that message I leave to adjudge if it be the letter of a madman bent upon self-destruction by strange means, or the gibe of a preternaturally clever scientist and the most elusive being ever born of the land of mystery—China.

For the present, I can aid you no more in the forming of your verdict. A day may come—though I pray it do not—when I shall be able to throw new light upon much that is dark in this matter. That day, so far as I can judge, could only dawn in the event of the Chinaman's survival; therefore I pray that the veil be never lifted.

But, as I have said, there is another sequel to this story which I can contemplate with a different countenance. How, then, shall I conclude this very unsatisfactory account?

Shall I tell you, finally, of my parting with lovely, dark-eyed Kâramanèh, on board the liner which was to bear her to Egypt?

No, let me, instead, conclude with the words of Nayland Smith:

"*I* sail for Burma in a fortnight, Petrie, I have leave to break my journey at the Ditch. How would a run up the Nile fit your programme? Bit early for the season, but you might find something to amuse you!"

ABOUT THE AUTHOR

Sax Rohmer was born Arthur Henry Ward in 1883, in Birmingham, England, adding "Sarsfield" to his name in 1901. He was four years old when Sherlock Holmes appeared in print, five when the Jack the Ripper murders began, and sixteen when H.G. Wells' Martians invaded. Initially pursuing a career as a civil servant, he turned to writing as a journalist, poet, comedy sketch writer, and songwriter in British music halls. At age twenty he submitted the short story "The Mysterious Mummy" to *Pearson's Magazine* and "The Leopard-Couch" to *Chamber's Journal*. Both were published under the byline "A. Sarsfield Ward."

Ward's Bohemian associates Cumper, Bailey, and Dodgson gave him the nickname "Digger," which he used as his byline on several serialized stories. Then, in 1908, the song "Bang Went the Chance of a Lifetime" appeared under the byline "Sax Rohmer." Becoming immersed in theosophy, alchemy, and mysticism, Ward decided the name was appropriate to his writing, so when "The Zayat Kiss" first appeared in *The Story-Teller* magazine in October, 1912, it was credited to Sax Rohmer. That was the first story featuring Fu-Manchu, and the first portion of the novel *The Mystery of Dr. Fu-Manchu*.

Novels such as *The Yellow Claw*, *Tales of Secret Egypt*, *Dope*, *The Dream Detective*, *The Green Eyes of Bast*, and *Tales of Chinatown* made Rohmer one of the most successful novelists of the 1920s and 1930s. There are fourteen Fu-Manchu novels, and the character has been featured in radio, television, comic strips, and comic books. He first appeared in film in 1923, and has been portrayed by such actors as Boris Karloff, Christopher Lee, John Carradine, Peter Sellers, and Nicholas Cage.

Rohmer died in 1959, a victim of an outbreak of the type A influenza known as the Asian flu.

APPRECIATING DR. FU-MANCHU

BY LESLIE S. KLINGER

The phrase "yellow peril," the stereotype of the threatening Asian, did not gain political currency until the epithet was popularized by Kaiser Wilhelm during the Sino-Japanese war of 1894-1895.[1] Yet the dangers of the East had already stirred the public's imagination. The terrible "Opium Wars" (1839-1842 and 1856-1860) had focused the attention of the British populace on China, as British expeditionary forces were sent from India (including Charles Gordon, later dubbed "Chinese" Gordon for his daring military exploits) to subdue the country and make it safe for English trade.

A generation later, the Boxer Rebellion in China (1898-1901), opposing foreign imperialism and Christianity, targeted white residents of the country. In Beijing, foreigners were forced into the confines of the Legation Quarter and kept under siege for fifty-

---

1   The Kaiser sent Tsar Nicholas II a scurrilously allegorical painting showing persons representing the European powers against a backdrop of storm clouds atop which rode a fiery image of the Buddha. The painting was entitled "The Yellow Peril."

five days, until an eight-nation force of 20,000 soldiers entered the country, crushing the Imperial Army and capturing Beijing.

In late nineteenth-century America, the Chinese, brought in to build the railways, found themselves displaced as the jobs were completed. They were forced to take low-paying servile employment. Then as the post-Civil War economy declined, anti-Chinese sentiments were fanned by labor leader Denis Kearney and his Workingman's Party, as well as by California Governor John Bigler, who blamed the Chinese for depressed wage levels.

The Chinese often refused to be assimilated into the population, clinging to their native religion and retaining their "foreign" language and appearance. As early as 1880, P.W. Dooner wrote a little-known novel titled *The Last Days of the Republic,* published in California—a hotbed of anti-Asian sentiment—and depicting a United States under Chinese rule. The novel describes how Chinese immigrants, purporting to be harmless laborers, were in fact undercover agents of the Chinese government working to overthrow the U.S. government.

Violence erupted in many places in the U.S., and in 1882 Congress passed a groundbreaking law excluding the Chinese from further immigration into the country. The law had the effect of forestalling the reunions of many families which had members already living there. Anti-miscegenation laws prevented Chinese men from marrying white women, further preventing the establishment of Chinese "families." The Chinese Exclusion Act was extended in 1892 and again in 1924, and Chinese were forbidden to apply for U.S. citizenship.

The Hearst newspapers, fueled by the personal prejudices of William Randolph Hearst, railed against the "yellow peril," and in 1911 G. G. Rupert, an influential religious figure, published *The Yellow Peril; or, Orient vs. Occident.*

The British press was filled with accounts of the ill-treatment of whites by Chinese in China preceding and during the Rebellion. Furthermore, the Chinese residents of London, who were gathered primarily in the dock areas of Rotherhithe and Limehouse, were commonly depicted in press accounts as denizens of slum housing and opium dens. Oscar Wilde's 1890 *Picture of Dorian Gray* horrified the public with Gray's dissolute visits to the dens, and in 1891 the *Strand Magazine*, home to the Sherlock Holmes stories and other popular tales, carried an influential (albeit likely fictional) first-person account of "A Night in an Opium Den," reflected in fiction by Conan Doyle's "Man with the Twisted Lip" in December 1891.

The evil Oriental genius first appeared in Western literature in 1892. *Tom Edison Jr.'s Electric Sea Spider, or, The Wizard of the Submarine World*, a "dime novel" published by the Nugget Library, features Kiang Ho, a Mongolian or Chinese—there is some confusion in the tale—who is a Harvard-educated pirate-warlord. Ho, who terrorizes the seas, is defeated by young Edison. He is succeeded in 1896 by Yue-Laou, an evil Chinese sorcerer-ruler featured in *The Maker of Moons* series by Robert Chambers. Yue-Laou is the first Chinese villain to combine black magic with rulership of a nefarious empire.

In 1898, M.P. Shiel wrote his most popular book, *The Yellow Danger*. The story tells of Dr. Yen How, a half-Japanese/half-Chinese villain ("he combined these antagonistic races in one man") who rises to power in China and fosters war with the West. Yen How is described as a physician educated at Heidelburg and was probably loosely based on the Chinese revolutionary Sun Yat Sen (also a physician). Yen How is defeated by the West in the person of Admiral John Hardy, a consumptive who overcomes his frailties to turn back the Yellow Danger.

Into this world was born one of the greatest evil geniuses of the 20th century.

* * *

It isn't known how much these earlier books affected the work of Arthur Henry Sarsfield Ward (February 15, 1883-June 1, 1959), better known as Sax Rohmer. Rohmer—who began as a comedy sketch and song writer for music halls—was fascinated by the East and told a story about a Ouija board that predicted that a "Chinaman" would be the source of his fortune. He worked as a reporter in London's Chinatown, and the *Encyclopedia of Mystery & Detection*, by Chris Steinbrunner and Otto Penzler, summarizes his account of that experience:

> [Rohmer's] research for an article on Limehouse had divulged the existence of a "Mr. King," an actual figure of immense power in the Chinese district of London. His enormous wealth derived from gambling, drug smuggling, and the organization of many other criminal activities. The apparent head of powerful tongs and their many unsavory members, Mr. King was never charged with a crime, and his very existence was in question. One foggy night, Rohmer saw him—from a distance; his face was the embodiment of Satan. This was Fu Manchu, the Devil Doctor.

In another version of the story, Rohmer said that his inspiration was a sighting in Limehouse. Waiting in an alley, Rohmer saw a shiny limousine pull up before a rude dwelling. Emerging from the car was "a tall, dignified Chinese, wearing a fur-collared overcoat and a fur cap... He was followed by an Arab girl wrapped in a gray fur cloak. I had a glimpse of her features. She was like something from an Edmund Dulac illustration of *The Thousand and One Nights*." (This tale is repeated in Cay Van Ash and Elizabeth Sax Rohmer's *Master of Villainy: A Biography of Sax Rohmer*.)

* * *

Whatever Rohmer's source material, Rohmer's short story "The Zayat Kiss" appeared in October 1912 in *The Story-Teller*, a popular British magazine. It was well-received, and Rohmer wrote nine more stories in the initial series. In 1913, the serialization was collected in book form as *The Mystery of Dr. Fu-Manchu* (published in America as *The Insidious Dr. Fu-Manchu*). The character appeared in two more series of stories before the end of the Great War, collected as *The Devil Doctor* (1916) (*The Return of Dr. Fu-Manchu* in America) and *Si-Fan Mysteries* (1917) (*The Hand of Fu-Manchu* in America)

Rohmer took a break from the evil Doctor and his colleagues then, penning dozens of short stories and novels with similar Eastern influences (Egypt was another favorite setting for his tales). In 1931, however, the Doctor reappeared, with *The Daughter of Fu-Manchu*. There were nine more novels, continuing until Rohmer's death in 1959, when *Emperor Fu-Manchu* was published. Four more stories, which had previously appeared only in magazines, were collected in 1973, as *The Wrath of Fu-Manchu*.

In the early stories, Fu-Manchu and his cohorts are the "yellow menace," whose aim is to establish domination of the yellow races over the white. Later, in the 1930s, Fu-Manchu foments political dissension in America among the working classes. As the wars in Europe and Asia threaten terrible disorder, destruction, and death, Fu-Manchu finds himself working to depose other world leaders and defeat the Communists in Russia and China, hoping to establish himself as the ruler of all nations.

Although the titular character is the center of attention of all of the Fu-Manchu stories, in fact there are other key characters: Dr. Petrie, who narrates the early tales; his friend Denis Nayland Smith (later knighted for his efforts), a Burmese police commissioner who has made the defeat of Fu-Manchu the lodestar of his life; Kâramanèh, the Eastern slave girl with whom Petrie falls in love and eventually marries; Fah Lo Suee, the daughter of Fu-Manchu, who vies for control of her father's empire; and later, Fleurette, the daughter of Petrie and Kâramanèh. Sir Lionel Barton, a Sinologist whom Smith and Petrie save repeatedly, also figures in several of the books, as does his daughter Rima and her fiancé anthropologist Shan Greville.

The mix of characters provides variety that raises the stories above many other works of the time.

Who was Fu Manchu, and why has his figure had such a powerful impact on Western culture? Rohmer describes him (in *The Mystery of Dr. Fu Manchu* and again using identical words in *The Devil Doctor*):

> Imagine a person, tall, lean and feline, high-shouldered, with a brow like Shakespeare and a face like Satan, a close-shaven skull, and long, magnetic eyes of the true cat-green. Invest him with all the cruel cunning of an entire Eastern race, accumulated in one giant intellect, with all the resources of science past and present, with all the resources, if you will, of a wealthy government—which, however, already has denied all knowledge of his existence. Imagine that awful being, and you have a mental picture of Dr. Fu-Manchu, the yellow peril incarnate in one man.

Yet the genius of the man is, at least in the early stories, confined to devising intricate means of killing those who stand in his way.

Some of Fu-Manchu's death plots depend on highly specialized knowledge of animals, insects, and poisons; others partake of what might be seen as supernatural means, "black magic," in the style of the Doctor's predecessor Yue-Laou. Fu-Manchu's successful efforts generally take place "offstage" but are reported to the authorities, and it is up to Petrie to discover how the murder was committed.

Many other episodes involve the discovery of a threat Fu-Manchu poses to one or more of the protagonists and the intervention of Smith, Petrie, or another lesser hero. Smith and Petrie in particular are frequently captured, threatened, tortured, and escape—occasionally by their own wits and frequently with the help of others—and poor Kâramanèh undergoes so many torments that it is a wonder that she desires to remain anywhere near her lover Dr. Petrie.

Even more telling than the Satanic descriptions of the Doctor's face are Rohmer's frequent references to the *eyes* of Fu-Manchu, which possess some sort of nictitating membrane and strongly suggest that the Doctor is *not human*. These simple elements reinforce the reader's fears and make for compelling tales. Not surprisingly, they have also formed the basis of numerous motion pictures, most famously the 1932 MGM film *The Mask of Fu Manchu*, featuring Boris Karloff as the Doctor. The film's success, along with the popularity of countless editions of Rohmer's books, made Fu-Manchu a household name, and Karloff's portrayal permanently linked the "Fu-Manchu moustache" to a figure of evil.[2]

---

2   Karloff was not the first to portray the Doctor on screen nor the first to wear the moustache; that credit goes to H. Agar Lyons, in *The Mystery of Dr. Fu Manchu* (1923), produced by Stoll Pictures. Lyons (1878-1944) was an Irishman who made a speciality of portraying Chinese villains; not only did he appear as Fu-Manchu in more than twenty films, he also starred later as Dr. Sin Fang (an obvious play on Rohmer's "Si-Fan") in a number of films. Stoll also produced a series of Sherlock Holmes films starring Eille Norwood.

Interestingly, Rohmer was not the only writer to make his fortune based on a "Chinaman." In 1913, an out-of-work Boston reporter named Earl Derr Biggers began to write fiction. His first book, *Seven Keys to Baldpate*, solidly established him as a mystery writer of note. However, it was his third novel, in 1923, *The House Without a Key*, that put him into the top echelon, with the introduction of Sergeant Charlie Chan. Biggers originally intended Chan to be a minor character, but the wise-cracking Chinaman soon came to dominate the stories and appeared in five more novels. Biggers knew well the prevailing stereotype of the "yellow peril" and set out to make Chan its polar opposite.

In 1931, Biggers went on record with his intentions: "Sinister and wicked Chinese are old stuff, but an amiable Chinese on the side of law and order has never been used."

His character found an audience, and Chan went on to appear in more than four dozen films (compared to a mere dozen or so for Fu-Manchu). Yet today, few of the Chan novels are remembered, while Rohmer's continue to attract new readers. The stories of Dr. Fu-Manchu appear as immortal as those of Sherlock Holmes.

Rohmer undoubtedly read the works of Conan Doyle, and there is a strong resemblance between Nayland Smith and Holmes. There are also marked parallels between the four doctors, Petrie and Watson as the narrator-comrades, and Dr. Fu-Manchu and Professor Moriarty as the arch-villains.[3]

But the similarities end there. The Fu-Manchu stories combine demonization of Eastern culture and denigration of effete

---

3 The resemblances were not lost on Cay Van Ash, former secretary to Rohmer, who, in 1984, published *Ten Years Beyond Baker Street: Sherlock Holmes Matches Wits with the Diabolical Dr. Fu Manchu*, a novel whose title says it all.

intellectualism with high adventure and gripping suspense. The emphasis is on fast-paced action set in exotic locations, evocatively described in luxuriant detail, with countless thrills occurring to the unrelenting ticking of a tightly-wound clock. Strong romantic elements and sensually described, sexually attractive women appear throughout the tales, but ultimately it is the *fantastic* nature of the adventures that appeal.

This is the continuing appeal of Dr. Fu-Manchu, for despite his occasional tactic of alliance with the West, he unrelentingly pursued his own agenda of world domination. In the long run, Rohmer's depiction of Fu-Manchu rose above the fears and prejudices that may have created him to become a picture of a timeless and implacable creature of menace.

As such, the tales of the Doctor and his worthy opponents will continue to offer comfort to those who want to believe that good will always eventually triumph over evil.

Leslie S. Klinger is the editor of the Edgar Award-winning New Annotated Sherlock Holmes *and the critically-acclaimed* New Annotated Dracula, *as well as numerous other books and articles on Sherlock Holmes, Dracula, vampires, and the Victorian age. His newest books are* In the Shadow of Dracula: Classic Vampire Tales, 1819-1914 *from IDW Books and* A Study in Sherlock, *co-edited with Laurie R. King, from Random House. His next work is* The Annotated Sandman *with Neil Gaiman for DC Comics, the first volume of which will appear at the end of 2011. He also reviews mystery-related books for the* Los Angeles Times. *He is former Chapter President of the So Cal Chapter of the Mystery Writers of America and Treasurer of the Horror Writers Association. Klinger is a tax and business lawyer who lives in Malibu with his wife Sharon, a large dog, and three cats.*

ALSO AVAILABLE

SAX ROHMER

CHAPTER ONE

A MIDNIGHT SUMMONS

"When did you last hear from Nayland Smith?" asked my visitor.

I paused, my hand on the syphon, reflecting for a moment.

"Two months ago," I said; "he's a poor correspondent and rather soured, I fancy."

"What—a woman or something?"

"Some affair of that sort. He's such a reticent beggar, I really know very little about it."

I placed a whisky and soda before the Rev. J. D. Eltham, also sliding the tobacco jar nearer to his hand. The refined and sensitive face of the clergyman offered no indication of the truculent character of the man. His scanty fair hair, already gray over the temples, was silken and soft-looking; in appearance he was indeed a typical English churchman; but in China he had been known as "the fighting missionary," and had fully deserved the title. In fact, this peaceful-looking gentleman had directly brought about the Boxer Risings!

"You know," he said, in his clerical voice, but meanwhile stuffing tobacco into an old pipe with fierce energy, "I have often wondered, Petrie—I have never left off wondering—"

"What?"

"That accursed Chinaman! Since the cellar place beneath the site of the burnt-out cottage in Dulwich Village—I have wondered more than ever."

He lighted his pipe and walked to the hearth to throw the match in the grate.

"You see," he continued, peering across at me in his oddly nervous way, "one never knows, does one? If I thought that Dr. Fu-Manchu lived; if I seriously suspected that the stupendous intellect, that wonderful genius, Petrie, er—" he hesitated characteristically— "survived, I should feel it my duty—"

"Well?" I said, leaning my elbows on the table and smiling slightly.

"If that Satanic genius were not indeed destroyed then the peace of the world may be threatened anew at any moment!"

He was becoming excited, shooting out his jaw in the truculent manner I knew, and snapping his fingers to emphasize his words; a man composed of the oddest complexities that ever dwelt beneath a clerical frock.

"He may have got back to China, Doctor!" he cried, and his eyes had the fighting glint in them. "Could you rest in peace if you thought that he lived? Should you not fear for your life every time that a night-call took you out alone? Why, man alive, it is only two years since he was here among us, since we were searching every shadow for those awful green eyes! What became of his band of assassins—his stranglers, his dacoits, his damnable poisons and insects and what-not—the army of creatures—"

He paused, taking a drink.

"You—" he hesitated diffidently—"searched in Egypt with Nayland Smith, did you not?"

I nodded.

"Contradict me if I am wrong," he continued; "but my impression is that you were searching for the girl—the girl—Kâramanèh, I think she was called?"

"Yes," I replied shortly; "but we could find no trace— no trace."

"You—er—were interested?"

"More than I knew," I replied, "until I realized that I had—lost her."

"I never met Kâramanèh, but from your account, and from others, she was quite unusually—"

"She was very beautiful," I said, and stood up, for I was anxious to terminate that phase of the conversation.

Eltham regarded me sympathetically; he knew something of my search with Nayland Smith for the dark-eyed, Eastern girl who had brought romance into my drab life; he knew that I treasured my memories of her as I loathed and abhorred those of the fiendish, brilliant Chinese doctor who had been her master.

Eltham began to pace up and down the rug, his pipe bubbling furiously, and something in the way he carried his head reminded me momentarily of Nayland Smith. Certainly, between this pink-faced clergyman, with his deceptively mild appearance, and the gaunt, bronzed, and steely-eyed Burmese commissioner, there was externally little in common; but it was some little nervous trick in his carriage that conjured up through the smoky haze one distant summer evening when Smith had paced that very room as Eltham paced it now, when before my startled eyes he had rung up the curtain upon the savage drama in which, though I little suspected it then, Fate had cast me for a leading rôle.

I wondered if Eltham's thoughts ran parallel with mine. My own were centered upon the unforgettable figure of the murderous Chinaman. These words, exactly as Smith had used them, seemed once again to sound in my ears:

"Imagine a person tall, lean, and feline, high-shouldered, with a brow like Shakespeare and a face like Satan, a close-shaven skull, and long magnetic eyes of the true cat-green. Invest him with all the cruel cunning of an entire Eastern race accumulated in one giant intellect, with all the resources of science, past and present, and you have a mental picture of Dr. Fu-Manchu, the 'Yellow Peril' incarnate in one man."

This visit of Eltham's no doubt was responsible for my mood; for this singular clergyman had played his part in the drama of two years ago.

"I should like to see Smith again," he said suddenly; "it seems a pity that a man like that should be buried in Burma. Burma makes a mess of the best of men, Doctor. You said he was not married?"

"No," I replied shortly, "and is never likely to be, now."

"Ah, you hinted at something of the kind."

"I know very little of it. Nayland Smith is not the kind of man to talk much."

"Quite so—quite so! And, you know, Doctor, neither am I; but"— he was growing painfully embarrassed—"it may be your due—I— er—I have a correspondent, in the interior of China—"

"Well?" I said, watching him in sudden eagerness.

"Well, I would not desire to raise—vain hopes—nor to occasion, shall I say, empty fears; but—er … no, Doctor!" He flushed like a girl—"it was wrong of me to open this conversation. Perhaps, when I know more—will you forget my words, for the time?"

The telephone bell rang.

"Hullo!" cried Eltham—"hard luck, Doctor!"—but I could see that he welcomed the interruption. "Why!" he added, "it is one o'clock!"

I went to the telephone.

"Is that Dr. Petrie?" inquired a woman's voice.

"Yes; who is speaking?"

"Mrs. Hewett has been taken more seriously ill. Could you come at once?"

"Certainly," I replied, for Mrs. Hewett was not only a profitable patient but an estimable lady—"I shall be with you in a quarter of an hour."

I hung up the receiver.

"Something urgent?" asked Eltham, emptying his pipe.

"Sounds like it. You had better turn in."

"I should much prefer to walk over with you, if it would not be intruding. Our conversation has ill prepared me for sleep."

"Right!" I said; for I welcomed his company; and three minutes later we were striding across the deserted common.

A sort of mist floated amongst the trees, seeming in the moonlight like a veil draped from trunk to trunk, as in silence we passed the Mound pond, and struck out for the north side of the common.

I suppose the presence of Eltham, and the irritating recollection of his half-confidence were the responsible factors, but my mind persistently dwelt upon the subject of Fu-Manchu and the atrocities which he had committed during his sojourn in England. So actively was my imagination at work that I felt again the menace which so long had hung over me; I felt as though that murderous yellow cloud still cast its shadow upon England. And I found myself longing for the company of Nayland Smith.

I cannot state what was the nature of Eltham's reflections, but I can guess; for he was as silent as I.

It was with a conscious effort that I shook myself out of this morbidly reflective mood, on finding that we had crossed the common and were come to the abode of my patient.

"I shall take a little walk," announced Eltham; "for I gather that you don't expect to be detained long? I shall never be out of sight of the door, of course."

"Very well," I replied, and ran up the steps.

There were no lights to be seen in any of the windows, which circumstance rather surprised me, as my patient occupied, or had occupied when last I had visited her, a first-floor bedroom in the front of the house. My knocking and ringing produced no response for three or four minutes; then, as I persisted, a scantily clothed and half awake maid servant unbarred the door and stared at me stupidly in the moonlight.

"Mrs. Hewett requires me?" I asked abruptly.

The girl stared more stupidly than ever.

"No, sir," she said, "she don't, sir; she's fast asleep!"

"But some one 'phoned me!" I insisted, rather irritably, I fear.

"Not from here, sir," declared the now wide-eyed girl. "We haven't got a telephone, sir."

For a few moments I stood there, staring as foolishly as she; then abruptly I turned and descended the steps. At the gate I stood looking up and down the road. The houses were all in darkness. What could be the meaning of the mysterious summons? I had made no mistake respecting the name of my patient; it had been twice repeated over the telephone; yet that the call had not emanated from Mrs. Hewett's house was now palpably evident. Days had been when I should have regarded the episode as preluding some outrage, but tonight I felt more disposed to ascribe it to a silly practical joke.

Eltham walked up briskly.

"You're in demand tonight, Doctor," he said. "A young person called for you almost directly you had left your house, and, learning where you were gone, followed you."

"Indeed!" I said, a trifle incredulously. "There are plenty of other doctors if the case is an urgent one."

"She may have thought it would save time as you were actually up and dressed," explained Eltham; "and the house is quite near to here, I understand."

I looked at him a little blankly. Was this another effort of the unknown jester?

"I have been fooled once," I said. "That 'phone call was a hoax—"

"But I feel certain," declared Eltham, earnestly, "that this is genuine! The poor girl was dreadfully agitated; her master has broken his leg and is lying helpless: number 280, Rectory Grove."

"Where is the girl?" I asked sharply.

"She ran back directly she had given me her message."

"Was she a servant?"

"I should imagine so: French, I think. But she was so wrapped up I had little more than a glimpse of her. I am sorry to hear that some one has played a silly joke on you, but believe me—" he was very earnest—"this is no jest. The poor girl could scarcely speak for sobs. She mistook me for you, of course."

"Oh!" said I grimly; "well, I suppose I must go. Broken leg, you said?—and my surgical bag, splints and so forth, are at home!"

"My dear Petrie!" cried Eltham, in his enthusiastic way—"you no doubt can do something to alleviate the poor man's suffering immediately. I will run back to your rooms for the bag and rejoin you at 280, Rectory Grove."

"It's awful good of you, Eltham—"

He held up his hand.

"The call of suffering humanity, Petrie, is one which I may no more refuse to hear than you."

I made no further protest after that, for his point of view was evident and his determination adamant, but told him where he would find the bag and once more set out across the moonbright common, he pursuing a westerly direction and I going east.

Some three hundred yards I had gone, I suppose, and my brain had been very active the while, when something occurred to me which placed a new complexion upon this second summons. I thought of the falsity of the first, of the improbability of even the most hardened practical joker practising his wiles at one o'clock in the morning. I thought of our recent conversation; above all I thought of the girl who had delivered the message to Eltham, the girl whom he had described as a French maid—whose personal charm had so completely enlisted his sympathies. Now, to this train of thought came a new one, and, adding it, my suspicion became almost a certainty.

I remembered (as, knowing the district, I should have remembered before) that there was no number 280 in Rectory Grove.

Pulling up sharply I stood looking about me. Not a living soul was in sight; not even a policeman. Where the lamps marked the main paths across the common nothing moved; in the shadows about me nothing stirred. But something stirred within me—a warning voice which for long had lain dormant.

What was afoot?

A breeze caressed the leaves overhead, breaking the silence with mysterious whisperings. Some portentous truth was seeking for admittance to my brain. I strove to reassure myself, but the sense of impending evil and of mystery became heavier. At last I could combat my strange fears no longer. I turned and began to run toward the south side of the common—toward my rooms—and after Eltham.

I had hoped to head him off, but came upon no sign of him. An all-night tramcar passed at the moment that I reached the high road, and as I ran around behind it I saw that my windows were lighted and that there was a light in the hall.

My key was yet in the lock when my housekeeper opened the door.

"There's a gentleman just come, Doctor," she began—

I thrust past her and raced up the stairs into my study. Standing by the writing-table was a tall, thin man, his gaunt face brown as a coffee-berry and his steely gray eyes fixed upon me. My heart gave a great leap—and seemed to stand still.

It was Nayland Smith!

"Smith," I cried. "Smith, old man, by God, I'm glad to see you!"

He wrung my hand hard, looking at me with his searching eyes; but there was little enough of gladness in his face. He was altogether grayer than when last I had seen him—grayer and sterner.

"Where is Eltham?" I asked.

Smith started back as though I had struck him.

"Eltham!" he whispered—"*Eltham!* is Eltham here?"

"I left him ten minutes ago on the common—"

Smith dashed his right fist into the palm of his left hand and his eyes gleamed almost wildly.

"My God, Petrie!" he said, "am I fated *always* to come too late?"

My dreadful fears in that instant were confirmed. I seemed to feel my legs totter beneath me.

"Smith, you don't mean—"

"I do, Petrie!" His voice sounded very far away. "Fu-Manchu is here; and Eltham, God help him … is his first victim!"

THE HARRY HOUDINI MYSTERIES

Daniel Stashower

Available now:
THE DIME MUSEUM MURDERS
THE FLOATING LADY MURDER

Coming soon:
THE HOUDINI SPECTER

In turn-of-the-century New York, the Great Houdini's confidence in his own abilities is matched only by the indifference of the paying public. Now the young performer has the opportunity to make a name for himself by attempting the most amazing feats of his fledgling career—solving what seem to be impenetrable crimes. With the reluctant help of his brother Dash, Houdini must unravel murders, debunk frauds and escape from danger that is no illusion…

A thrilling series from the author of *The Further Adventures of Sherlock Holmes: The Ectoplasmic Man*.

Praise for Daniel Stashower:

"Magician Daniel Stashower pairs [Sherlock Holmes] with Harry Houdini (who was a friend of Conan Doyle) in a romp that cleverly combines history and legend, taking a few liberties with each. Mr. Stashower has done his homework...This is charming... it might have amused Conan Doyle." —*New York Times*

"In his first mystery, Stashower paired Harry Houdini and Sherlock Holmes to marvelous effect." —*Chicago Tribune*

"Stashower's clever adaptation of the Conan Doyle conventions—Holmes' uncanny powers of observation and of disguise, the scenes and customs of Victorian life— makes it fun to read. Descriptions and explanations of some of Houdini's astonishing magic routines add an extra dimension to this pleasant adventure." —*Publishers Weekly*

SHERLOCK HOLMES: THE BREATH OF GOD
Guy Adams

A body is found crushed to death in the London
snow. There are no footprints anywhere near it. It is
almost as if the man was killed by the air itself.

Sherlock Holmes and Dr Watson travel to Scotland to meet with
the one person they have been told can help: Aleister Crowley.
As dark powers encircle them, Holmes' rationalist beliefs
begin to be questioned. The unbelievable and unholy are on
their trail as they gather a group of the most accomplished
occult minds in the country: Dr John Silence, the so-called
"Psychic Doctor"; supernatural investigator Thomas Carnacki;
runic expert and demonologist, Julian Karswell...

But will they be enough? As the century draws to a
close it seems London is ready to fall and the infernal
abyss is growing wide enough to swallow us all.

A brand-new original novel, detailing a thrilling new
case for the acclaimed detective Sherlock Holmes.

PROFESSOR MORIARTY:
THE HOUND OF THE D'URBERVILLES
Kim Newman

Imagine the twisted evil twins of Holmes and Watson
and you have the dangerous duo of Professor James
Moriarty—wily, snake-like, fiercely intelligent, terrifyingly
unpredictable—and Colonel Sebastian 'Basher' Moran—
violent, politically incorrect, debauched. Together they
run London crime, owning police and criminals alike.

A one-stop shop for all things illegal, from murder to high-
class heists, Moriarty and Moran have a stream of nefarious
visitors to their Conduit Street rooms, from the Christian
zealots of the American West, to the bloodthirsty Si Fan and
Les Vampires of Paris, as well as a certain Miss Irene Adler...

"*The Hound of the d'Urbervilles* is a clever, funny mash-up
of a whole range of literary sources... It is extravagantly
gruesome, gothic and grotesque..." *The Independent*

"It's witty, often hilarious stuff. The author portrays the scurrilous
flipside of Holmes's civil ordered world... and ventures into more
outré territory than Conan Doyle even dared." *Financial Times*

ANNO DRACULA

Kim Newman

It is 1888 and Queen Victoria has remarried, taking as her new consort Vlad Tepes, the Wallachian Prince infamously known as Count Dracula. His polluted bloodline spreads through London as its citizens increasingly choose to become vampires. In the grim backstreets of Whitechapel, a killer known as 'Silver Knife' is cutting down vampire girls. The eternally young vampire Geneviève Dieudonné and Charles Beauregard of the Diogenes Club are drawn together as they both hunt the sadistic killer, bringing them ever closer to Britain's most bloodthirsty ruler yet.

"Compulsory reading... Glorious."—Neil Gaiman

"Anno Dracula is the definitive account of that post-modern species, the self-obsessed undead."—*New York Times*

"Anno Dracula will leave you breathless... one of the most creative novels of the year."—*Seattle Times*

"Powerful... compelling entertainment... a fiendishly clever banquet of dark treats."—*San Francisco Chronicle*

THE FURTHER ADVENTURES
OF SHERLOCK HOLMES

Sir Arthur Conan Doyle's timeless creation returns in
a series of handsomely designed detective stories.
The Further Adventures of Sherlock Holmes encapsulate the most
varied and thrilling cases of the world's greatest detective.

THE ECTOPLASMIC MAN
by Daniel Stashower

THE WAR OF THE WORLDS
by Manley Wade Wellman & Wade Wellman

THE SCROLL OF THE DEAD
by David Stuart Davies

THE STALWART COMPANIONS
by H. Paul Jeffers

THE VEILED DETECTIVE
by David Stuart Davies

THE MAN FROM HELL

by Barrie Roberts

SÉANCE FOR A VAMPIRE

by Fred Saberhagen

THE SEVENTH BULLET

by Daniel D. Victor

THE WHITECHAPEL HORRORS

by Edward B. Hanna

DR. JEKYLL AND MR. HOLMES

by Loren D. Estleman

THE ANGEL OF THE OPERA

By Sam Siciliano

THE GIANT RAT OF SUMATRA

by Richard L. Boyer

THE PEERLESS PEER

by Philip José Farmer

THE STAR OF INDIA

by Carole Buggé

WWW.TITANBOOKS.COM